THE GODS
HELP THOSE

PRAISE FOR *FORTUNE'S FOOL*
BY ALBERT A. BELL, JR.

"Bell reinforces his place among those who are pushing the mystery beyond genre, toward the literary."

—*Foreword Reviews*

"This series is an exemplary blend of fact, fiction, scholarship, and imaginative and convincing reconstruction. A must-read for all ancient Rome aficionados."

—Ward Saylor, *CrimeThruTime*

"...this sixth installment hits the ground running...a clever and highly readable whodunit."

—*Kirkus Reviews*

"...this marvelously written book...sets a high standard for mysteries in the time of the Caesars."

—*Mystery Scene Magazine*

"Bell does a fine job of juggling his various characters and storylines and pays great attention to period details. The relationship between Pliny and Tacitus, with their bantering humor and teamwork in solving the cases, continues to entertain."

—*Historical Novels Review*

ALSO BY ALBERT A. BELL, JR.

HISTORICAL FICTION

The Flute Player

CASES FROM THE NOTEBOOKS OF PLINY THE YOUNGER

All Roads Lead to Murder

The Blood of Caesar

The Corpus Conundrum

Death in the Ashes

The Eyes of Aurora

Fortune's Fool

The Gods Help Those

CONTEMPORARY MYSTERIES

Death Goes Dutch

Murder My Love

Death by Armoire

FOR YOUNGER READERS

The Secret of the Bradford House

The Secret of the Lonely Grave

NONFICTION

Perfect Game, Imperfect Lives

Exploring the New Testament World

THE GODS HELP THOSE

A SEVENTH CASE FROM THE NOTEBOOKS OF PLINY THE YOUNGER

ALBERT A. BELL, JR.

MMXVIII

PERSEVERANCE PRESS · JOHN DANIEL & COMPANY

PALO ALTO / MCKINLEYVILLE, CALIFORNIA

A Perseverance Press Book
Published by John Daniel & Company
A division of Daniel & Daniel, Publishers, Inc.
Post Office Box 2790
McKinleyville, California 95519
www.danielpublishing.com/perseverance

Distributed by SCB Distributors (800) 729-6423

Book design: Eric Larson, Studio E Books, Santa Barbara
www.studio-e-books.com

Cover painting:"The Gods Help Those" © by Chi Meredith
Egg tempera on panel
www.sites.google.com/site/meredithchiartist

10 9 8 7 6 5 4 3 2 1

LIBRARY OF CONGRESS CATALOGING-IN-PUBLICATION DATA
Names: Bell, Albert A., Jr., (date) author.
Title: The gods help those : a seventh case from the notebooks of Pliny the Younger / by Albert A. Bell, Jr.
Description: McKinleyville, California : John Daniel and Company, 2018.
Identifiers: LCCN 2018003085 | ISBN 9781564746085 (pbk. : alk. paper)
Subjects: LCSH: Pliny, the Younger—Fiction. | Murder—Investigation—Fiction. | GSAFD: Mystery fiction.
Classification: LCC PS3552.E485 G63 2018 | DDC 813/.54—dc23
LC record available at https://lccn.loc.gov/2018003085

THE GODS
HELP THOSE

I

THIS MAKES THREE DAYS of rain without *any* let-up," Tacitus groused. "And no sign that it's going to stop any time soon. It must be about the sixth hour—although who can tell—and it just won't stop."

The rain had not been especially heavy, but Tacitus was right. It simply would not stop. Autumn can be a wet season in Rome, but this September was well beyond anything I could remember. We were sitting under the colonnade that runs around the garden of my house on the Esquiline Hill, watching the fish pond fill up and overflow. I was reading some poetry written by my friend Caninius Rufus, who had asked for my comments on some passages about the eruption of Vesuvius. The topic still sends shivers down my spine, even six years after I witnessed the disaster and my uncle died there, but I had promised to give Caninius my reaction.

In a corner of the colonnade to our right sat my wife, Livia, and her mother, Pompeia Celerina, along with several of their servant women. They were here at my mother's invitation—certainly not mine—to celebrate my upcoming birthday. Pompeia has been in my house on several occasions recently, but this was the first time I'd seen Livia in nearly four months. She and I have reached what I can only describe as an uneasy truce in the fiasco that we call our marriage. She lives on her estate in Umbria, a legacy of her first husband, and I keep my relationship with my servant Aurora in the background.

My mother and her most trusted servant and confidante, Naomi, sat in the corner of the colonnade to our left. Naomi was reading something to my mother and a few other servant women.

Tacitus stood up, stretched, and held out his hand to feel the rain, as though he hoped it might prove to be an illusion. "Three...*days.*" The volume of his voice made us aware of his impatience, but, out of deference to my mother, he left out the sort of colorful adjective with which he would normally have modified "days."

"Three days?" my mother called to us. "That's nothing. Imagine it raining for forty days and forty nights."

I got up from my seat and Tacitus and I walked over to the women. Except for Naomi and my mother, they stood.

"Forty days and forty nights?" I said. "That amount of water would submerge most of Rome. Another day and the Tiber will be flooding the lower part of the city. We're lucky to be on this hill. Where did you get such an absurd number?"

Naomi rolled up the scroll from which she had been reading, but Mother put her hand on it. "It's all right, dear," she said. When she looked up at me I noticed the sadness in her eyes that has become a permanent fixture. "It comes from the story Naomi was reading us, about a man who survived a flood."

"Oh, yes," Tacitus said. "Deucalion and his wife, Pyrrha. But I don't remember any mention of forty days and forty nights, or any particular period of time." He scratched his chin.

"No, this is a different story," Mother said. "It comes from a book"— she looked at Naomi—"What's it called again, dear?"

"In Greek it's 'Genesis,' my lady," Naomi said quietly, "a book about beginnings. It's one of the sacred books of my people."

Naomi and her son Phineas, my most able scribe, were taken captive when Jerusalem fell to Titus and his army fifteen years ago. She and my mother have become more like sisters since they discovered that they both lost a daughter at birth at about the same time and have both lost a brother in recent years. I worry that Naomi is influencing my mother with her bizarre beliefs. Mother has gone with her to their synagogue and given money to decorate the place. It's her money, so I can't do anything to stop her. To keep peace in the house I don't voice my objections, though I certainly have some.

"May I see that?" I held out my hand and Naomi grudgingly gave me the book, like a child whose favorite toy was being taken away.

The script, which I recognized immediately as Phineas' work, was larger than usual. I would have to talk to him about his use of my materials. Or I could confiscate the scroll and keep it in my library. I wondered how many others he had copied. Naomi did say "one of" her sacred books.

"Rather large script, isn't it?" Tacitus said.

"Phineas does that to make it easier for me to read," Mother said.

"Where is the story about a flood?" I asked.

"It's about five pages in," my mother said.

I unrolled the scroll far enough and Tacitus looked on as I read about a god getting angry at the human race and deciding to annihilate us by means of a flood. One man was told to build a boat and take his family and numerous animals aboard.

"Wait a minute," Tacitus said, pointing to two passages. "This passage says one pair of each animal, but back here it says one pair of every *un*clean animal and seven pairs of every clean animal. Which animals are clean and which unclean?"

"It's a question of our law, my lord," Naomi said, still seated. Her close friendship with my mother has given her privileges that no other slave in my house, except for Aurora, enjoys. "Some animals are acceptable for sacrifice. They're the clean ones, but others are unclean."

"So how many animals were on the boat?"

Naomi raised her hands in a gesture of ignorance. "I don't know, my lord. A huge number, I'm sure."

"Must have been a damn big boat!" Tacitus laughed. "Where did this Noah live?"

"I believe he lived in southern Mesopotamia, my lord."

"Have you ever been there?" Tacitus asked.

"No, my lord."

"Well, I have. There are no trees in southern Mesopotamia, or anywhere in Mesopotamia. That's why they build things out of mud bricks."

"This happened a long time ago, my lord. There must have been trees there then."

"I believe it's always been a desert."

"This says," I put in, "that Noah took only his wife, three sons, and their wives on board."

"Yes, my lord."

"And everyone else drowned?"

"Yes, my lord."

"But then, after the flood they would have been the only humans, meaning that the entire human race today is descended from that one family. That's positively incestuous." I wrinkled my nose.

"Well, it could account for some of the crazy behavior we see every day," Tacitus said, with a jerk of his head toward Domitian's house on the Palatine.

"I'll grant you that." Everyone knew that Domitian, in addition to the other bizarre behavior he demonstrated, was having an affair with Julia, the daughter of his deceased brother Titus. I thought it best not to dwell on that. "But how do you account for Ethiopians and Indians and other races? Greek and Roman women don't give birth to any kind of children except Greeks and Romans, unless the father is from somewhere else."

Tacitus nodded. "The story of Deucalion and Pyrrha makes more sense. Or less nonsense. It happened in a place where there are trees, so they had material to build a boat. And afterwards, they repopulated the earth by throwing stones—the 'bones of their mother,' Gaia—over their shoulders. The stones became people—males from Deucalion's stones and women from Pyrrha's."

"Nothing incestuous about that," I said. "Nothing logical, but certainly nothing incestuous."

Before we could carry the discussion to any further degree of absurdity, my steward, Demetrius, came out of the house. "My lord, forgive me, but someone is here to see you."

"Do you know what's it about?" I was afraid it was bad news, if someone had come out in this weather.

"No, my lord. He says he needs to talk to you."

Tacitus and I, with Mother and her servant women trailing us and Livia and Pompeia joining the crowd, went into the atrium and found three rain-soaked men standing just inside the door, one slightly in front of the other two. They wore the uniform of the *vigiles urbani*, the watchmen who patrol the city. Their primary responsibility is to look for fires, but that couldn't be why they were in my house now. Rain dripped from their crested helmets and glistened on their polished metal breastplates.

"Good afternoon," I said.

"Good day to you, sir," the man in front said, with a quick nod of his head. He had a somewhat spectral appearance, with a thin, hooked nose and deep-set eyes. "Are you Gaius Pliny?"

"Yes, I am. What can I do for you?"

"Sir, I'm Lucius Macronius of the second century of the fourth cohort. I'm afraid I bring bad news. The storehouse you own on the banks of the Tiber has collapsed."

"By the gods!" I said. "What caused that?"

"The rains have swollen the river, sir. It washed away the ground under the building."

Pompeia gasped. "Is that the building you and I bought together, Gaius?"

"I own three warehouses along the Tiber," I reminded her. My worst fear, though, was that ours *was* the one that had collapsed. In an effort to improve my relationship with my mother-in-law, I had offered to find some property for her to invest in. She isn't a poor woman, but she will never be able to buy business property in Rome out of her own resources, so I had offered to match whatever sum she wanted to put up.

I turned back to Macronius. "Where was this warehouse?"

"At the south end of the island in the Tiber, sir."

Pompeia groaned loudly. I did too, but inwardly. That had to be our building.

"I'm ruined!" Pompeia cried.

"No, you're not." I tried to sound hopeful. "I told you I would reimburse anything you might lose if this investment didn't work out."

For me, though, this would mean a sizeable loss. We had bought the place two months ago and made a few repairs. We were expecting to start receiving shipments as soon as the rain let up. There's always a rush of business in the autumn, just before the sailing season ends, and ships are looking for places to unload their cargos. That's when storehouse fees go up. But I couldn't make anything from a pile of rubble and, to compound the problem, I would have to give Pompeia sixty thousand *sesterces* as well as losing ninety thousand from my accounts. I hadn't told her the actual cost of the building.

"Gaius," my mother said, "what are you going to do?" She leaned on Naomi's arm, as she seemed to be doing more and more these days.

"Well, there's nothing to be done about it right now, Mother. When the rain lets up, I'll go down and look the situation over."

"Ah…sir," Macronius said reluctantly, "our centurion wants you to come *now*."

"In this weather? Why? What's so urgent about a building collapsing?"

"It's not just the building, sir. There were six people in it. They're all dead."

"By the gods, Gaius!" Livia wailed behind me. "I see you for the first time in four months and now somebody is dead, just like the last time we were together. What sort of curse have the gods put on you?"

I wanted to say, *Having you as my wife*, but I bit my lip just in time.

"Livia, this is an unfortunate accident, unlike that incident last summer. These poor wretches were probably just seeking shelter from the rain. There's nothing sinister about it."

"I don't care." Livia stamped her foot and folded her arms over her chest. "Mother, I'm going home tomorrow. I urge you to do the same."

"But what about Gaius' birthday?" Pompeia reached out to Livia, who drew back from her. "It's not for two more days. We can't just leave without—"

"You'll be amazed at how fast I can leave in the morning." She turned to one of her servant women. "Go, start packing. Tell the others we'll be leaving at dawn."

"In the rain, my lady?"

"Rain, snow…volcanic eruption." She sneered at me. "Nothing is going to keep me here another day." Gathering her cloak around her short, stocky body as if she needed protection from more than just the rain, Livia walked quickly toward her rooms, with her mother pleading in her wake.

—⁓⁓—

Letting out a huge sigh, I told Demetrius to gather a few servants to accompany me. "You know the ones I like to have with me." I touched the lobe of my right ear. An assailant had once nicked Aurora in that spot. Demetrius and I used the gesture as a signal when it seemed unwise to speak her name. I didn't care which other servants he recruited, as long as she was among them.

"Certainly, my lord. Give me just a few moments."

In the several days that Livia had been in the house, Aurora had become virtually invisible, eating in the kitchen and bathing with the other servants, which was not her usual habit. But then she would appear at my door during the night. Knowing how much Livia hated her, she had suggested I send her to my estate at Laurentum while Livia was here, but I refused. Livia had promised that she would not make any objection to my relationship with Aurora as long as I did not flaunt it in front of her, as some men do to their wives—as her first husband did to her with his favorite boy. I could not bear the thought of a lengthy period away from Aurora, so I was determined to make Livia live up to our bargain.

"The loss of your warehouse may not be such a disaster after all," Tacitus said, "if it rids you of Livia as well."

I glared him into silence as we waited for half a dozen of my servants and a few more of his to assemble in the atrium. Normally I would travel with a larger entourage. With the weather keeping most people indoors, though, I thought ten or twelve men would enable us to move through the streets easily enough, and we would have the *vigiles* with us. Aurora was wearing a drab cloak with a hood pulled over her hair. Our eyes met and my breathing quickened, but we did not exchange any other sign. As we went out the front door, she fell in between Tacitus and me. Our arms touched, the only form of affection we could share. The others formed a cordon around us. Macronius and the men accompanying him walked in front of us. Their cloaks were leather; ours were wool coated with animal fat to repel the rain.

"Demetrius didn't tell me what has happened," Aurora said as soon as the door closed behind us. "Just that you wanted me to accompany you somewhere."

Because she was trying so diligently to stay out of Livia's sight, I hadn't seen her since the previous evening. I took a moment to refresh my sensation of her—the olive skin, the dark eyes and hair—before I could find my voice. "One of my warehouses on the river has collapsed, the one I bought with Pompeia."

"Oh, my, that's terrible. I'm sure she's hysterical. But why do you have to go down there now in this awful weather?"

I jerked my head toward Macronius. "He says his centurion wants me down there. They found six people dead in the wreckage."

"Oh, dear gods! But you're not responsible."

"No, but I do want to see the scene before they move everything around."

"They'll probably just throw the bodies into the Tiber," Tacitus said from the other side of Aurora.

"I hope not before I've at least had a chance to look at them."

Aurora shook her head. "Surely you don't think—"

"Foul play? No. Not with six people. The poor wretches just wanted to get out of the rain, I'm sure. But I would like to verify that."

"You and your damnable curiosity," Tacitus said.

"Make way!" a voice behind us commanded. "Make way for Marcus Aquilius Regulus. Make way."

Regulus lives farther up the Esquiline than I do. He hated my uncle and now hates me, a sentiment that has always been returned with relish from our side. I was surprised that he was out in this weather, but I knew he would have a large contingent of servants, so I motioned my men to one side.

A dozen servants filed past us. Then came Regulus himself, in a large litter borne by eight Nubian behemoths, clad only in loincloths and wearing silver collars and bracelets on their wrists and ankles, instead of the iron ones that slaves usually wear. They were followed by another dozen as a rear guard. Regulus never misses a chance to show off his wealth—and his lack of taste. His slaves dress more fancily than most people in Rome below the noble class.

The Nubians' overseer walked just in front of them, directing them with a short staff, since Regulus had had their eardrums punctured to deafen them and insure his privacy. The four in front had the poles supporting the litter on their shoulders while the four in back had their arms straight down to keep the poles just above their knees. Even with that arrangement, the litter tilted forward. The poor fellows were having great difficulty with the weight of their burden—both the litter and its occupant—and the slippery road leading down the hill.

Someone inside the litter gave the order to halt. The overseer's staff went straight down, bringing the litter to a stop. Regulus poked his head out of the curtains on the side closer to me and my little entourage, huddled up against the wall of a house. His dyed, thinning hair was slicked down with a perfumed unguent that I could smell even over the stench of the garbage and waste in the street, which smells so much worse when it's wet. I'd been fortunate enough not to have seen him in a while, and his round face seemed puffier than I remembered, his eyes even beadier.

"Well, neighbor Pliny," he chortled, "what brings you out on a day like this?"

"Business at one of my warehouses on the river." I didn't ask where he was going because I didn't care and didn't want to prolong the conversation.

"I'm on my way down to the river as well," Regulus said. "Perhaps I'll see you there." A woman's bare arm and hand emerged from inside the litter and played with one of Regulus' ears. "You know, Gaius Pliny," Regulus said, "you really should follow your uncle's example and use a litter." As he kissed the woman's hand and drew his head back inside the curtain, he gave me one of his oiliest smiles. "Well, have a pleasant *walk*."

On a day like this I could almost agree with Regulus. My uncle—and adoptive father—had always had himself carried in a litter instead of walking. He was a heavy man, as is Regulus, and had difficulty breathing. He made good use of his travel time by having a scribe read to him or take notes as my uncle dictated. Regulus finds other ways to pass the time. Like Livia and me, he and his wife, Sempronia, have a marriage in name only, but Sempronia flaunts her affairs as brazenly as Regulus does his. To her credit, Sempronia has given him a son, and it

almost certainly is his, since Sempronia prefers the company of other
women and the child already has a reputation as a despicable brat.
Sempronia, at least, is a striking woman and, I'm sure, capable of arous-
ing any partner. I wish I could say as much for Livia, on either count.

"It would be a shame if his bearers slipped," Aurora said as we
resumed walking.

"No, it wouldn't," Tacitus said. "And you know it. The sight of Regulus tumbling down the hill—just imagining it makes me want to laugh."

Aurora looked him right in the eye. "I was thinking of his servants,
my lord. They might be injured, and I'm sure they would be severely
punished for something that was no fault of theirs. By the gods, those
poor Nubians have already been mutilated."

"Yes, of course, you're right." Tacitus bowed his head slightly. "Regulus' treatment of his servants borders on the barbaric."

"He crossed that boundary a long time ago, my lord. Just ask Gaius
Pliny's friend Lorcis." The audacity that Aurora has cultivated with me
now extends to Tacitus.

All Tacitus could do was nod. He knew the story of the former
slave of Regulus, a flute player, who had suffered abuse at his hands
and those of his wife. She and a previous owner had been my uncle's
guests at Misenum when Vesuvius erupted. In return for her bravery
on that occasion I had been able to play a small part in helping her gain
her freedom and enjoy a better life on a small farm north of Rome.

We fell silent, concentrating on placing our feet securely on the
slippery stones. The Esquiline isn't a particularly steep hill, but the
rain had turned the ever-present muck in the street into a perilous,
stinking slime.

"I think I'll just throw these sandals away when I get home," Tacitus
muttered, "and I'm not sure my feet will ever really be clean again." He
groused a bit more, then let out a loud oath as his feet went out from
under him and he slid several paces. Aurora and I helped him up, barely
keeping our own balance against his weight.

"Damn!" he said. "Now I'll have to throw away this tunic as well."

"But you were right, my lord," Aurora said. "It was funny."

—◈◈◈—

When we reached the site of my warehouse I was disappointed to see Regulus' litter sitting in the street behind the building next to mine, or the ruins of mine, to be precise. My warehouse shared a wall with that building on one side. I'd had no idea it belonged to him. On the other side a narrow alley ran between my building and the next one, giving access to the Tiber. The centurion would not let us go around to what had been the front of my building.

"It's too dangerous, sir," he said. "The water's still washing away the ground. Your dock and about half the building have fallen into the river." His size and the scar across his chin made it unlikely that anyone would argue with him.

So there would be no chance of rebuilding on this site. The Tiber had washed away one hundred and fifty thousand *sesterces* along with the lives of six people.

"Where did you find the people who were in there?"

He pointed to the door opening off the street. "They were in the rear, just inside this door, sir."

"Were they all men?"

"Four men and two women, sir."

"Were there any children with them?" Aurora asked. It was a question I would never have thought to raise.

The captain eyed her, obviously uncertain how to address her. Her simple dress and hairstyle and her lack of jewelry marked her as of the lower class, but he couldn't figure why she was out with me and standing so close to me. Finally he erred on the side of caution and said, "None that we've found…my lady."

"Where are the bodies now?" I asked.

"Right where we found them, sir. We checked to see if any of them were still alive, then we sent for you right away. I didn't know if you knew they were here."

"I certainly did not. I assume they're just homeless wretches trying to get out of the rain."

"I would have thought that about five of them, sir, and wouldn't have bothered you, but the other one is wearing an equestrian stripe on his tunic, just like yours."

II

THE EMPTY WAREHOUSE had measured thirty paces in length and twenty across before the river began gnawing away at it. Normally it stood above the river by the height of a man; today the distance was about half of that. One side of the building was occupied by shelves and bins for storage of goods that needed to be up off the ground, even though the floor was paved with tufa stones. The other side was bare, to allow for storage of oversized items or goods that could be safely stacked. The dock, now on its way downriver, had been large enough to accommodate two ships at a time.

"What a disaster!" Tacitus said as we stepped through the rear door. Beams lay across one another amid stones from the walls that had been pulled down by the beams.

"My examination of the bodies is going to have to be cursory," I said, as the building creaked around us and the rain splattered us where the roof was gone.

"Why do you have to examine them at all?" Tacitus asked, and the centurion added his voice, urging me to get out.

"I need some sense of what happened and who these people were, in case I might ultimately face some liability for their deaths." I also knew what the guards were going to do with the bodies as soon as I would let them.

"We can be done more quickly," I said to Tacitus and Aurora, "if you'll help me. Look for anything that might tell us who they are or where they came from."

The centurion and his men had removed the beams that had fallen and killed the victims. Three men and two women were huddled together. I thought four of them were in their twenties, around my age. One man appeared to be older, perhaps approaching thirty. Except for one of the women, they appeared to be in reasonably good health. Their teeth were present and solid. They had had enough to eat. Their clothing was adequate and not patched or frayed. I would have guessed that they were a local family of shopkeepers, except that the three men and one woman had an Eastern look to them, while the other woman gave every indication of being Roman or Greek.

One man had his arms around one of the women. "Could they be husband and wife?" Aurora asked.

"Or lovers," I said. "Have you seen any sign of slave bracelets or manacles?"

Neither Tacitus nor Aurora had seen anything of that sort, nor did the victims' hands show signs of hard labor, though they were somewhat discolored.

"They might have worked with dyes," Tacitus suggested.

"This man has a long scar on one arm," Aurora said, holding the limb up for me to see. "A knife wound, I think, and poorly healed."

The centurion stepped forward, his face betraying even more puzzlement now at Aurora's role. "Sir, may my men and I be of any help?"

I waved him back. "My friends and I know what to look for. You and your men would just confuse things." In the last few years I've had occasion to investigate several scenes where crimes have been committed, so I know that the more people who trample on the area, the less information I can glean, and a half dozen or so of the *vigiles* had already been in here.

While Tacitus and Aurora continued to examine the other five, I turned my attention to the man with the stripe on his tunic. He was apart from the rest, half-sitting close to the wall. The injuries on his face and head from the collapse of the building did not appear as severe as the other five. In fact, there was no blood around the injuries. The most peculiar thing was that his lips had been sewn together and his bloated mouth seemed to be filled with something hard. Almost as strange was the fact that the stripe on his tunic had been slashed so that it hung in ribbons.

I tried to move him to lay him down and found that his body was not rigid. He had been dead long enough for the death stiffness to pass. He fell over on his stomach. My attention immediately went to a large bloody spot on the back of his tunic.

"Look at this." I motioned for Tacitus and Aurora to join me. We raised the tunic above his waist. Aurora has long since lost the squeamishness most women would display at the sight.

"He's been stabbed," she said. "Twice, from the look of it, and they're not fresh wounds."

"His body is no longer stiff," I said. "He's been dead longer than any of the rest of them." In his copious unpublished notebooks my uncle had recorded his observations about what happens to bodies after death. Based on what he learned from dead slaves and dead soldiers under his command, he concluded that after a few hours the body begins to stiffen. After a day or so it relaxes again. "Unlike the others, he was dead before the building collapsed. That's why there's no blood where the beams hit him."

Tacitus wrinkled his nose. "You mean the rest of them sat here with a dead man in front of them?"

"Possibly, for a day or more."

"Do you think one of them killed him?" He looked over his shoulder at the rest of the bodies.

"At this point I can't answer that."

Aurora shook her head. "It's possible that they ducked in here and found him like this."

"If you came in here and saw him," Tacitus said, "would you stay?"

"It might depend on how desperate I was to find some shelter," I said. "And they could have come in here just before the building collapsed. Think how dark it must have been. They might not even have noticed him."

"Their clothing and hair aren't wet," Aurora said. "They've been in here for a while, at least as long as that man has been dead."

I glanced at her with admiration at her deductive skills. "I certainly can't dispute that possibility. Did either of you see a knife?" They both indicated that they hadn't. "I wish we had the time to do a thorough search."

The building creaked again. "Sirs," the centurion said, "we've got to get on with our business so we can get out of here."

"Well, go then," Tacitus said. "We'll be out in a moment."

"He's going to throw the bodies into the Tiber," I said to Aurora. I turned to the centurion. "Isn't that what you've been ordered to do?"

"Yes, sir. It's the only way to keep down decay from rotting corpses. That could spread disease, you know. And the rats would have a feast, and then there would be more of them." He looked apologetic. "We've no way to burn them in all this rain."

"But Ostia is downstream," Aurora said.

"Then they'll be Ostia's problem, not ours, won't they, my lady? The river's high enough and the current's strong enough that they should just wash on out to sea."

"Unless they get caught on something," Aurora said.

"My lady, I've got my orders. All I can do is follow them." The centurion motioned for his men to remove the bodies.

The Tiber has long been the disposal method for masses of dead bodies in Rome. When Tiberius put down Sejanus' conspiracy, Sejanus and over three hundred of his followers were executed and dumped into the river. But I needed to know what had happened to the man with the stripe on his tunic and his lips sewn shut. I stood in front of him. "I want this man taken back to my house."

"Then your fellas will have to carry him, sir. I can't spare any men."

The centurion supervised as his men picked up the first two bodies— the man and woman who were embracing—and carried them to the edge of the river, the new edge which the current was still scooping out. "Careful, lads," the centurion said. "The ground's none too steady here."

They returned to pick up another man and the other woman. As they touched her, the woman's arm moved.

"Wait!" I cried. "She's alive."

"Well, barely," the centurion said.

"She is alive. Put her back by the door. I'll take her to my house."

The centurion turned to his men grudgingly. "You heard his lordship."

The woman turned her head slightly. "Look there," I said. "She is definitely alive."

"I doubt she will be by the time you get her home," the centurion said. "Do you have enough men to carry two bodies?"

That was what I was considering, but I couldn't see any alternative. I needed to examine the body of the dead man to see if I could determine who he was. If the woman could be revived enough to talk, she might help me understand what had happened in my warehouse.

I was watching two of my servants remove the man with the stripe when I realized I had lost sight of Aurora. Looking around, I saw her working her way through fallen beams and debris toward the front of the building.

"Hey, what are you doing?" I called. "Get back here."

She looked at me over her shoulder. "Don't you hear that?"

"Hear what?" All I could hear was the rushing of the river and the pelting of the rain.

"A sound," she said. "A little cry."

"Probably just some trapped animal," I said. "We've got to get out of here."

"But I heard—" She dropped to her knees and crawled a little farther, wriggling under a beam. Lifting a few blankets that were lying in a pile, she looked under them. "My lord, it's a baby! I can almost reach him."

The building made ominous noises and another beam crashed to the floor.

"Get back here, now!" I called to her.

"But it's a baby. We can't leave him." The upper half of her body disappeared under the blankets. When she re-emerged and stood up, she was cradling a naked infant in her arms.

"Get out of there!" I yelled. The centurion gestured vehemently.

Aurora had taken two steps toward me when the ground was washed out from under her and, like a performer in the arena dropping through a trapdoor in the floor of the amphitheatre, she and the baby plunged into the Tiber.

———✹———

"Grab a rope!" I yelled at Tacitus as I scrambled over fallen beams and stones from the collapsing walls. I scraped my leg—badly, I suspected—but I couldn't worry about it. "Go to the warehouse next door, downstream."

"What are you—"

I didn't hear the rest of what he said as I shed my cloak and jumped into the river, feet first. Aurora and I used to swim together when we were children—nude until we were nine, then in our tunics, at our mothers' insistence. We learned that dropping straight down into the water can trap a bubble of air under the tunic and help a person stay afloat for a few moments. We used to make a game of it, but never in a current like this.

Shaking my head to get the water out of my eyes, I saw Aurora a short distance ahead of me, clinging to something that had gotten lodged against the bank of the river. The current carried me to her. The body of the woman whom the guards had thrown into the river had struck a beam that fell into the water. Aurora was clinging to the corpse and trying to keep the baby's head above the water. I clutched the beam beside them with one arm and held Aurora with the other. "You're going to be all right," I assured her.

Given the strength of the current, I wasn't nearly as confident as I tried to sound.

"Gaius Pliny!" Tacitus called from above us. I saw his face peering over the edge of the riverbank. "Where are you?"

I yelled and let go of Aurora long enough to wave. Tacitus spotted me and lowered the rope. But the current caught it and drew it away from me. "Try again! Drop it farther upstream and closer to the bank!"

On the second toss the current worked with us instead of against us and I was able to catch the rope. Tacitus had tied a loop in one end. I managed to get it over the arm with which Aurora was clutching the baby and over her head.

"This next part will be tricky," I told her. "You need to let go with your other arm so I can slip the rope all the way around you."

"Gaius, I'm scared! The current's so strong."

I positioned myself beside the dead woman's corpse, using her like a dam, so that Aurora would not be washed away if she let go for a moment. "Just trust me. I'm right here, but you have to let go with your other arm. I'll count to three and you let go."

As soon as I got the rope around her, it went taut and Tacitus and his helpers began to pull her up. The baby cried weakly; at least it was still alive and this was not all for naught. Now I just had to hold on until they could get the rope back down to me.

"Gaius! Look out!" Aurora cried from above me.

Because all of my attention was focused on Aurora's ascent up the bank, I didn't have time to react before a large chunk of debris hit me and jarred me and the dead woman loose from our mooring. I felt myself starting to float downstream, along with the corpse. I had to push her away from me. I'm a strong swimmer, but I couldn't fight the raging current. I was looking for something on the bank to grab hold of when a roof beam plunged into the water in front of me. I wrapped my arms around it and looked up to see one of Regulus' Nubians on the other end.

The black giant handled the beam as easily as a soldier handles his spear. He began pulling it up and was joined by one of his fellows. In just a moment I was hoisted back onto the ground. The Nubians helped me to my feet and we hurried away from the river, toward the door at the rear of a warehouse, where Regulus stood. At the sight of him my joy at being rescued lessened.

"Well," he said smugly, "I see my men have done a little fishing. I guess their catch is large enough to keep."

"Is this your warehouse?" I asked.

"Yes, it is. Or was. It's joining your building on its way downriver, bit by bit. So we'd better get out of here."

I turned to the Nubians and tried to express my thanks for their help. "Is there any way I can communicate with them?" I asked Regulus.

"They understand the whip," he said.

I grimaced and faced the Nubians again, trying to convey my gratitude in signs and facial expressions, and patted them on their shoulders. Only then did I notice the welts left by a whip. The scars did not show against their dark skin.

—⁓—

We gathered on the street beside Regulus' litter, exhausted. Even those who hadn't been in the river were soaked, no matter what sort of cloak they were wearing. The Nubians' black bodies glistened, the way stones gleam when wet. Their silver collars and manacles shone like stars against the cloudy sky. I asked Aurora if she was all right and put my arm around her, as a master might comfort a shivering slave who had just been rescued from danger, but I could not embrace her the way I longed to. It would have been awkward, at any rate, with her clinging to the baby.

"Thank you for saving me, my lord," she said. "We need to go home now. We have to take care of this baby."

"And we have two victims to carry with us," I said. "It's going to be a slow trip."

"Let me make it easier for you," Regulus said. He reached inside his litter and pulled his traveling companion, squealing and wriggling, out by her blond hair. Instead of a woman's wool *stola*, she was wearing a flimsy dinner gown that began to reveal her body as soon as the rain hit it—not that it concealed much even when dry. With a magnanimous gesture Regulus pulled back the linen curtain on the litter. "Your servant, the baby, and the injured woman are welcome to use my litter."

Not even waiting for me to thank Regulus or give my consent, Aurora climbed into the litter and drew one of the dry blankets over herself and the baby, but she continued to shiver, as much from fear as from cold, I suspected.

"Thank you, Marcus Regulus," I said. It was the most sincere thing I'd ever said to the man.

"Not at all. I'm not the ogre you think I am, Gaius Pliny." He pulled a blanket out of the litter and laid it over my shoulders. "And this should take care of your leg until you can get home." He ripped a piece off the girl's dinner gown and gave it to me to wrap around my bleeding leg.

My servants loaded the injured woman from the warehouse in beside Aurora and covered her as well. "Pay attention to her," I told Aurora. "She might say something. She's our only hope of learning what happened in there."

Regulus called his Nubians and their overseer to the litter. They picked it up and we set off at a good pace. Regulus' clients and slaves cleared the street in front of us with brutal efficiency. My men trailed behind us, burdened by the body of the man wearing the equestrian stripe. Regulus had ordered one of his people to drape a blanket over the man to cover his disfigured face. "You can burn it with him," he said.

—◦◦◦—

"It's all right. You're safe now." I cradled the tiny infant to my breast, trying to warm and comfort him. He was in fact a boy, I noticed, although his tiny mentula looked odd. He settled in my arms and we both gradually stopped crying as the litter rocked. "Yes, sweetheart, you're safe. I'll never let you go."

I laid my head back on one of Regulus' scented pillows, too exhausted even to worry about what might have happened on it. Having a baby in my arms felt incredible enough to overwhelm any other emotion. As best I could estimate, the baby I lost would have been just about the age of this one by now, not more than a month old.

Was one of the women in the warehouse his mother? Could it be the injured woman sharing the litter with me? Would she want the child when she recovered? But some instinct told me that the dead woman in the water was his mother. By giving me something to grab onto, she might have been making a last-ditch effort to save her child. I touched the Tyche ring on its leather thong around my neck, a lucky charm Gaius and I had found when we were children. We traded it back and forth. I was wearing it now because we didn't want Livia to notice it on Gaius and ask what it was.

"Am I being ridiculous?" I said to the baby. "I would never say anything like that to Gaius. He would tell me that when you're dead, you're dead."

I stroked the baby's head and he peed on me. I laughed. "That's the thanks I get for saving you? Well, I hope it won't be the last time it happens."

Would Gaius be willing to keep this child? I didn't know the legal ramifications of this situation. People abandon and expose unwanted children, who are often picked up and raised by others. Was this child unwanted? I turned him so I could see his beautiful little face. "How could anyone not want you?" I patted him on the back. "You need a name, don't you? Let's see. You came out of the Tiber, so I could call you Tiberius, but that's not a very popular name in Rome these days." I held him more tightly. "I'll have to give it some thought."

The injured woman groaned and I put a hand on her shoulder. "It's going to be all right," I said. "We're going to take care of you."

She opened her eyes, but I wasn't sure she was seeing anything. I put my face close to her ear. "You're in a litter," I said. "We're going to Gaius Pliny's house. I know you don't know him, but you'll be safe there."

I hadn't paid much attention to her until that moment. Now I saw that she had a couple of bad wounds on her head, caused by collapsing roof beams, no doubt. Her skin, like mine, was browner than is considered beautiful in Rome. Gaius' wife, Livia, and her sister are "blessed" with light skin, but aristocratic women who aren't light enough will resort to all kinds of trickery—powders and bleaches—to make themselves appear fairer. I'm thankful that Gaius doesn't care. I think he would love me if my skin were green.

The woman made another noise—not words that I could understand, just a noise. Then her eyes rolled up under her lids and her head fell to one side. I placed my hand over her heart and felt it still beating. I also felt how thin and bony she was.

—◦◦◦—

Tacitus, Regulus, and I pulled the hoods on our cloaks up as far as they would go, but the rain still pelted our faces. The black dye that Regulus uses on his hair was beginning to run down the sides of his head. I don't think he had planned to expose himself to the rain. His burst of generosity served only to make me more suspicious of him. He must want something.

"So, Gaius Pliny," he asked me, "how are you going to deal with this little addition to your *familia*? Do you have a wet nurse in your house?"

"No. None of my women has given birth recently." I couldn't help but realize that, if Aurora had not lost our child, she would be nursing a baby right now.

"One of my women's baby died just recently," Regulus said, a bit winded because of the pace his men were setting. "You could send the baby up to my house."

"I don't think Aurora will let me do that."

Regulus raised an eyebrow. "Oh, I thought you were the master in your house, Gaius Pliny. Well, never mind. I'll lend the woman to you."

I had no desire to have one of Regulus' servants—a potential spy— in my household for an indefinite period of time, but I saw no way to refuse the offer. "Thank you, Marcus Regulus. You're most generous."

"The little fellow has had a difficult start to his life. Perhaps we can make things better for him. Who knows? He might be a god in disguise. Isn't that what the myths always tell us?" Laughing at his own joke, he pulled one of his servants closer to him, said something in the man's ear, and sent him off in a hurry. "The nurse will be at your house when you arrive."

That prompted me to send one of my servants to tell my steward to have a room ready for the injured woman, another for the baby and the nurse, and to prepare a place at the back of the house where we might deposit the man wearing the stripe. We would have to dispose of his body in another day, two at the most, but I wanted to have a secure place, and one away from my family, where I could examine him more thoroughly before we did.

I parted the curtain on the side of Regulus' litter and smiled at Aurora. "How are you doing?"

"I'm fine, my lord, just fine. We're fine." She looked at me expectantly. Did she want me to touch the baby? Since she lost her baby she has been different in some way. She's sad, aloof.

"Isn't he beautiful, my lord?"

I didn't know if Regulus could hear us over the rain—his Nubians couldn't, of course—but I was glad she had addressed me properly. "Yes, he is." I touched his head lightly. That seemed to satisfy her. "Has this woman said anything?"

"She has made a few sounds, my lord, but nothing I could understand. I believe she's badly in need of something to eat. So is the baby."

"Regulus is going to lend us one of his women as a wet nurse."

Aurora's eyebrows rose in surprise. "Well, that's…generous of him, my lord."

"That's what I thought." I stood back. "You rest now. We'll be home shortly."

Everyone fell quiet as we negotiated the last corner before starting up the Esquiline. We were distracted by the woman whom Regulus had hauled out of his litter. She had given up trying to cover herself. With her flimsy dinner gown completely soaked, she might as well have been naked. Regulus' clients and servants and any man we passed on the street ogled her with open appreciation.

Once we had our feet securely under us, Regulus said, "You've stumbled into quite an enigma, Gaius Pliny. Dead bodies, one of them an equestrian with his mouth sewn shut, a baby that someone was trying to hide. All of them in *your* warehouse."

"That doesn't mean I know anything about them or have any responsibility for them."

"True, but you took on the responsibility as soon as you picked them up and carried them home. I would have tossed them all in the Tiber and been done with them."

"Even the baby and the woman who wasn't dead?"

Regulus put an arm around my shoulder. "Who would miss them, Gaius Pliny? Who would *ever* miss them?"

There was the Regulus we all know and hate.

"I daresay, though," Regulus continued, "that questions are going to be raised. Not about the woman and the baby, of course, but a dead equestrian can't be ignored, especially one with his mouth crammed full of something and sewn shut."

"As to that point," Tacitus said, "I have a couple of questions."

I glared at him, even though it meant looking up and getting more rain in my face. "You're not going to prosecute me in court, are you?"

"What? Oh, my word, no! I'm just curious about two things. First, this man is wearing the equestrian stripe—albeit one that has been cut to ribbons—but I don't recognize him. Do either of you?"

Regulus and I shook our heads. "It does seem unlikely," Regulus said, "that there could be an equestrian in Rome that not one of us knows."

"Exactly," Tacitus said. "That makes me think he's not someone who lives in Rome. After all, there are members of the order who prefer to pass a humdrum life on their estates."

Regulus and I nodded our agreement. *Humdrum?* I thought. *Or pleasant, free from close association with noxious people like Regulus?*

"There is another possibility, though," Tacitus said. He paused for effect, the way a skilled orator—which he is—would do in court. "What if...what if he isn't equestrian?"

I raised a hand in protest. "But he's wearing—"

"Yes, he's wearing the stripe on his tunic. But what if it isn't his tunic? Have either of you ever had a garment stolen while you were in the baths?" Before Regulus or I could even respond, Tacitus went on. "Well, I have. I was in a hurry one day—the young man was *so* beautiful—and I hired one of the attendants in the bath to watch my clothes. He went to sleep—or he may have been in on it—and I came out to find a filthy rag in the niche where I had left my tunic and a little bit of money."

"But it would be very risky," I said, "to wear a tunic with the stripe if he wasn't entitled to it. There are penalties for that kind of fraud, you know."

"Perhaps he took it with the intention of removing the stripe," Regulus said. "Then he would have probably the nicest tunic he'd ever worn."

I wished Tacitus had waited until we separated from Regulus to start this conversation. "So, if we're going to identify him, we'll have to rely on his signet ring."

"What signet ring?" Tacitus said. "Haven't you noticed?" He paused to let the surprise register on our faces. "He's not wearing one."

III

WE HAD ARRIVED at the door of my house, so we had to put Tacitus' troubling observation aside for the moment. My mother, my mother-in-law, and my wife were waiting in the vestibule, along with Naomi and a woman I did not recognize. My steward, Demetrius, hovered behind them.

"Gaius," my mother said before I could even get out of the rain, "this woman says Marcus Regulus sent her to us to be a wet nurse for the baby. What is she babbling about? What baby?"

I took Aurora's hand to help her get out of the litter. "This baby. We found him in the warehouse. Aurora rescued him just before the place collapsed. He's very hungry. Regulus has been kind enough to help us out by lending us a wet nurse."

Regulus stepped to the door. The woman nodded and said in Greek, "My lord."

Regulus acknowledged her by raising a bejeweled hand and addressed us in Greek. "This is Merione. She will make an excellent nurse for this child, I've no doubt. She does not speak Latin. I hope that won't be too great an inconvenience." Merione was short but comely, with reddish brown hair, suggesting a Thracian background. Her dark eyes latched on to the baby in Aurora's arms.

I turned to Aurora. "Why don't you and Merione take the child to your room and tend to him? You can get yourself a dry gown as well."

"Yes, my lord." Aurora started into the house. Merione reached for the baby, but Aurora clutched him to her. "This way," was all she said. She and her nominal husband, Felix, another of my servants, share a room off the garden next to mine.

33

"Now, let's get this injured woman in the house," I said, "so Marcus Regulus can have his litter back and get home as well."

Tacitus picked up the woman, who groaned softly. Regulus peered into his litter where the two women had been lying. Wrinkling his nose, he closed the curtain and waved his entourage forward, walking with them up the hill. His less squeamish playmate climbed into the litter and wrapped a blanket around herself.

"Bring her in here, my lord," Demetrius said, snaking his way through the crowd of women. They parted to let Tacitus pass with his burden.

"Who is she?" Pompeia demanded.

"I don't know," I said. "She was injured when the warehouse collapsed, so we need to take care of her."

"What about the others? The messenger said there were others, didn't he?"

"Sadly, they were all killed. The guards are…taking care of them."

Just then my other servants arrived, carrying the body of the man with the stripe. "Oh, take him around to the back gate. Demetrius will show you where to put him."

"Who is that?" Livia asked.

"We found him in the warehouse."

She looked at the blanket draped over him and her jaw dropped. "Is he…dead?"

"Yes."

The pitch and volume of her voice rose. "Why did you bring him here?"

"Because he wasn't killed when the building collapsed. He had been stabbed in the back before that. I want to know what happened." I decided not to mention the matter of his mouth.

"By the gods!" Livia cried. "Murder! Death! It follows you everywhere you go. And now you're bringing it into your own house." Her eyes widened. "Mother, I said I was leaving tomorrow morning. I've changed my mind. I will not spend a night under the same roof with a dead man. I'm going over to your house. I'll leave from there. Gaius, tell your men to get the litter ready. Now!"

Pompeia's house is on the other side of the Caelian Hill. She and

Livia had come over here in Pompeia's litter, which was gone now. Mine is smaller. It can be carried by four men. I hated to send any of my servants out on such a useless errand, but if it would get Livia out of my house, I had to do it. I would send a different group than the ones who had accompanied me to the warehouse; they had been subjected to enough of this miserable weather for one day.

"Let's get everyone inside, out of the rain," I said, "and I'll take care of it. We need dry clothes and something to eat."

Mother seemed to notice my wet tunic for the first time. "Why, yes. You look like you fell into a puddle. And, Cornelius Tacitus, you must have been rolling around in the mud."

"Something like that," I said.

———∞∞∞———

We found a clean tunic that would fit Tacitus, although one without the stripe, and he and I, after washing up, sat down in my library to drink some warm broth, eat some bread and cheese, and talk over the day's events.

"I'm not sure which is more surprising," Tacitus said, "the collapse of your warehouse, the death of our putative equestrian friend, or Regulus' generosity."

"The first is a natural phenomenon, the second is a mystery I hope to solve, but the last is absolutely inexplicable. Regulus doesn't do anything without some motive that leads to a benefit for himself."

"Does his interest in the baby strike you as odd?"

I dipped a piece of bread in my broth. "Exceedingly. I wasn't about to let him get the child into his house, but I don't understand what some cast-off infant means to him."

"If the child *is* a castoff." Tacitus swirled his broth around in the cup before taking another sip. "One or two of those people in the warehouse could be his parents."

"But why was he hidden under those blankets?"

"That is only one of several questions you have to answer, my friend. What do you intend to do about the child?"

"I'll let him stay here as a kind of guest for the time being, I suppose. I don't believe his chances of survival are very good. You saw how small he is. He can't be more than a month or two old and hasn't been well cared for, I would say."

"So many children in Rome die in infancy," Tacitus said quietly. "We seem to hear of another one every day, and that's just among the people we know."

I knew he was thinking of the child his wife, Julia, had lost at birth. My own mother lost a child in the same way when I was too young to understand what had happened. "It's always been that way, sadly. Remember Cornelia, mother of the Gracchi. She had twelve children, and only three survived."

Tacitus clapped me on the shoulder. "Yes, my friend, but those children didn't have Aurora to care for them. You couldn't see her face when we dragged her out of that water. She wouldn't even let me take the baby from her to make it easier to pull her out."

"But it's not her baby."

"Gaius, she lost a child and now she's found one. I strongly suspect that he'll be hers—and therefore yours—for as long as you live. Whatever you do, don't let her name it."

I snorted. "It's my house. I'll have something to say about what happens to the child, don't you think?"

He shook his head. "Not if you're smart."

"But we don't know anything about the child. Is he slave or free?"

"Such cases don't come up every day," Tacitus said, "but in the ones I'm familiar with, where a child's status is uncertain the law tends to favor freedom. Better to mistakenly free the child of a slave than enslave the child of a free man. This might even be the child of the stranger with the stripe. If I were arguing this case, I would point out that none of the people in that building showed any signs of slave status—no brands, no manacles, no marks from a whip. The woman who survived has hands that show no sign of heavy work."

"I hope she'll recover enough to help us sort this out—and soon. The disfigured mouth, the lack of a signet ring, and the tattered stripe are most puzzling. Someone who wears the equestrian stripe is certain to have a signet."

Tacitus took a sip of his broth. "Whoever killed him must have stolen it when they sewed his lips together. Having a man's signet would allow someone to falsify documents. You use your uncle's ring. If you weren't the upstanding person that you are, you could put that seal on letters that purport to come from him. Petronius went so far as to break his signet ring before he committed suicide to keep Nero from using it to incriminate people. We all worry about that."

I chuckled. "Leave it to you to bring in a historical example."

"You mentioned Cornelia and her children."

"Well, yes, I guess I did."

"That's what history is for, isn't it—to teach us what to do and what not to do?"

"I thought it was to help us get to sleep at night by providing such boring reading."

Tacitus sat back, obviously offended by my jab at his favorite type of book. "Perhaps I should write some history, just to show you how interesting it can be."

"You're an orator, not a historian, and a fine one." He seemed mollified.

We fell silent for a moment, until an idea occurred to me. "This may be outlandish, but what if the man was being held for ransom by the others in the warehouse? They might have taken his ring to send to his family as proof that they had him."

"That's certainly been known to happen," Tacitus said, "but he wasn't restrained in any way. And none of them had a signet of any kind."

"Perhaps there's another person involved, someone who wasn't in the warehouse when it collapsed. Maybe he was out trying to collect ransom."

"But, if they were hoping for ransom, why was the man killed?"

My shoulders slumped as I felt the weight of these questions pressing down on me. "I want to go back to the warehouse, if there's anything left of it. We didn't get a chance to examine the place thoroughly. But the first thing I have to do is find out what's in his mouth."

—◈—

When I opened the door of the library I almost ran into Pompeia, standing with one hand raised, ready to knock. She is short and heavyset, like my wife. Livia has learned to soften her appearance by wearing lighter colors and less makeup. Pompeia, unfortunately, must use a mason's trowel to paint her face and favors bold colors like the scarlet *stola* she was wearing now.

"My lady, what can I do for you?" I asked.

"Gaius, I…I think I should go back to my house, to be with Livia. She was so upset when she left here."

I tried not to show my pleasure. "Yes, that sounds like a good idea. I'm sorry that my concern over this matter distresses her so much."

"Before I leave, could I talk to you?" She glanced at Tacitus and at the door. "In private?"

Tacitus nodded to her and headed for the garden. "Let me know when you're ready to go back to the warehouse," he said over his shoulder.

"Why are you going down there?" Pompeia asked as we entered the library and I closed the door behind us.

"I want to look the place over once more, before it all falls into the Tiber. If I'm to understand what happened to that man, I need to know as much as possible about the place where it happened."

"Well, the warehouse is one thing I wanted to talk to you about."

I knew it wasn't the building but her investment in it that concerned her. "I assure you that you will get your money back. It may take me a couple of days to raise the full amount, but you will have it."

"I have every confidence in you, Gaius. The money does mean a lot to me, I must admit. I'm not a wealthy woman, and I was looking forward to earning some interest on that investment."

"I was anticipating about a twenty-five-percent return," I said. "I will pay you that in addition to returning your money."

Pompeia drew in a quick breath and put her hand over her bosom. "That would be wonderful! Thank you, Gaius. But how can you afford it?" She sat down at the table where Tacitus and I had just been sitting.

"You needn't worry about that." I sat down across from her, already trying to calculate where I could draw together seventy-five thousand *sesterces* in only two days. "You said the money was one thing you wanted to talk about. What else is on your mind?"

Pompeia folded her hands on the table in front of her and sighed heavily. "It's Livia. I'm worried about her."

I sat back in surprise. "Is she ill?"

"Not that I know of. I worry about her because she's so unhappy, and I don't know what I can do to make her feel better."

"I'm sorry that I, as her husband, have not been able to make her happy." I almost choked on the words.

"It's not your fault. She recently confided in me about how her first husband treated her, what he demanded of her and inflicted on her." Pompeia kept her eyes down, and her voice softened, showing her trouble in talking about a difficult subject. "When I arranged that marriage, I had no idea Liburnius was such a monster." She looked up at me. "Has she said anything to you about it?"

"Enough that I understand…and sympathize. I hope you know that I would never treat her—or any woman—in such a fashion."

Pompeia took my hands in hers. "Dear boy, of course you would never be capable of such a thing. Poor Livia has had so much misfortune in her life. She adored her father, and he doted on her. When he died, it was a great loss to her, greater than it was for me, I think. I don't believe she's ever fully recovered from it. And perhaps I haven't been as kind and understanding a mother as I should have been."

If I ever needed an example of an understatement, there it was. Everyone had seen Pompeia criticize Livia harshly and compare her—always unfavorably—to her younger sister, the child of Pompeia's second husband. "It's difficult for me to console her. I assume she said something to you about the conditions she has imposed on our marriage as a result of her experience with Liburnius."

"Yes, and I'm sorry. I know your mother desperately wants a grandchild, and Livia is unwilling to do her duty. That must disappoint you, too, even though she's no great beauty, and that's the gods' own truth. I wouldn't blame you if you divorced her and found someone else. You would be within your legal rights."

"We're young, and we have time. Anything could happen." I had to pretend that I didn't know my mother was dying. From Pompeia's expression I could see that she knew, but my mother must have told her not to say anything to me. "I have no intention of divorcing Livia. I would not embarrass her or you."

"I'm relieved to hear that," Pompeia said.

It wasn't that I *would* not divorce Livia. I *could* not. She had threatened to spread calumnies about Aurora and me if I did so. I could not risk letting her embarrass my family—my mother in particular—like that. Divorcing her would also impose a heavy financial penalty on me because I would have to return her dowry, which I had invested.

I stood, signaling an end to the conversation. "I need to get back down to the warehouse."

Pompeia stood and kissed me lightly on the cheek. "Your mother is quite enchanted with this baby you've pulled out of the Tiber. As soon as the nurse was finished feeding him, Plinia insisted on holding him until he fell asleep. I think she and your girl Aurora are going to have to learn to share him."

"Your girl" was the kindest thing Pompeia had ever said about Aurora, whom she blames for the difficulties in my marriage to Livia. Although Pompeia, who has twice been widowed, is my mother's cousin, I had little contact with her while I was growing up. During those years she preferred to live on her estate at Narnia, north of Rome, and my mother and I moved around with my uncle. My relationship with Pompeia has always felt...wintry. Maybe, I thought, this was the beginning of a new season.

—◈—

The rain was letting up as Tacitus and I crossed the garden to the storage room where we had stashed the man with the equestrian stripe. I was carrying a knife to cut the threads that had been sewn through his lips. Tacitus had sent a servant to his house to fetch a clean tunic. His wife, Julia, had brought it herself. She and Aurora, who are about the same age, have become friends, in spite of the differences in their social status, and Julia wanted to hear about Aurora's harrowing escape and see the baby she had saved. Julia lost a child right after its birth two years ago. She and Tacitus have not yet been able to have another.

We couldn't help but hear the chatter of the women who had gathered around the baby, as though they had nothing else to do. The foundling had immediately become the center of attention for my mother and all the other women in my house. Merione's nursing of him had to take place in the *exhedra*, where there was enough room for everyone to watch and be out of the rain.

"It amuses me," Tacitus said, "to see how women go into ecstasies over a baby, even one that's not their own."

"Wasn't it Xenophon who said that the gods gave women a stronger attraction to children than men have, because it's up to the women to raise them?"

"I suppose there's a lot of truth to that." Tacitus sounded wistful.

"Do you still think about the child you and Julia lost?"

"Once in a while, especially, like today, when I see another baby and see how Julia reacts. What about you? Do you think about Aurora's child?"

"Probably not as much as you do about Julia's." I wanted to word my answer carefully. "Remember, I only found out about the child at the moment when Aurora had the miscarriage. There was no anticipation, no build-up of expectations. It was all very unreal to me. I know the experience has changed her, though. Her mood is often like this weather."

Tacitus looked up at the clouds. "Women are like that anyway, aren't they? I believe it was Semonides who said their moods change like the sea, from peaceful and calm to stormy, without any warning."

"Aurora has never been *that* unpredictable, but I've definitely noticed a change. At times she seems to sink within herself."

"Julia was that way when our baby died. For a month she hardly got out of bed. Give Aurora time. She won't ever be the same, but she will become more like her old self. It has taken me some time to accept the loss, too, as I'm sure it has you."

I tested the blade of the knife on my thumb as I thought about my response. "I grieved the loss of the child, of course, but his birth and survival would have brought us enormous complications, unlike the joy you and Julia would have experienced. I try to focus on work and business."

I had assigned Aurora's husband, Felix, to watch the door of the storage room. He stood as we approached. There probably wasn't any reason to post a guard on a dead man, but in the last few years I've

learned to expect the unexpected—even a dead man can disappear—
and to try to take precautions.

"Is everything all right?" I asked.

"Yes, my lord." Felix smiled. "He's a very quiet fellow. He raises a
stench, but he is quiet."

"I certainly hope so." Tacitus knew what I meant, but Felix looked
at me as though I was babbling. I felt some relief when I opened the
door and saw the man lying where we had put him. As I pulled back
the blanket covering him, the smell made my eyes water. Tacitus stayed
close to me, but Felix retreated to the doorway. I resolved to act quickly.
I sent Felix to get a bucket to catch whatever fell out of this man's
mouth.

"Now," I said, cutting the threads and touching the man as little as
possible, "let's see what's puffing his cheeks out. Whatever it is, it's hard."

People like Regulus, who enjoy flaunting their wealth, like to present their dinner guests with animals stuffed with all sorts of unexpected
items—a roast boar crammed full of live chicks, for instance. I'm not
sure what I'd expected to find now, but it wasn't the *denarii* and the
maggots that began dropping out of the man's mouth. I didn't want to
touch the small silver coins, so I let them plop into the bucket.

"Get me a bag of some kind," I told Felix, "and something to clean
these things off with. Some water and some wine, I think."

By the time Felix returned with a bowl of water mixed with wine,
a cloth, and a leather bag, the cascade of coins had stopped. A few
more maggots crawled around his mouth. I could tell that some coins
were still lodged in the back of the man's mouth and throat, so I pried
them out with my knife. Without being told, Felix gathered them up,
dropped them in the water and wine, and wiped them with the cloth.
As he placed them in the bag we counted them.

"Thirty *denarii*," Tacitus said as we finished. "Are you sure that's all?"

Expressing silent apologies, I probed around in the man's mouth
with my knife. "That's all."

"Thirty *denarii*?" Tacitus jingled the coins in the little bag. "Why
thirty and why *denarii*? It's a piddling sum."

Felix had stepped closer to the door, showing signs of revulsion
at the smell that permeated the small room and at the sight of the

maggots. "It's more than enough, my lord, to pay Charon for the soul's passage across the river Styx, although I think the old boatman might demand more for this stinking cargo." He disappeared and we heard him vomiting.

"It is an odd sum," I said, trying not to step on the wriggling maggots that had fallen to the floor. "The myths say that Charon expects only one small coin in a dead man's mouth. Thirty *denarii* is more like a month's wages for a laborer."

"But hardly significant for a man wearing the equestrian stripe."

The man's open mouth allowed another vent for the stench of his rotting body to escape. I threw the blanket back over him and Tacitus and I escaped into the garden, where we found Felix leaning against a tree.

"I'm sorry, my lord. I couldn't help myself." He wiped his mouth on the sleeve of his tunic. "I'll clean this up immediately."

"Don't worry. It's a perfectly natural reaction. I don't feel so well myself. Why don't you go sit down until you feel better? Thank you for your help."

With a hand on his stomach Felix headed for his room. Tacitus and I proceeded to my library, where we found Phineas copying a scroll.

"Would you like me to leave, my lord?" he asked.

"That won't be necessary," I said as I emptied the bag of coins onto a table and spread them out. Tacitus and I sat down and leaned over the table. "Do you see any pattern?" I asked.

"They're all *denarii*, so they're all silver. Those are the only common factors I can see." He moved them around to form groups. "A number of them have Vespasian's head on the front; a couple have Titus'. The rest of them are Domitian's coins."

"That's what you'd expect from any random group of coins these days, isn't it? Domitian's our current *princeps*. Titus was in power for only a couple of years. Vespasian had ten years, so he put a lot of money into circulation." I turned the coins over. "Is there any common feature on the reverse sides?"

Tacitus ran his hand over the coins, picking up a few for closer examination. "None that I can see. Maybe the common feature is just that they're all *denarii*."

"And thus all silver, no gold or bronze. It would have been easier to put this amount of money in his mouth if you used a few *aurei*."

"So the sum may not be as important as the individual pieces, the thirty."

"But what does 'thirty' mean? The man was obviously older than thirty."

"Thirty days in a month?" Tacitus suggested.

"Some months have thirty days, others don't."

"Excuse me, my lord," Phineas said. "I couldn't help overhearing. There is a passage in one of our holy books that says, if an ox gores a slave, the owner of the ox must pay thirty pieces of silver to the owner of the slave."

I cocked my head. "How is that relevant? This man wasn't a slave." Phineas, like most Jews I've known, thinks there is some line, some saying, in their holy books, that applies to any situation. They're worse than Romans who open a scroll of the *Aeneid*, close their eyes, put a finger on a line and chart the course of their day by whatever they read there.

"No, my lord," Phineas countered. "Perhaps he wasn't a slave. But he was gored, in a manner of speaking."

—⟶⟵—

"What do you think of Phineas' explanation of the thirty *denarii*?" Tacitus asked as we walked down the Esquiline.

"I don't see how it can 'explain' anything. That man wasn't a Jewish slave."

"We don't know who he was, do we? He had no signet ring, and we both know he could have stolen the tunic. And the number of silver coins in his mouth must mean something."

"Perhaps we should have counted the number of maggots as well."

The watchmen were still on duty outside the warehouses when we arrived. The man who had come to summon me that morning greeted us and asked if there was anything he could do for us.

"We just want to look at the damage in my warehouse," I said. "We were in rather a hurry earlier."

"Certainly, sir. Go right ahead."

"Is the centurion here?" I said. "I'd like to ask him a couple of questions."

"No, sir, he's not here right now. He and a detachment of men are farther downriver."

"Well, perhaps you can tell me what I need to know. You're Macronius, as I recall."

"Yes, sir." He nodded once, obviously pleased that I had remembered his name.

"It's not so much a question, Macronius, as just wanting to hear an account of what happened this morning before I arrived."

He placed a hand on the belt holding his scabbard and sword. "I suppose I could tell you that, sir, as well as anyone. I am second in command."

"I would appreciate any information you can give me."

Macronius straightened his shoulders. "Well, sir, when we saw how heavy the rain was at dawn, the captain said we should check the warehouses along here. Because of the bend of the river and the way the island turns the river toward the bank, the current can get strong at this point."

"I wish I'd thought about that before I bought this place."

"Yes, sir. It is a shame about your loss."

"Thank you. So you sent men to notify the owners of property along here?"

"Well, first we looked in each of the warehouses. In this kind of weather we do find people taking shelter, like the ones in your place."

"Did you find anyone else?"

"Two men in that place on the other side of yours. We rousted them out and sent them along."

I immediately wondered if they could have seen or heard anything that went on in my warehouse, but we would never be able to find them. "And then you came to notify me?"

"Well, sir, first the centurion himself went to speak to Marcus Regulus."

I looked at Tacitus and could see that he was as surprised—and concerned—as I was.

"Your centurion went to Regulus first?" Tacitus said.

"Yes, sir. When he got back, he sent me and a couple of men to Gaius Pliny's house and three more men to the fellow that owns the next warehouse beyond Regulus'. I'm afraid I don't recall his name."

"It doesn't matter," I said. "Let me make sure I understand. Who went into my warehouse and saw the people who were in there?"

"The centurion, myself, and two other men," Macronius said, pointing to two of the men standing behind him. "We saw the ones who were huddled together right away because there was a bit of light coming in there, what with the roof being collapsed. Then the centurion noticed that other fella, the one with the stripe. It was darker over where he was, and he was sitting up against the wall."

"How did you decide that they were dead?" Tacitus asked.

Macronius looked at him as though he'd never heard such a stupid question. "Well, sir, we poke 'em with a sword, maybe a gentle tap with a boot. If they don't move or say anything, they must be dead."

"Or they may just be unconscious," I said, "as that one woman was."

Macronius shrugged. "Sometimes we make mistakes, sir. We all do. That's what makes us human, not gods."

Gods have been known to make mistakes. Just look at the hippopotamus. "Who checked on the man with the stripe?"

"The centurion did, sir, seeing that he was a gentleman, a narrow-striper like yourself."

"Did the centurion poke him or kick him?"

"No, sir, not that I saw. He got down on one knee and checked to see if he was breathing. Like I say, it was dark over there, and I was paying more attention to the others."

"Did you notice if the centurion took anything off the man's body?"

Macronius drew himself up, as though deeply offended. "Centurion's no thief, sir. Me and my men aren't thieves neither."

"I didn't mean to imply—"

"If that's all, sir, we've got rounds to make. The rain may be letting up, but we've still got to look after things." He saluted and turned back to his men, who followed him upstream.

Tacitus and I entered the remains of my warehouse before we said anything. The rain had stopped, but water still dripped from broken beams and stood in puddles on the floor.

"I saw the look on your face," Tacitus said. "You're thinking what I'm thinking. The centurion could have removed that man's signet ring."

"But why? And, the bigger question, why did he go straight to Regulus' house after that, before he notified me?"

—⁓⁓—

Tacitus and I both fell into our own thoughts as we walked back to my house. We were taking a circuitous route along the base of the Viminal Hill, to avoid the Subura. I was pulled back into the world around me when we passed a house with signs of mourning on the door and Tacitus prodded me with an elbow.

"That's Lucullus' house, isn't it?" Tacitus said.

"Yes."

"Julia and I were visiting her parents at their villa when Lucullus was killed. Do you know anything about it?"

"Just that Lucullus was scheduled to hold a consulship in January. Domitian was going to be his colleague at the beginning of the year."

Tacitus' eyebrows went up. "That's quite an honor."

"Or a disgrace, depending on how you look at it."

"Yes. How does Lucullus rate such treatment?"

"He's the cousin of Regulus' wife."

"So it could be an honor or a disgrace."

I laughed. "I suppose so. He'd been living in Syria for some time, probably doing Regulus' dirty work over there. Regulus persuaded Domitian to give him the consulship, so Lucullus moved his household to Rome and bought that house. He would have become a member of the Senate after his consulship, of course."

"And they think it was one of his slaves who killed him?"

"So I've heard. Domitian showed his 'clemency' by not executing the rest of the slaves in the house."

Roman law requires that, if a slave kills his or her master, the entire household must be executed. The reasoning—if it can be called that—is that the other slaves should have protected the master. It's an ancient law, rarely enforced, but a ruler can make himself appear kind by invoking it and then setting it aside.

"I haven't heard that they've captured anyone yet," Tacitus said.

I waved a hand. "Oh, the culprit's probably across the Alps by now."

Tacitus raised an eyebrow. "Or he could be right under our feet. You know there are probably half as many people living beneath us, in the sewers and tunnels, as there are living around us. They come out after dark, like bats rising out of their caves."

"That's true." The city's sewers are so large and extensive that Vespasian once surveyed them, riding in an ox-drawn wagon. "But my only concern right now is with the people we found in my warehouse."

IV

IT'S AMAZING how much excitement the arrival of a baby creates in a house, even a half-starved, cast-off, naked baby. Our steward, Demetrius, and his wife have two daughters; the younger is eight. It has been that long since there was an infant among our servants. Some masters encourage "breeding" among their slaves, just as if they were cattle. Gaius doesn't do that. He doesn't put any prohibition on coupling among his slaves—some are even married to one another—but he has told me he's glad there haven't been any children from those unions. A servant with children to care for, he says, finds it difficult to keep up with her work.

I dried off the crying baby and wrapped him in a blanket before handing him to Merione. I thought we would just stay in my room, but Plinia, Naomi, and so many other women in the house wanted to see him—and Julia had come all the way from her house—that Merione had to nurse him in the exhedra so there would be enough room for the "audience." She obviously enjoyed the attention, just like a performer on the stage. All I could do was sit there and watch with Julia and the rest of them while she unfastened the brooch on her shoulder, lowered her gown and put him to her ample breast.

Julia and I linked arms. "He's quite small, isn't he?" she said in a low voice.

"He's probably been hungry for a few days. He even tried to nurse on me when we were in Regulus' litter." I hadn't pushed him away. The sensation of him sucking on my breast had sent an ache all the way through me.

When he was finished and falling asleep in Merione's arms, Plinia took him. She and Naomi cooed over him as the other women crowded around them. Naomi started to hand him back to Merione when I reached for him.

"I'll take him."

Merione tried to reach over me. "I'm the nurse," she said sharply. "The baby is my responsibility."

"You're the wet nurse." I clutched the child to me. "You don't even belong in this house. You were sent here to feed him. You've done that, and I thank you. I'll take care of him until you're needed again."

Naomi pulled the child away from me, rocking him gently. "This reminds me of a story in one of our holy books," she said. I rolled my eyes, but, with Plinia's blessing, Naomi continued. "There once was a wise king over Israel. His name was Solomon. Two women, who lived in the same house, came before him. They had both had babies. One of the children died. That child's mother was trying to claim that the living child was hers. No one had been able to settle the dispute. Solomon said, 'We'll cut the child in half and give half to each woman.' One of the women immediately said, 'No, give him to her.' Solomon knew then who the real mother was."

"I don't see your point," I said. "I know I'm not his mother, but she isn't either. I found him and saved him from drowning in the Tiber."

"That's not quite how we heard the story," Naomi said. "I believe Gaius Pliny had something to do with it."

I blushed. Several of the other women around us giggled behind their hands. "Yes, of course, but I found him. He wouldn't even be alive if it weren't for me."

Merione took a step toward me, with her hands cupping her breasts. "And these tits are going to keep him alive. Can you do that?"

Plinia stepped between us. "Stop it, both of you! Gaius will be very unhappy to hear of such discord in his house. Aurora, you did a very brave thing, but you have duties in this household. Merione is here just to take care of this child. We must let her do that. It's what is best for him."

Merione smirked at me and reached to take the baby from Naomi.

"Oh, my," Naomi chuckled. "We're going to need something dry to wrap him in." She unwrapped the blanket I had put around him, which was now quite wet, and her brow furrowed. "Hasn't anyone noticed that he's circumcised?"

—⁓—

Julia was waiting for us in the atrium when we returned from the ruins of my warehouse. She took Tacitus by the arm. "Tacitus dear, Gaius Pliny, come quickly. You must see this."

She refused to answer any questions as we hurried across the garden to the *exhedra*, where we found Naomi holding the lost baby amid a crowd of my servant women and the ones Julia had brought with her.

"It looks like your servants have declared a holiday," Tacitus said.

"What is going on?" I asked my mother. "Don't these women have work to do?"

Mother ignored my question and guided me to stand beside Naomi, who started to stand, but my mother put a hand on her shoulder. "It's all right." She unfolded the blanket in which the baby was wrapped and pointed to his tiny genitals. "Look, Gaius. Look at that."

Tacitus stood behind me, gawking over my shoulder, which is easy for him to do because he's a head taller than I am. I've seen a few circumcised men in the baths, but most Jews are embarrassed to be seen there because of their disfigurement. They bathe at home in private.

"Why would anyone do that to a baby?" Tacitus asked.

"It's the mark of our covenant with God, my lord," Naomi said.

"Your god must have quite the sense of humor," Tacitus said. "What do women have cut off?"

"Nothing, my lord."

"Of course, you women always get the easy part."

"Give birth to a child, my lord, and then tell me that." Her place as my mother's friend has given her too much liberty. I would have to say something to Mother in private.

"Does this necessarily mean the child is a Jew?" I asked, just to steer the conversation somewhere else.

My mother took the baby from Naomi. "I believe he is. We've sent Phineas to their synagogue to ask their priest to come over here. They should arrive shortly."

Phineas is a few years older than I am and—though I've never thought much about it—must also be circumcised. The synagogue to which they belong, and which my mother has occasionally attended, is in the Subura, the most dangerous part of Rome, at the foot of the Esquiline behind the Forum. I can't stop my mother from going there;

all I can do is insist that she be accompanied by a large enough number of servants to insure her safety.

"We thought our rabbi, Malachi, might know something about this child, my lord," Naomi said.

"What is a rabbi?" Tacitus asked.

"A teacher, my lord. We no longer have priests since the destruction of the temple in Jerusalem. Our priests made sacrifices, and the only place where they could sacrifice was the temple. Once you Romans destroyed the temple, there could be no sacrifices and thus no need for priests. Our gatherings in the synagogues are led by rabbis, learned men who study our holy books, but they are not priests."

"I've met this Malachi," I said. "He seems an honorable man."

Malachi had helped me and some of my clients and servants escape from an ambush a couple of years ago when, out of necessity, we were passing through the Subura on our way to the Forum. His Greek was somewhat limited and he spoke no Latin, but with Phineas to assist us we ought to be able to find out if he knew anything about the baby.

—◦◦◦—

While we waited for Phineas to return with Malachi I asked for something to eat. The rain had finally let up, but the clouds still hung low and heavy, threatening to resume the deluge at any moment. Tacitus and Julia decided they needed to return home while they could do so without getting soaked again. From the expression on Julia's face, I suspected that being around the baby had awakened some urge in her to have her own child. I promised I would send word immediately if Malachi gave us any helpful information.

"I'll be back later," Tacitus assured me, "although probably somewhat drained of energy." Julia blushed and laughed.

I closed the door to my room and wished I was at my house at Laurentum. Because this house is in the middle of the city, I have no space to expand it as I've done at Laurentum. There I was able to build a suite of rooms for myself, apart from the main house and connected to it only by a long portico. Those rooms provide a sanctuary from the constant noise of a large household. Their only disadvantage is that Aurora's room isn't immediately next to mine.

What would it have meant if Aurora's child had lived? I certainly want to have a child or two. My uncle adopted me because he had no children—at least none he could acknowledge—and I was my father's only legitimate, surviving child. I inherited considerable wealth from my father and my uncle, but, if I died tomorrow, to whom would I leave my estate? Livia, as my wife, would try to claim most of it, but my will provides for funds to go to my hometown of Comum, to my mother, and to various of my servants.

It's not just about money, though. A man achieves immortality—the only immortality he can have unless he wins a battle or writes a great epic—through his children, especially his son. A son bears his name and passes it on to his son. A daughter marries into another family and provides heirs for her husband and that family, not for her father. The grandsons of Scipio Africanus, one of Rome's greatest heroes, bore the name of Sempronius Gracchus because they were the sons of Scipio's daughter and her husband. Scipio's sons had no sons by birth, so his branch of the family lived only through an adopted son, like me, who gave most of his inheritance to his birth mother and died childless. Would that be my fate? The fate of my family?

On the other hand, if Aurora gave me a son, could I emancipate them, marry her, and adopt him? I sighed. Certainly not while my mother was alive.

I heard a knock on my door. I would have ignored it if it had not been the knock that Aurora and I have used as a signal since we were children—two quick taps, a longer tap, a pause and then two more quick taps. I opened the door to let her in.

"Gaius," she said, clutching the front of my tunic like a desperate supplicant, "I need to talk to you."

"Of course. What's wrong?" I took her hands in mine, pulling them off my tunic, and had her sit down in the chair at my writing table. She had not combed her hair since we hoisted her out of the Tiber. Her eyes were wild, nervous, like a Maenad one sees in paintings of Dionysus and his crazed followers. I assumed she was still reacting to nearly drowning.

"It's Merione." She glanced toward the door, as though the nurse was standing there.

"What about her?"

"She wants the baby."

"It looked like every woman in the *exhedra* wanted that baby."

"No, I mean she wants to take him away from me."

I sat down on the bed and put my arms around her. She crossed her arms over her chest so I could not pull her too close to me, something she has often done since she lost her own baby. As gently as I could, I said, "Aurora, he's not your baby."

Tears welled in her eyes. "But I found him, Gaius, and we saved him."

"Yes, and we're going to take care of him until we can find out more about him—who his parents are, that sort of thing. The injured woman that we brought back here may be his mother."

Aurora shook her head vigorously. "No, she's not. I'm sure of it."

"How can you be?"

"I believe that other woman—the one whose body kept me from being washed downstream—she's his mother. She was doing everything she could to protect him."

"Aurora, darling, you have to keep your wits about you. That woman was dead. Her body happened to get lodged against a beam that had fallen into the water."

"I know, that's your explanation for everything—it just happened. And I've always held to that. But what if we're wrong? What if there is some order, some purpose, in what happens to us, even if we don't understand it right now?"

"A purpose decided by whom?" I snorted in derision. "The gods?"

Aurora pulled her hair back out of her face. "That might be one name for them."

"But that would mean they intended for you to be sold into slavery and…to lose your baby."

"If I hadn't been sold into slavery, I never would have known you, Gaius. If I hadn't lost my baby, I wouldn't understand how important it is to save this one. Naomi says her people have learned that their god sometimes puts them through hardships in order to strengthen them. Iron has to endure the forge and the hammer to make it strong, she says."

"By the—" I pounded my fist into my other hand. "She's not infecting you now, is she?" As my mother has gotten older, she has seemed more susceptible to superstitions masked as religion. The eruption of Vesuvius and the death of her brother there left her shaken and frightened about the future. She spends most of her time with Naomi, whose influence in such matters, I'm afraid, is becoming pernicious.

Aurora took my face in her hands. "I just know that I feel so much stronger after what happened to me last summer, no matter how difficult it was at the time. I want—no, I *need*—to take care of that baby, and he needs me. But now your mother has turned him over to Merione, and I don't trust her, not for the blink of an eye."

"What do you think she's going to do?"

"She's going to take the baby, as soon as she has a chance."

"And do what with him?" I stood up, wishing I had room to pace. Aurora's hands fell to her lap.

"She'll give him to Regulus. I'm sure of it."

My voice betrayed my impatience. "With his wealth and influence, why would Regulus want a Jewish baby that someone threw away? He made a generous gesture. Uncharacteristic, I'll grant you, but generous."

"Gaius, have you ever known that man to do anything that didn't have *his* advantage as its ultimate goal?"

My mother knocked on my door and called for us to come into the garden. Aurora's question echoed in my mind as we crossed the garden to the *exhedra*. The baby was now lying on a small table, with several people standing around him. At least my servant women had been sent back to their tasks. Malachi stood on the other side of the table, facing me as I entered the *exhedra*. With his long, mournful face and deep-set eyes, he looked like a man who needed more sleep than he typically got. His dark hair and beard, his unshaved forelocks hanging down over his ears, along with his Eastern-style tunic, set him apart in any crowd.

"Welcome, Malachi," I said.

"Good day, sir. It is honor to be receive in home of noble Gaius Pliny and noble lady Plinia." His Greek was still labored.

"Thank you for giving us your time." I pointed to the baby and spoke slowly. "Can you tell us anything about this child?"

Naomi held the baby up, unwrapping him for inspection.

Malachi didn't have to look long. "I'm afraid not, sir. I did not perform circumcision. I have not done one in two months or so. This one is…not done neatly. I know of no woman in my synagogue who gives birth in last month."

"Is that how old the child is?"

"I believe so, sir. By our law, circumcision we do on eighth day after child is born. This one is healed up, the way I would expect after few weeks."

"'Weeks'? What are weeks?"

At a loss, Malachi turned to Phineas, who cleared his throat and said, "We keep track of time in periods of seven days, my lord, which we call weeks. The seventh day of each week is the Sabbath, our day of rest."

"What day is this?" I asked.

"It's the fourth day of this week, my lord, and the twenty-first day of this month."

"Your birthday is in two days, Gaius," my mother said. "That would be the twenty-third day of September by their count."

I waved my hand to dismiss this nonsense. "My birthday is on the ninth day before the kalends of October. It always has been and always will be." Aurora had no idea when her birthday was. Her mother knew the year but only that it happened in the autumn, if there is even such a season in the desert climate of North Africa where Aurora came from. She and I had developed the habit of observing her birthday on the day after mine. She felt it would be presumptuous to put it on the same day.

"You Jews are in Rome now," I said, "even if not by your own choice. I suggest that you adapt to Rome's ways."

After an awkward moment of silence my mother asked Malachi, "Is there anything else you can tell us about this baby?"

"No, noble lady. I'm sorry."

"Do you know," I said, "of anyone else—perhaps someone not in your synagogue—who might be able to help us?"

"There are several other synagogues in the city. I know leaders of two others. I will ask them if they have performed circumcision lately."

"Thank you. You've been most helpful. Now, if I can impose on you for a bit longer, I need to ask you about a couple of other people."

I motioned for him to follow me. My mother, Aurora, and several of our servants trailed behind us.

When we came to the room where the injured woman was being kept, the servant who was sitting by the door to watch her—a young woman named Thalia—stood up. My mother said, "We cleaned her up, Gaius, and put a new gown on her. We did not see any evidence that she had recently given birth."

"Has she said anything?"

My mother turned to Thalia, who shook her head. "She moans and reacts a bit when we touch her or move her, my lord, but she has yet to open her eyes or speak."

"She needs to eat, my lord," Aurora said. "I could feel her bones when we were in the litter."

"I've tried to get her to swallow a bit of broth," Thalia said, speaking to Aurora. "She spits it out. She acts like it's poison."

"Keep trying," I told her.

I had everyone stand aside so Malachi could go in with me. Holding a lamp close to her face, I asked, "Do you recognize her?"

While he took a moment to study her I also examined her closely for the first time. Her breathing was shallow and slow. Her hair was black; her thin, almost emaciated face had a mole on the right cheek, near her upper lip—what most Roman women would consider a mark of beauty. Her sunken cheeks, though, would not be envied. It was clear she had not eaten much recently. I lifted one of her eyelids and saw that her eyes were dark.

"I am sorry, noble sir," Malachi said. "I do not know her."

"That's all right. It was an improbable chance that you would. There is one other person I need to ask you about."

"I will do what I can."

I dismissed my mother and the other women. Accompanied by Phineas and Aurora, we walked to the storeroom at the very back of the garden where the body of the man with the equestrian stripe was being kept. Boards had been placed between the seats of two chairs, since his comfort wasn't an issue. The blanket was still draped over him, but the odor of death was becoming more noticeable.

Malachi stopped at the door. "Is this man dead?"

"Yes, he is."

"Then, noble sir, I cannot touch him or get any closer to him. It would defile me." He drew back from the doorway.

"I don't need for you to touch him, just look at him and see if you recognize him."

Phineas held a lamp close to the body and Malachi leaned into the room, as though he could not even cross the threshold. I turned the body so that it faced Malachi.

"I believe I have seen him," the rabbi finally said.

I was surprised. "At your synagogue?"

"Yes. He has been there several times. I have not talked with him and do not know his name."

It was one thing for an aristocratic woman like my mother to take an interest in some peculiar religious cult, but a man of the equestrian class? "Why would he be at your meetings?"

"Some Roman men come to synagogue. We call them 'God-fearers.' This man attended our worship recently but always stayed in background. His was not only stripe we saw. Some even with broader stripe." He made a gesture, with his fingers farther apart, as though running his hand down the place on a tunic where a senatorial stripe would be affixed. "Many of you Greeks and Romans admire our way to live, but, for grown men, circumcision they cannot think of it."

"If a woman wants to become a Jew," I asked, recalling Naomi's comment that they didn't have anything cut off, "what would she have to do?"

"A woman takes a purifying bath, what we call *mikvah*."

A moment of uncertainty seized me. My mother could have done that and I would never know. There would be no change in her appearance. I shook my head to restore some sanity. "So you know this man."

"I have seen him. I do not know him," Malachi said.

"I recognize him, too, Rabbi," Phineas said.

"You have seen him at synagogue?"

"Yes. Two Sabbaths ago he seemed to be arguing with another man outside the synagogue."

"Did you know the other man?" I asked.

"No, my lord."

"Was the other man wearing a stripe?"

"No, my lord."

"Can you describe anything about him?"

Phineas shrugged. "He had black hair and a beard, my lord. There was nothing exceptional about him."

"Could you tell what they were arguing about?"

"No, my lord, but it seemed heated. This man finally pushed the other man away and stomped off."

"In which direction?"

"Into the Forum, my lord."

I had hoped I might get some idea about which part of the city the man lived in, but "into the Forum" was no help.

"Is he circumcised, my lord?" Aurora asked.

"That's a good question. I haven't looked. Phineas, I hate to ask this of you, but would you please check?"

Blocking Aurora's view and with his face registering his disgust, Phineas lifted the man's tunic with only his thumb and forefinger and immediately said, "He is, my lord."

I turned to Malachi. "So he's not one of your 'god-fearers' after all," I said.

Malachi stroked his beard. "I am in surprise, sir. This man never act like Jew around us."

"Why would he not have joined in with you, identified himself as one of you?"

"Some of us want to be not one of us."

I had to take a moment to parse that sentence.

Malachi, shaking his head, took a long look at the dead man. "Some Jews who live among you Romans begin to forget who they are."

"How can they, if they're circumcised? They must look at…that several times a day."

"To look at something is not always to see it." He examined the man's face more closely. "What is wrong with his lips? They're swollen…and those marks?"

"His lips were sewn together. Someone had crammed coins into his mouth."

Malachi's eyes widened. "How many coins? What kind?"

"We counted thirty *denarii*," I said. "We still have them, in a bag."

"Thirty silver coins? About the number…you're sure?"

"Yes. Does that mean anything to you?"

"No. It's just…unusual number."

The nuances of language and facial expression make it difficult for a person to lie in a foreign language. This man was lying, but I couldn't see how to challenge him.

"What will you do with him?" Malachi asked.

"I want to see if the body can tell me any more about how he died. Then, in a day or two, we'll have to burn it, if the rain will let up and we can find enough dry wood for a pyre."

"If you are willing, sir, may I bury him by Jewish customs?"

"But you don't even know who he is."

"He bears circumcision, sir. That is all I need to know."

Letting Malachi deal with the body would solve a big problem for me. "All right, I'll send Phineas to tell you when I'm done with him. You can come and get him." I would be glad to let someone else haul a corpse across town. It would also mean that the body wouldn't be burned, destroying any evidence it might still yield. Jews place their dead in an underground chamber and let the flesh decay. Later they put the bones in a box.

"Thank you, sir." Malachi made a quick nod that was almost a bow. "I cannot touch him myself, but I will send someone."

"Well, I guess that's all," I said, announcing that it was time for him to leave. As I turned to walk with him toward the front of the house, I said, "By the way, do you know a man named Flavius Josephus?" I had met the historian a couple of years ago at Domitian's palace, where he lives, and I knew he was not popular among his own people. My library contained my uncle's copy of Josephus' history of the war between the Jews and Romans. Given my mother's increasing interest in those people and their presence in my home, I vowed to read it soon. "Do you think he, as a Jew with connections in high places, might know—"

Malachi spat on the ground. "Do not call that dog a Jew, noble sir. He lost claim to be one of us when he betray us in war."

V

AS PROMISED, TACITUS returned later that day. While we prepared to examine the dead man's body, I told him how Malachi had reacted to the mention of Josephus' name.

"That's no surprise," Tacitus said. "The Jews vilify him. And I can understand why. He surrendered when others killed themselves rather than surrender or be captured. He took on Vespasian's family name, like a freed slave, and his history of the war is simply an apology for the Romans. I know his book. You've met him. What sort of man is he?"

"He's quiet, studious. I think he regrets being a man without a country, so to speak. His own people reject him, as you say, while the Romans among whom he lives are suspicious of him. I can't help but think, though, that he might be acquainted with another Jew wearing an equestrian stripe—one who, for some reason, did not make his identity known to others of that religion. Josephus has been forced to the edge of their group. Was this man drawing back by his own choice, or was he a kind of exile as well?"

"Why don't you invite Josephus over here?"

"I was thinking that very thing. I'll send a messenger when we finish here. But now we'd better learn what we can from this poor fellow."

"I suppose he's starting to get odiferous."

"I had the servants burn some incense. Still, I think we'd better hurry."

Phineas took notes for us, using a portable scribe's box that he has designed to hold papyrus, pens, ink, and a stone to smooth the papyrus. The top provides him with a firm writing surface and a strap around his neck holds it in place.

We had to step outside several times to get our breath while we examined the body. The stab wounds on the man's back were his only injuries. His arms bore a few small scars, long since healed, the sort of scrapes and nicks anyone collects over time. I placed his age at no more than thirty-five.

"His hands show no sign of hard labor," Tacitus said, "nor does he bear the marks of a whip. None of those found with him appeared to be slaves either."

"None of them, though, had what you'd call an aristocratic bearing." We Romans have inherited from the Greeks the conviction that one's social class is evident in one's physical appearance. Homer always has noble lords looking like noble lords, and a peasant like Thersites is unmistakably a peasant. "This man certainly doesn't look noble. His head is small, and his ears too large to fit it."

"He's not what you'd call handsome, is he?" Tacitus said. "But he doesn't look like a Jew."

Behind us, Phineas cleared his throat. "Excuse me, my lord, but what does a Jew look like?" He can be downright impertinent at times.

"We saw plenty of them when we served in Syria," Tacitus said. "On the short side, black hair, with a tendency toward large noses."

"My mother has dark hair and eyes, it's true, my lord, but a quite dainty nose. I have red hair and green eyes. I know some Jews, right here in Rome, who are almost as blond as Germans and have as Roman a nose as anyone in the Senate."

"How do you account for that?" I asked.

Phineas straightened his shoulders. "We didn't all come here as slaves after the war, my lord. My people have been scattered around the Mediterranean for over five hundred years, since our first temple was destroyed by the Babylonians. We were in Rome more than a hundred years ago, in the days of Julius Caesar. We've mixed with native populations. There are Jews who've never set foot in Judaea. This man may be one of them."

"Or he may be one of us Romans who wasn't afraid of circumcision." I turned to face Phineas. The dead man wasn't going anywhere, and Phineas knew things I needed to know. "I think I've heard you say that you reckon Jewishness from the mother, not the father."

Phineas rested his hands on his scribe's box. "Yes, my lord. You always know who a child's mother is. The identity of the father can be…less certain. If a woman goes to the *mikvah* and lives by our law, she becomes a Jew. Then her children are Jews."

"Has my mother done that—gone to this *mikvah*?" I hoped to catch him off-guard.

Phineas answered quickly. "No, my lord. I assure you, she has not. She would also need to study our Scriptures for a while, under the direction of someone like Malachi, and would have to observe our laws, for instance, about what foods to eat or to avoid. Your mother has done none of those things."

"If she did become a Jew, would that make me one?"

Phineas laughed and put his hand over his mouth to cover it. "Excuse me, my lord. I mean no disrespect. It's so rare that I hear you say something so…so foolish. No, you would not become a Jew. Only a child born after a woman's conversion would be a Jew."

"Just as, under Roman law," Tacitus said, "only a child born *after* a slave is emancipated is considered free."

"Yes, my lord, just so."

Relieved to hear that, I took a deep breath and regretted it as the stench of death began to overwhelm the smoldering incense. I pulled the blanket up over the dead man. "I don't think we're going to learn any more this way. It's getting late. I'll try to get Josephus here as early as possible tomorrow; then we'll tell Malachi that he can come and remove the body."

Tacitus turned to leave. "Let me know what you work out with Josephus so I can be here."

———⟨∾∾⟩———

The rain came down in such wind-blown torrents the rest of that day, overnight, and into the next day that it was almost impossible to do anything. The atrium, with the *compluvium* in the roof, gets damp and slippery whenever it rains, even the least bit. Sometimes I wonder why we continue to build our houses with a huge hole in the roof. We connect our houses to the aqueducts now, so it's not as though we need to collect rain water anymore. In this storm the floor had water

standing on it. Lightning was another incentive just to stay inside.
Josephus had replied to my message with word that he could not see
me until the day after tomorrow. I pitied the slave who had to deliver
the note.

I was stymied. When someone has been murdered, the clues that
might lead to the killer need to be investigated right away. But the man
with the tattered stripe had been dead for at least a couple of days,
and the site where he was murdered was floating down the Tiber by
now. In my house I had one living person who might know what had
happened, but she was incoherent. She refused to eat the broth Thalia
tried to feed her. Naomi suggested a lentil soup, and the woman did
swallow some of that.

Since I could not make any progress in my investigation, I decided
to spend a stormy day writing. What would I write? Tacitus is always
hinting that he might write history, but that seems to me dangerous. If
one chooses to write about the distant past, probably no one will read
it, as Livy himself admits in his introduction to his massive work. Writing something no one reads is a waste of time and effort. As Catullus
said, "If no one is reading you, you aren't writing." On the other hand,
if one writes about more recent history, one will probably have readers
looking for scandalous stories, but one risks offending powerful people
for whom that past is not entirely past.

Poetry might be another option. Ten years ago I wrote a Greek tragedy. At the time Aurora, the only person to see it, expressed admiration
for it as we read it to one another. Now we both read it only when we
want to amuse ourselves.

I decided to stay where I feel most comfortable and revise one of
my speeches to send to Caninius Rufus when I return his volume
of poems. If I can comment on his poetry—which was actually quite
good—I might expect him to return the favor. I don't yet enjoy Tacitus' reputation as an orator. The only way I might hope to someday
equal him is to solicit the opinions of people whose literary judgment
I respect, and Caninius is certainly one of those.

The speech I selected was one I had made last year in an inheritance
case in the Centumviral Court, in which I was defending a client against
a claim brought by Regulus. Unfortunately, I lost the case, which cost

my client quite a bit of money and enriched Regulus. As I read the speech I wondered how I could have made a stronger case. Regulus has told me that he thinks I try to cover too many points. He describes his own technique as grabbing the case by the throat and not letting go. I had a copy of his speech which Phineas had taken down in Tironian notation and then transcribed for me. I read it, once as I would deliver it and again trying to imitate Regulus' florid style. I could see now that he had indeed latched onto something but not the throat, something much less essential. And yet he had won the case.

On days when I can't see the sun I lose all sense of time. I guess that's true for most people. Aurora brought me some lunch and told me the servants had been sweeping water out of the atrium into the street all morning. She sat with me for a while, but clearly her attention was on the baby and our conversation was desultory. Demetrius came in a few times with questions, none requiring serious thought, thankfully. Late in the afternoon Phineas made a clean copy of the speech and I dictated a letter to go with it.

At supper everyone's attention was on Merione and the baby. I could see that Aurora was seething over Mother's decision to give Merione full supervision of the child. I might need to intervene in the matter at some point, if I could do so without appearing to favor Aurora unduly. But, as I closed the door to my room behind me, I decided I would leave that problem for another day.

—◦◦◦—

I sat up in bed and pulled the blanket up to my chin. "I can't believe Plinia took the baby away from me and gave him to Merione! Just because she has those big sagging tits, like a cow's udders. Moo!"

Felix rolled over, showing me his back. "There's nothing you can do about it," he said over his shoulder. That was his signal that he didn't want to talk anymore. Gaius had to arrange this marriage to mollify Livia. In spite of that, Felix is a kind husband, more like a father, but his patience does have a limit.

The conversation wasn't done, though, as far as I was concerned. I lit the lamp beside the bed. "Why can't she see that she's playing right into Merione's hands, and into Regulus'?"

Felix turned back to me, propping himself up on one elbow. "Aurora, you are becoming obsessed about this. It's not your affair."

"But I found him, Felix. I saved his life—"

"And almost lost your own."

"I would do the same thing again, without a moment's hesitation."

Felix put his hand on mine. In the dim light I could barely see the tenderness in his eyes, but it came out in his voice. "What's come over you, Aurora? Ever since you were injured this past summer, you've been like a different person."

I've never told Felix the true nature of the "injury" I suffered a few months ago. The fewer people who know the truth, the easier it will be to conceal it. And I have to conceal it. I got up from the bed. "I've got to protect that child."

"Where are you going?"

"I can't sleep. I'm going out in the garden to think about this. There's got to be something I can do."

The garden of Gaius' house has a small arbor back in one rear corner with a bench under a vine-covered trellis. In summer the blossoms on the vine provide a perfume. Unfortunately, they were finished for the year, and the odor of the murdered man in the nearby room was growing stronger by the hour.

Still, the arbor is one of Gaius' favorite places to sit and contemplate. If you sit there quietly, you become practically invisible. Whenever I see him there I wish I could sit down beside him. Perhaps put my head on his shoulder. But, of course, that could never happen in a place where others could see us.

The clouds were thinning, letting the moon show through a bit. On a pedestal next to the bench is a marble bust of his uncle, and it's an excellent likeness. As I sat down I found myself looking the old man in the eye, and for some reason I wondered if my mother had loved him. Or had her relationship with him been simply a way of improving her status in the household—and mine as well? Did she trade her body for our benefit? In the crudest terms, was my mother a whore?

For that matter, was I doing the same thing?

I shook my head. I believe Gaius loves me, just as much as I love him. We became friends the day I entered this house when I was seven, and we *have grown closer every day since. And I think the old man did love my mother. His grief when she died seemed genuine. He lived six years after her death, and he did not take up with another woman before he died.*

I didn't know how long I'd been sitting under the trellis when I saw someone come down from the upper level of the house—the slaves' quarters—and work his way across the garden. At first I thought it was a man, but I wasn't entirely sure because the figure was wearing a cloak drawn up over his head. He kept to the shadows on the edge of the garden, and he was clutching something close to his chest. Then that something squirmed and let out a small cry.

It wasn't a "he." It was Merione, and she was stealing the baby! Looking around while still in the shadows, she checked to see if she was being watched, then stepped over to the rear door of the garden and put her hand on the latch.

Bolting from my seat, I grabbed Merione from behind and spun her around, slamming her up against the door.

"What are you doing?" I demanded. "Where are you taking that baby?"

"I don't have to answer to you," she sneered.

"You're taking the baby to Regulus, aren't you? Why? What does Regulus want with him?"

Merione laughed. "Regulus? You're not nearly as clever as everybody thinks you are, you bitch. Why would Regulus want him? Now, get out of my way or I'm going to scream." She took a breath.

I clamped my hand over her mouth and knocked the back of her head against the door. She let out a moan and slumped to the ground. The baby started to cry, but I picked him up and snatched Merione's cloak off her, wrapping it around both of us.

"It's all right, sweetheart. I've got you now. Nobody's going to hurt you. Nobody."

—✺—

I came out of my room the next morning—the first rainless, though still cloudy, morning in five days—to find my mother and Naomi in the garden, along with several other servant women, hovering over someone who was sitting on the ground by the back gate.

"Are you going to be all right?" I heard Mother ask.

I could see now that she was talking to Merione, who nodded and put a hand to her head.

"I think so, my lady, but my head really hurts."

The other women stood back as I approached. "What happened?" I asked.

"Oh, Gaius," Mother said, "someone attacked Merione last night and took the baby."

I stood in front of Merione as two of the servants helped her to a bench. "Tell me what happened. Who did this?"

"I don't know, my lord. The baby was restless, so I thought I would walk with him to settle him down. That's the last thing I remember."

My mother looked at a few of the women around her. "Your rooms are near Merione's. Did any of you hear anything unusual last night?"

Heads shook all around.

I examined the back of Merione's head, the spot she was rubbing. "There's a bit of blood. Someone get water and a bandage."

While the women were tending to Merione, Felix came up beside me and said softly, "My lord, may I speak with you?" He gestured with his head toward the door to his room.

"What is it?" I asked, matching the volume of my voice to his.

"I don't know where Aurora is, my lord," Felix said quietly as we stepped away from the women.

I lowered my voice a bit further. "She's not in your room?"

"No, my lord. She couldn't sleep. You know she's been very moody lately, even morose at times. She said she was going to sit in the garden to clear her head. I thought she might have come to your room."

Aurora often does come to my room at night, though less often since her miscarriage. We're always careful that she returns before dawn to the room she and Felix share. That's why I gave them the room next to mine, instead of a place in the servants' quarters.

"I was afraid she had stayed too long with you, my lord," Felix said.

"I haven't seen her since yesterday evening."

Aurora had tended to me at dinner, as she always does, but she had obviously been distracted. Mother had insisted on Merione and the baby sitting behind her place on the middle couch during dinner, beside Naomi. They might as well have had Merione sitting in front

of us, in the center of the *triclinium*, as though she and the child were
the evening's entertainment. Even Demetrius' daughters got permission to sit with Merione and shower attention on the baby, who still
seemed sluggish and not particularly responsive. I hoped a few days at
Merione's breasts would restore his health. The girls took turns holding
the child and suggesting names for him. Naomi told us one of her stories about a baby being pulled from a river. Aurora had been especially
interested in that one.

"What should I do, my lord?" Felix asked.

I was certain now that Aurora had taken the baby and left the
house. "I'll send a few men out to places around here where Aurora
might have gone. Josephus is coming at the third hour—Tacitus as
well—so I can't leave before then."

I had a strong suspicion that I knew where Aurora was, and I suspected that Merione was lying about what had happened to her, but
I needed to see if Josephus knew anything about the poor fellow who
was rotting in the room at the back of my garden. There was a certain
urgency about that. Once he was disposed of, I could join the search
for Aurora.

But before any of that, I had to know why Merione was lying to
me. I returned to where the women were tending to her and examined
the place where she had been on the ground and gave close attention
to the gate, which was locked from the inside. There was now enough
light to see what I needed to see.

"I'd like to talk to Merione alone," I said, waving my hand to dismiss
the rest. My mother's face showed her displeasure, but she complied.

I sat down next to Merione. "Tell me what really happened," I said.

She wouldn't look directly at me. "My lord, as I told your mother,
someone knocked me senseless and took the baby."

"And you didn't see who it was?"

"No, my lord. They came up behind me."

I took her hand and led her to the gate, putting my finger next to a
spot on the doorpost. "Do you see that?"

Merione peered closely. "Yes, my lord."

"That's blood," I said. "And when I stand you up beside it"—which I
did—"it matches the spot on the back of your head. Someone slammed

you up against the doorpost, so they were in front of you, not behind you. You must have seen who it was."

"It was dark, my lord."

I grabbed her arm. "I'll have the truth out of you, woman, one way or another."

Fear flickered in her eyes for an instant, but I suppose she had heard others in the household describe me as mild-mannered. She did not back down. "Are you sure that's what you want, my lord? What if I told you it was your woman, that Aurora, who attacked me? Would you want me to say that?"

I let go of her arm. "If that's the truth, then that's what you should tell me. It will be up to me to decide what to do about it, but I must have the truth."

"That is the gods' own truth, my lord. She was lurking somewhere over there"—she pointed to my arbor—"and jumped on me for no reason. And you're right. She did give me a good crack up against the doorpost. I was wearing a cloak—my pretty blue one that my lady Sempronia gave me—and carrying the baby. She must've taken them both."

"You said you were walking in the garden to calm the child. Why were you all the way back here by the gate?"

She hesitated. "I didn't want to disturb anyone, my lord. The tyke was fretful."

She still wasn't telling me the whole truth. "Are you sure you weren't about to leave the house? Perhaps to take the child to Regulus?"

"*Pssht!* What would Regulus want with him, my lord? He's got a son of his own—insufferable little brat that he is." She clapped her hand over her mouth. "I'm sorry, my lord. I shouldn't speak so of my betters."

She had just expressed the opinion held by everyone who'd ever met Regulus' pampered, overindulged son.

"As you can see, my lord, the latch is still in place. I did not open the gate. I don't see how your girl Aurora could have either, and left it latched like it is."

—◈—

I sent Merione to her room with one of the other servants to keep watch on her. We would need her to feed the baby when we found him, as I was sure I would do as soon as I was free to search. With clouds hanging low, the sundial in the garden was useless, but it felt like it was close to the third hour when Tacitus arrived, with Josephus only moments behind him. Tacitus was accompanied by half a dozen servants, while Josephus risked walking the streets by himself. I hadn't seen him in a couple of years. His face was as downcast as it had ever been any time I'd been around him before. His gray-and-white beard accented the melancholy that seemed to hang over him. His olive skin and general Eastern appearance contrasted with his Roman toga bearing the equestrian stripe.

Tacitus knows more about Josephus as a historian than I do. My uncle had done his best to inculcate in me an interest in history—while Vesuvius erupted I was copying passages from Livy that he'd assigned me—but oratory and poetry crowded out other growth in my literary garden.

"What are you writing now?" Tacitus asked after we exchanged pleasantries.

Josephus, in his sad, deep voice, said, "I've begun a large-scale study of Jewish history, based on our holy books and other sources."

"I look forward to reading it," Tacitus said.

"You may be the only one," Josephus replied. "Domitian's entirely against the idea. My servant has heard rumors that he may even throw me out of my rooms. I'm not sure how much longer he'll feel obligated to maintain me as Vespasian and Titus did."

Tacitus and I exchanged a glance when we caught the singular "servant." Since his surrender to Domitian's father, Josephus had been living in the imperial residence on the Palatine. Vespasian had treated him as an honored guest, Titus more like a family member. Domitian treats him like a tenant he wants to evict. He turned to me. "You said you needed my assistance, Gaius Pliny. How can I help you?"

"A man was found dead in my warehouse when it collapsed the day before yesterday." I decided not to mention how he died. Being asked to identify a dead man is not as frightening, or as incriminating, as being asked to identify a murder victim. "I thought you might know who he is."

"Why would you think such a thing? This must be more than just a random dead man."

"He is circumcised, and he wears an equestrian stripe. There can't be that many Jews in our class in Rome."

Josephus nodded once and pursed his lips, as if pondering some philosophical problem. "Can you not identify him from his signet ring?"

"He wasn't wearing one."

"We think someone removed it before we got there," Tacitus offered.

"Well, that is certainly curious. I might even call it ominous." Josephus stroked his beard. "Where is the man?"

I turned toward the room at the back of the garden. "He's back here. I must warn you, he is getting to the point that we're going to have to dispose of the body very soon."

"Today," Tacitus said with a grimace. "Yesterday would have been better."

Josephus drew himself up. "Let's make this quick then. The odor of rotting flesh has never sat easy on my stomach." Maybe that was why he surrendered and tried to urge those defending Jerusalem to surrender.

That odor seemed to be advancing toward us as we approached the room. Josephus put a hand over his mouth. As quickly as I could, I opened the door to the room and pulled the blanket down far enough that Josephus could see the man's face. He took a quick look and stepped away, waving for me to close the door.

Tacitus and I followed Josephus as he hurried to the fish pond in the middle of the garden. Kneeling, he picked up a handful of water and rubbed it over his face, then repeated the process and blew air out of his nostrils.

"Are you all right?" I asked.

"I just need to get rid of that stench."

I summoned the first servant I saw and told him to tell Phineas to take a message to Malachi that he could come get the body.

"May I offer you some wine?" I asked Josephus.

"No, thank you. I think I'll be all right." He moved to a bench at the opposite end of the garden from the room where the dead man lay and sat down. "I heard you mention Malachi."

"Two of my servants attend his synagogue. Do you know him?"

"I know *of* him. He would never speak to me or allow me in his synagogue. You know all about that, of course."

I nodded. Josephus' story was well-known, and I had talked with him about it on the couple of occasions our paths had crossed. He always brought up the subject. I waited, then asked, "Can you tell us anything about that man?"

"Well, to begin with, his name is Julius Berenicianus."

"Bere—" Tacitus stuttered.

"Berenicianus, son of Berenice."

"Titus' mistress? *That* Berenice?"

Josephus nodded. "Julia Berenice. She's the only one I know of."

We sat down beside him. "This sounds like something of a story," Tacitus said with anticipation. It did to me, too, but I had almost hoped for a simple "no" so I could get on to finding Aurora and the baby.

"I saw Berenice when Titus brought her back after the war," Tacitus said. "She was quite a striking woman. Somewhat older than Titus, though, wasn't she?"

Josephus nodded. "By about ten years, although precise information about her is hard to come by. I believe she was born in the fourteenth year of Tiberius' reign."

"So that would make her about fifty-seven."

"I believe so. She was the daughter of Herod Agrippa the Elder. She had a brother of the same name and a sister named Drusilla, along with two or three other siblings. Berenice is a beautiful woman, but Drusilla was quite stunning. Berenice was jealous of her and did everything she could to interfere in her life and make her miserable."

"You're using the past tense. Is Drusilla dead?"

"Yes. And this will interest you I'm sure, Gaius Pliny. Drusilla was in Pompeii when Vesuvius erupted. She and your uncle are the only two people, out of the thousands who died there, whom anyone has been able to identify by name."

"Back to Berenice," Tacitus said. "From what I've heard, she had an incestuous relationship with her brother, the younger Herod Agrippa."

"That is entirely likely," Josephus said. "Her brother never married. Berenice, after the death of a husband—and she lost several—would always return to Agrippa's court. I've been told that they adored one of our holy books, a love poem attributed to King Solomon. It contains lines such as 'You have ravished my heart, my sister, my bride' and 'I come to my garden, my sister, my bride.'"

I wanted to get this story back on track. "This Julius Berenicianus wasn't Titus' child, was he?"

"Oh, no," Josephus said quickly. "As I said, Berenice was married several times. The first time, as one might expect, was when she was about fourteen, to a member of a prominent family in Alexandria. He died after a couple of years." Josephus stroked his beard. "I'm sorry to be so vague about dates and ages, but information about this family is not easy to come by. A few years later Berenice was married again, this time to her uncle, also named Herod. He was the father of the poor fellow who's stinking up your back room, and of another son, Julius Hyrcanus. There is no record of him since the early days of Rome's war with the Jews. He—that is Hyrcanus—simply disappeared."

"Killed?"

"Most likely, but I can't prove it or disprove it."

"The dead man," Tacitus said. "How old was he?"

"He must have been about thirty or so."

That would fit with my estimate of his age. "Why was he named after his mother?"

"Berenice was a wealthy, strong-willed woman. If Titus could have married her, she would have made herself queen of Rome, just like Nero's mother tried to do."

I chuckled. "My tutor, Quintilian, once told me that, during Titus' time in power, he appeared in court to speak in a case on behalf of Berenice, only to find her sitting as a judge in the case."

"That doesn't surprise me at all," Josephus said.

"You said she *was* wealthy," Tacitus said. "So she's dead?"

"I don't actually know," Josephus said. "No one, so far as I can determine, has seen her for almost five years. She left Rome, as I'm sure you know, because people disapproved so strongly of her relationship with Titus that he had to send her away. I have no idea what happened to her after that. I'm also quite surprised to learn that one of her sons was here in the city."

"'One of'?"

"Yes. She had several. One died in his teens, I believe. Two of them were her sons by her uncle, who was also her husband. One of those disappeared by the end of the war. The other I have only tidbits of information about."

"Do you know if her son was married or had any children?" I asked.

Josephus shook his head. "Getting information about him is even harder than uncovering anything reliable about his mother."

"Then it should interest you to know," I said, "that in the warehouse, along with this man and several others, we found a male child who had been circumcised."

Josephus' eyebrows arched with interest. "Was the child alive?"

"Yes, he is."

"Where is he? May I see him?"

"We brought him here," I said, "but at the moment I...I—"

"What Gaius Pliny means to say is that...well, he's lost him," Tacitus said with a smirk.

"Now, it's not that simple, and you know it."

Josephus' interest turned to agitation. "You've got to find him, Gaius Pliny. Considering how wealthy Berenice was—or perhaps is—that child could be the heir to an immense fortune."

That might explain why Regulus wanted him, I thought. *Could it also be why his father—if that's who he was—had been stabbed twice in the back?*

—◦◦◦—

Tacitus invited Josephus to see his library and to talk more about Josephus' proposed history of the Jews. I assured him that I did not need his assistance to find Aurora and would let him know as soon as she and the baby were back in my house.

"Do you want me to send Julia over here?" he asked before joining Josephus at the door. "Aurora's behavior obviously has something to do with...what happened last summer. Julia could be some help to her."

"I don't think that will be necessary, but thank you for offering."

As soon as the door closed behind them, I headed for the rear gate in the garden. Merione may not have been able to imagine how Aurora could have gone through the gate while leaving it latched from the inside, but I knew exactly how she did it.

As children, one afternoon we had listened to my uncle and some of his friends talk about how a crime might be committed in a room with all the doors and windows locked or barred from the inside. They proposed a contest, with a prize of an amphora of Falernian for the first one to devise a method. Taking up the challenge, Aurora and I had noticed the crack in the rear door of the garden, just above the latch, which was a piece of wood that fit into a U-shaped bracket. We figured out how to use a slip knot on a piece of string that would fit through the crack. Once outside, we could drop the latch into place and then pull hard enough that the knot would come untied and the string could be drawn through the crack. We never revealed our secret to my uncle, and none of his friends ever claimed the prize.

Now, taking three servants with me, I went out the gate and turned right. The street behind the house is barely more than a narrow lane to allow deliveries of supplies to the houses. I stopped at the third house down the hill from mine and told my servants to wait on the street. This house did not extend quite all the way back to the narrow lane. As children, Aurora and I had learned from an elderly servant that, at some time long-past, there had been a well here, for the common use of all the houses in this block. All of these houses now had water piped in from the aqueducts, so the well had been covered over and forgotten. But the flat stone covering the opening wasn't difficult for an adult—or two children—to push aside. As soon as I did, I heard the fretting of a baby.

I squeezed past the stone, leaving enough of an opening to provide some light. Several step-like ledges ran around the shaft of the well. That's where Aurora was sitting, in tears, with the child sucking on one of her breasts and crying intermittently. I hardly recognized her in the dim light, with her long hair streaming over her shoulders and her eyes wild, maniacal.

"I can't feed him, Gaius," she cried. "He's so hungry, and I can't feed him."

I sat close beside her but did not touch her. "My darling, I know you're grieving over the baby you lost—"

"You lost him, too, Gaius. Don't you ever feel that you lost him, too?"

Her voice was rising, frantic. I kept my own voice calm, trying to reassure her. "Of course I do. It was our child."

"He wasn't an 'it.' He was *us*." She slapped me, then looked at me in horror, drawing back slowly. "Oh, Gaius, my lord! What have I done? Please forgive me!" Still holding the baby, she fell at my feet, a precarious perch on the narrow ledge. "I think I'm going mad."

I took her arms and pulled her up, but she wouldn't go any farther than her knees. When I lifted her chin, her face was contorted with tears.

"I know what would happen to me, my lord, if I did that to any other master in any other house in Rome, and I know you have to punish me. I'll accept whatever you decide." She turned her face down again, drawing the baby so close to her I was afraid she might smother the child.

Pulling her up to sit beside me, I wrapped my arms around her and tried to loosen her grip on the infant. "How could you think I would ever hurt you? No one saw what just happened here. I know it will never happen again."

"No, my lord. I swear it, and I beg your forgiveness."

"You have it." I kissed her forehead and stroked the baby's head. "This is not between master and slave. It's between us. I know you're deeply distraught over the loss of our child. But you knew you were carrying him. You'd been thinking about him for a while, without telling me. I didn't know anything until the moment you had the miscarriage. I clearly didn't appreciate just how much it has affected you."

"It has, Gaius. No one else knows about it, except Tacitus and Julia, and that's two people too many. I have no one to talk to. Any time I start to feel sad about it, I have to choke it down."

She let me pull her closer beside me. "Felix knows, doesn't he?" I asked as tenderly as I could.

She shook her head. "He knows I was hurt, but I never told him all of it. The only time I can let my feelings out is at night, when I'm with you. That's why I cry so much."

"We could have found a baby for you to raise. There are dozens of them abandoned every day in Rome."

Aurora looked at me in disbelief. "How can you even say that? Nobody would understand if I suddenly wanted a baby. Forgive me, Gaius, but that was a stupid thing to say."

I could feel my ears burning. "Yes, I guess you're right."

"Besides, it's not just a matter of a baby, any baby. I feel—no, I *know*—that I was meant to find *this* baby and to care for him."

"Wouldn't it be easier all around if you told Felix about your miscarriage? He would support you if he knew the whole story."

"No, absolutely not. Anyone who knows could let a careless word slip and Livia could find out. If she did, there would be nothing you could do to protect me, or yourself."

"So you keep holding it back—"

"Until it spews out, like Vesuvius erupting."

"And woe to anyone in the path." I hugged her. "Men and women, I guess, express their feelings about such things differently."

She stroked the baby's head and kissed him. "I'm not sure men even have feelings about their children. If they did, how could they discard them or sell them as slaves, the way my father did?"

I could not argue with her on that point. It would be better to get her focused on the baby. "You said the child was hungry. He needs to be fed. Let's go home and let Merione take care of that, if she's still willing after you attacked her."

"She was leaving the house! I had to stop her."

"She says she was just walking around in the garden, trying to settle the child and get him to sleep. She happened to be by the rear gate and you over-reacted."

Aurora shook her head vigorously. "She's lying. I was watching her from the arbor. She looked around to make sure no one could see her and then she headed straight for the gate. She had her hand on the latch. Another moment and she would have been gone. I don't trust her, Gaius. She is, first and foremost, Regulus' servant. Can't we get someone else?"

"I'll do my best to find someone." We sat quietly for a few moments until her breathing became lighter and steadier. "Are you ready to go home now?"

"I think so." As we stood she pointed to a spot on the wall. "Do you remember when we did that?"

"I'll never forget it. I hope it's prophetic."

On the wall beside the steps, when we were twelve, we had scratched the word SEMPER vertically into the rock. We attached PLIN to the P and AUR to the R, with the word ET between us. "Pliny and Aurora always."

$$
\begin{array}{l}
S \\
E \\
M \\
P\ L\ I\ N \\
E\ T \\
A\ U\ R
\end{array}
$$

At that time we meant it as a gesture of friendship, because we couldn't imagine being more than friends. I wonder, though, if we did not, even then, somehow sense that there was more of a connection between us.

"I just hope Livia never sees it," Aurora said.

VI

REGULUS' *IANITOR* BOWED and stepped aside to allow Merione and me to enter the atrium of his master's house, followed by four of my servants, who stopped just inside the door. I motioned for Merione to stay with me.

Like everything else about Regulus, the atrium was large and overstated. His oratorical style is florid, tending toward what he thinks is dramatic but is in fact merely bombastic. The atrium revealed the man. It was so large that it required columns at each corner of the *impluvium* to support the roof. Today the space was filled with scaffolding and workmen, busy painting new frescoes. They had finished one side and were conferring with Regulus about something near the back of the atrium.

Regulus turned away and crossed the atrium. We met beside the *impluvium*.

"Welcome, Gaius Pliny, my good neighbor. I apologize for the mess, but what do you think?" He spread his arms to indicate the walls on the finished side.

"Impressive," I said. And it was, since even something dreadful can be described with that word. Between the doors of the rooms opening off the atrium, frescoes depicted scenes from early Roman history, the era of the kings. Because his name means "little king," Regulus was within his rights to choose such a theme, as long as he did not show himself as a monarch. Instead, the kings tended to look like Domitian. "Did the *princeps* himself serve as your model?"

Regulus laughed. "We're using the bust at the rear of the atrium. It's a good likeness."

His son, now about five years old, was playing with a boat on the other side of the *impluvium*, which was quite full due to all the rain we'd been having. I remembered doing the same thing when I was a child. What I did not remember was giving orders to a servant whose task it was to retrieve the boat when it floated out of reach. The boy's whining caused Regulus and me to look in his direction. He had a silver rod with which he prodded the servant. When the man slipped and fell in the water, young Regulus let out a cascade of nasty laughter, which his father echoed before turning back to me.

"Well, Gaius Pliny, what brings you to see me?" Regulus rested his hand on his belly.

"I've come to return your servant, the wet nurse you so graciously lent me." I took Merione's arm and brought her up beside me.

Regulus pursed his lips and examined Merione's bandage, turning her head so he could see it better. "You're returning damaged goods, it seems, Gaius Pliny." He addressed Merione. "What happened?"

"I slipped in the garden, my lord," Merione said. "It was dark, the stones were wet and I wasn't familiar with the place." That was the story we'd agreed on so she wouldn't have to explain how she'd failed in her mission to kidnap the baby—I still believed that was her assignment—and I wouldn't have to reveal that one of my servants had attacked her.

"Is the baby all right?" Regulus asked with some actual concern in his voice.

"The child is fine," I said.

"She hasn't run dry then?" Regulus pinched Merione's breasts, causing her to flinch. Instinctively she started to bring her hands up to protect herself, but Regulus slapped them away.

"No," I said. "Merione did her job admirably."

"Then why are you bringing her back? And why in person? Why not just send one of your servants?"

"I wanted to thank you in person, but also to tell you that I've decided I don't want a spy in my house."

Regulus chuckled and put a clammy hand on my shoulder. "We're surrounded by spies, Gaius Pliny. Why, every time I send old Nestor on an errand, I know the first place he stops is your house."

Nestor is Regulus' steward. He's Jewish, and his real name is Jacob, which is what I call him. We became acquainted several years ago, through our shared concern over Regulus' slave, the flute player Lorcis. Naomi and Phineas will have nothing to do with Jacob because he is some different sort of Jew—what's called a Christian. I'm not sure Regulus knows that, and I'm not quite sure of the full significance of the name, even though I've encountered a few of them recently. Whatever it means, Jacob is absolutely trustworthy. He's no spy of mine and has never told me anything incriminating about Regulus, but I'm not about to disabuse Regulus of the notion that he is a spy.

"So, how do you plan to feed the child?" Regulus asked.

"One of my servant women has found a nurse." When Malachi brought some men to take away Berenicianus' body, Naomi had asked him if he knew of anyone who could help us. Within the hour a woman who spoke only Hebrew was at my door. Naomi was convinced that the milk of a Jewish woman would nourish a circumcised baby better than "Gentile" milk. The child could also hear lullabies in his people's tongue.

"Very well, then," Regulus said. "I know you distrust me, Gaius Pliny. I hope for once you can accept that sending the wet nurse was simply an act of kindness."

I blinked but gave no other reaction.

"Do you think I'm entirely incapable of such a thing? Perhaps now you'll give me the benefit of the doubt."

Or perhaps you're trying to make me doubt my own opinion of you so that I'll be caught unawares in your next plot, I thought.

"May I offer you some refreshment? You must be tired after your long and arduous trek to the top of the hill." As thoroughly as I despise the man, I had to appreciate the sarcasm. I hadn't walked fifty paces. I managed to smile.

"No, thank you." Over my shoulder I noticed Jacob talking to my servants. It was not out of place for him to do so, but I turned back to face Regulus again, to distract him so he would not have further reason to suspect Jacob. "Do you have any idea of your losses in the warehouse?"

"I'm still figuring them up. Unlike yours, my warehouse was nearly full."

"Is that why you got an earlier warning than I did? Is it why the captain of the *vigiles* removed the dead man's signet ring and brought it to you?"

Regulus gave me his oiliest smile. "You're a man of the world, Gaius Pliny, though a young one. Surely you know how the *vigiles* work."

I knew perfectly well. Everyone in Rome expects to be paid over and above their salary just to do what they're paid to do, but I wanted to see if Regulus, while he was gloating, would let anything drop about Berenicianus or the signet ring that the captain of the *vigiles* had brought to him. "I thought they guarded our property, but I must be too naive."

"Well, they, like anyone else, appreciate some 'recognition' of their work. And those who give them more 'recognition' get more service. I've told them that I want to know of anything unusual or suspicious that happens around my property. A dead man wearing an equestrian stripe qualifies."

"May I see the ring? It might help to identify him. Since he was found in my warehouse, not yours, I think I have a right to know who he is." I didn't have to tell Regulus that I already knew his identity.

Regulus shook his head. "His ring won't help you. All it had on it was a couple of odd marks. In this case the 'recognition' wasn't any help."

"What's the going rate for 'recognition' these days?"

Regulus waved his bejeweled hand. As rich as he is, bribes must be of little concern to him, a minor cost of doing business. "I'm sure the captain will be happy to discuss the matter with you. Before you go there is one more matter I need to talk over with you."

I hadn't realized I was going. I guess he was being more polite than pointing me toward the door and giving me a push, but barely.

"What might that be?"

"We're planning the funeral for Lucullus. I assume you know that he is my wife's cousin and he was murdered a couple of days ago."

"By one of his servants, I've been told."

"As far as we know, yes. Since he only recently moved to Rome and bought that house, he does not have a large *clientela*—hardly any, in fact. It would be embarrassing for Sempronia and me if the turnout at his funeral was small. After all, he was a consul-designate and would have had Domitian as his colleague. I'm bringing my clients, and she will have hers there. Would you be willing to attend with as many of your people as you can muster? You can consider it a return on my favor of a wet nurse, even if she did not work out to your satisfaction. My intentions were honorable."

As my friend, the poet Martial, likes to say, every gift from a wealthy man has a hook hidden in it. I didn't see that I had any choice but to open my mouth and bite down.

"A consul-designate certainly deserves a respectable funeral," I said. "When will Lucullus' be held?"

"The pyre has been built in the Licinian Gardens—named for some distant relative of his—and covered to keep it dry. Lucullus' body is below ground here. It's the coolest place we know of. We hope the rain will let up enough by tomorrow to allow us to proceed. We don't want to just dump him in the Tiber. I will do the eulogy, of course."

"He didn't have a son?" Delivering the eulogy was usually the responsibility of the deceased man's son, if he was old enough. I had not been old enough to speak at my father's funeral, but I had delivered what I thought was a fine eulogy at my uncle's funeral.

"No," Regulus said. "He had very young children by his current wife. By an earlier wife he had a daughter, who must be about eighteen by now. But no one has seen her since her father was killed."

"Isn't anyone concerned about her?"

"From what I understand she's a very unpredictable person. She has a poor relationship, to say the least, with her stepmother. We believe she'll turn up when it suits her. So, may I count on you and your clients?"

"All right. I'll be there with my people."

"Thank you." He put a hand on my shoulder and did in fact turn me toward the door. "Now, I need to get back to my workmen. Good day, Gaius Pliny."

When we were out of sight of the house, I turned to my servants. "What was Jacob talking to you about?"

One of them handed me a piece of papyrus, folded and sealed. "He gave me this and asked me to give it to you once we were away from the house."

The wax seal lacked any insignia. I broke it and opened the note. Jacob had written, "The signet ring bore two Hebrew characters, *yodh* and *beth*, equivalent to *J* and *B* in Latin letters."

Perhaps I did have a spy in Regulus' house after all.

———

When I reached my house Tacitus was waiting in the garden, with a rolled-up scroll in his hand. I had sent him word, as I promised to do, when I found Aurora and the baby. On a bench beside the *piscina* the Hebrew woman was nursing the baby, with Naomi on one side of her and Aurora on the other. I had countermanded my mother's order and put Aurora in charge of the baby's care. Demetrius' daughters, Hashep and Dakla, sat on the ground in front of the bench, touching the baby's feet and cooing to him. As Tacitus and I approached them, Naomi and Aurora started to stand, but I motioned for them to remain seated.

"How is he doing?" I asked.

"He's well, my lord," Naomi said. "This is Miriam. She speaks no Greek or Latin, but she seems to have a plentiful supply for the little fellow."

Miriam must have recognized her name. She smiled and nodded, apparently not at all self-conscious. I nodded back to her.

"We've been thinking, my lord," Naomi said, "that the baby ought to have a name."

"That seems reasonable."

"'Lucius' and 'Publius' are common names in Rome," Tacitus said. "You don't have either in your house. Would one of those do?"

Naomi smiled at him the way one smiles at an impertinent child. "We think, my lord, that he ought to have a Hebrew name."

I sighed. "I see. Well, we already have Egyptian names"—I patted the girls on their heads—"and Hebrew names floating around here, so one more won't hurt, I guess. What did you have in mind?"

Naomi looked at the others, as if to be sure of their agreement, then said, "We like Joshua, my lord."

I pronounced the name a couple of times. "I don't particularly like it, but it doesn't matter to me, as long as the word has no political overtones—'death to the king,' anything like that."

Naomi put a hand on her heart. "Oh, certainly not, my lord. It's just an old and honorable name. It was my father's name."

"Very well, then. Joshua he shall be."

Naomi bowed her head. "Thank you, my lord."

As Tacitus and I turned away, he lowered his voice and said, "I warned you, Gaius Pliny. 'If you let them name that child,' I said, 'you'll never get rid of it.'"

"He's not an 'it,'" I snapped, though I feared his prediction might come true. "Now, what's in that scroll?"

"I had a scribe take down everything Josephus could tell me about Berenice and her family. It's a lot to sort through, with her various marriages. And he was quite certain she lived as a wife with her brother. No matter how many marriages were arranged for her, she always went back to her brother, if you understand me."

"I do, as revolting as that idea is. May I see this?"

Tacitus was about to hand me the scroll when I saw Thalia, the servant woman who was watching over the injured woman from my warehouse, approaching.

"My lord," she said, "I believe the woman is waking up. Her eyes are open. Do you want to see her?"

"By all means." Tacitus and I followed Thalia back to the room. Several lamps hung from a lamp tree, making the room reasonably bright.

The woman was still lying on her back, but her eyes were open and her head moved slowly from side to side. She gasped when she saw us.

"Who are you?" she asked slowly. "Where…where am I?"

"It's all right," I said, not standing too close to the bed. I didn't want to make her any more afraid than she already was. "My name is Gaius Pliny. You were in my warehouse when it collapsed. Now you're in my house. We're going to take care of you. You're safe now."

"What happened to the others?"

I sat down in the chair Thalia had been using and placed my hand on the woman's arm. Aurora had been accurate. The arm was one of the scrawniest I'd ever touched. "I'm afraid they were all killed when the building collapsed."

The woman let out a keening wail. "Oh, gods! No!"

When she was quiet again I asked, "What is your name?"

"My name is...Clymene." She raised her head off the pillow.

"Who were the people with you?"

"They were my father and his wife and my two brothers."

"You say your father's wife. Was she not your mother?"

"No, sir. My mother died some years ago. This wife was near my age. She was more like a sister to me than a stepmother." She laid her head back down, her breath coming in short, rapid gasps.

"We have some soup here. You need to eat."

"No meat, please. That's how I was raised."

"You spat out the broth we tried to feed you. This is lentil soup."

"Thank you, sir."

I stepped aside so Thalia could bring the bowl close to the bed and spoon-feed the poor woman.

After Clymene had swallowed a few spoonfuls Tacitus said, "Probably better not to give her too much at one time. I suspect she's not eaten in days. Her stomach may not be able to hold a full meal."

Thalia wiped Clymene's mouth and stepped back so I could sit by the bed again. "Can I ask you a few more questions? Then we'll let you eat a bit more and get some sleep, if that's what you need."

"Yes, sir. I'd like that."

"All right. What do you know about the baby we found in the warehouse? Whose was he?"

"Baby? What baby, sir?"

"You didn't see or hear a baby?"

"We didn't see one, sir. We heard what we thought were the squeaks of an animal, most likely rats. We just hoped they would stay away from us."

That wasn't an unreasonable assumption. "How did you come to be in my warehouse?"

"We were trying to find passage on a ship, sir."

"Passage to where?"

"Back to Spain, sir. That's where we came from."

"You didn't have any money on you when we found you."

"No, sir. We were robbed. My father and brothers hoped they could find work on a ship to pay our passage. That's why we were staying close to the docks, but we couldn't afford any place to stay, or anything to eat."

"Why were you in Rome?" Tacitus asked from behind me.

"Six months ago, sir, my uncle—my father's brother—wrote and said we should come here. There was more work here than in Cadiz. That's where we lived."

"What sort of work?" Tacitus asked. I let him take the lead while I studied the woman's facial expressions and the movements of her hands and body. Such things can often reveal how truthful a person is being when answering questions.

"My father is…was a fuller, sir." She wiped away tears. "My brothers worked with him."

"That confirms your deduction about the stains on their hands, from the dyes," Tacitus said, turning to me.

I nodded. I had never known a cloth-worker whose hands didn't immediately reveal his occupation. Nothing in Clymene's expression or movements made me suspect she was lying, but my experiences of the past few years have left me basically mistrustful of anything people tell me. "Would you like more to eat?"

"Yes, sir. Please."

Tacitus and I stepped back while Thalia gave Clymene a few more spoonfuls of soup. "Thank you," she said. "That tastes good." She laid her head back.

"Just a couple of more questions," I said. "Then we'll let you rest. Why were you trying to get back to Spain?"

"Nothing was going right, sir. The fullers' guild was demanding that my uncle pay more in dues because he had more people working with him. We had arguments with the guild leaders. My father was accustomed to running his own business without that sort of interference. We argued with my uncle. And Rome is such a big, ugly place. My father and my brothers finally decided they couldn't take it anymore. We all just wanted to go home. But with the rain and the river overflowing, we couldn't find a ship."

"The sailing season is about over," I said. "I doubt you'll find a ship sailing as far as Spain until next spring."

Clymene moaned. "We tried to stay near the river, just in case we could find a boat. Then, a few days ago, we were robbed."

"Could you tell anything about the men who robbed you?"

"No, sir. It was dark and raining hard. They were on us before we knew what was happening. After that, all we wanted was someplace that was dry so we could figure what to do. Maybe a place to die. The door to your warehouse was unlocked."

"Are you sure you didn't 'unlock' it?" Tacitus asked.

Clymene tried to raise her hand. "No, sir. I swear it. We were trying doors on several buildings and yours was the only one that wasn't locked. It seemed like a gift from the gods. At least we could get out of that accursed rain."

"Was the man with the stripe on his tunic someone you knew?"

"No, sir. We didn't realize he was there until the next morning. It was dark as the inside of a cave. We were so tired we just fell asleep. I could hardly stop shivering from being cold and wet. It wasn't until daylight that we saw that man on the other side of the building."

"What did you do when you saw him?"

"My father called to him, said we meant no harm. But he didn't move or say anything back. My father told my brothers to stay with his wife and me and he went over to the man. But he still didn't move. My father touched him and the man slumped over a little bit, but he didn't say anything. My father came back to us and said the man was dead."

"What did you do then?" I asked.

"My father wanted to dump him in the Tiber rather than give up the only dry place we'd been able to find. He said, if anyone found us there with him, they'd accuse us of killing him." She coughed. "My brothers refused to touch him. They said we should just leave."

"Did you move him or take anything from him?" Tacitus asked.

"No, sir. Not after that first time my father touched him and realized he was dead. We were still trying to convince my father that we should leave, but the building collapsed on us before we could get out."

I patted her arm. "We'll let you rest now."

"What are you going to do with me, sir?"

"We'll worry about that when you're feeling better."

When we were out of sight of her door Tacitus said, "You don't believe her, do you?"

"Is it that obvious?"

"You don't do a very good job of hiding what you're feeling, Gaius."

"Aurora tells me the same thing. No, I don't believe her. It's a very convoluted story, and she obviously isn't related to any of those people. Remember, they were all Eastern-looking, especially the one she calls her father. She's as Roman as you or I."

"But why would she be lying?"

"I don't know, but I'm sure she is."

———∽∾∽———

I held Joshua up to my shoulder, with my left arm under his tiny bottom and my right hand on his back supporting his head. After a long time at the wet nurse's breasts he seemed satisfied and content to sleep. In Hebrew, Naomi had explained to the nurse that, according to Gaius' order, I was to be in charge of caring for the baby, with whatever assistance I needed from the other women.

"I'll be glad to have the help," I said softly to him, "and you'll be glad of it, too, because I don't know anything about taking care of a baby. I would be more comfortable if you were a horse."

I had settled on the bench in Gaius' arbor, the quietest, most secluded place in the garden. Admittedly it was brazen of me to take that seat, but I had seen Gaius and Tacitus go into the room where the injured woman was waking up. I was tempted to follow them and listen to what was said, but that would have meant leaving Joshua with the other women, and I wasn't sure when I would get him back. Since Gaius had put me in charge of him, I wanted to assert myself right away. I was enjoying every sensation—his little body pressed to mine, his breath on my neck. I could have sat there for the rest of the day. I hadn't given him life, but I had saved his life. To that extent, he was mine.

Now Gaius and Tacitus came out of the woman's room, talked for a moment, and Tacitus handed Gaius a scroll. They clasped hands, and Tacitus summoned his servants and headed for the door. Gaius looked around until he saw me, then turned in my direction. As he drew nearer I prepared to stand, even though it might mean waking Joshua, but he motioned for me to remain seated. I was quite surprised when he sat down beside me, laying the scroll in his lap.

I slid over to make more room for him on the bench. "Forgive my impertinence," I said softly. "I know this is your—"

"What impertinence?" He kept his voice down, too. "This is the best

place in this entire garden to sit with a sleeping baby. You're just doing what I asked you to do."

We sat without saying anything for a few moments. I couldn't help but feel that this was what it would be like to be his wife. We could sit here, holding our first child. He might even put his arm around me, not worrying about who would see us....

I shook my head. I had to stop thinking like that. "What is that?" I asked.

Gaius unrolled the scroll. "It's a record of what Josephus told Tacitus about Berenice and her family. It's a complicated story. When I have time I'll sit down and puzzle it out. I'm hoping there might be a clue in here about who would want to kill Julius Berenicianus. For that matter, if we could just figure out what he was doing in Rome, in my warehouse, it might be a step toward a solution."

"What if he was the random victim of some thug or gang of thugs on the street? He was in a very dangerous part of Rome, you know."

"Then we'll probably never know who killed him. But we have to find out why he was in that area. I can't believe it was a random killing, not with the coins stuffed in his mouth."

"And why did he have a baby with him?"

"I'm not convinced he brought the baby. And I don't think he was killed in my warehouse."

"You could be right. There was no blood."

"At least not in the part of the building we saw before it fell into the Tiber."

"So you think he was killed somewhere else?"

Gaius nodded. "I do. Considering his wounds, there must have been a lot of blood."

"But why would someone put his body in your warehouse?"

"Either because it was the only unlocked door they could find or because they wanted to implicate me in the crime."

"And why was Joshua there?" I patted the baby's back as he stirred slightly, gave a sigh, and settled back down. "Did that woman's story tell you anything?"

Gaius shook his head. "Not much. If what she said is true, there's no connection between her and the people she calls her family and Berenicianus.

Apparently they just happened to end up in the same place because the door wasn't locked."

"But that sounds like a coincidence, and I know how you feel about coincidences."

Gaius grimaced. "For the first time, I may have to accept one. What I really don't understand is how the baby got there and why he was hidden away from everyone else. Because of the circumcision I have to think there's some connection between Berenicianus and...Joshua. But, if Berenicianus was in fact killed somewhere else, who brought this child into the warehouse?"

"Oh, that reminds me. When I stopped Merione from leaving, I accused her of taking the baby to Regulus. She said I was wrong. Regulus had no interest in him."

Gaius gave me a disappointed, almost accusatory, look. "I wish you had told me that before I took her back to Regulus. She said something of the same sort to me. If I had known she said it to you, too, I certainly would have questioned her more closely to see what she meant."

"I'm sorry, Gaius. Things were happening so fast and I was so distraught that I completely forgot what she'd said."

Gaius placed a hand on my leg, a gesture no one else could see. "It's all right. I know you were very upset." He patted Joshua again.

"Wouldn't you like to hold him?" One of the hardest things I had to learn about Latin is that questions can be asked in different ways, depending on the answer one expects. The way I phrased my question meant that I was telling Gaius to answer "yes."

"Ah, well, yes, I suppose so. Aren't you afraid he'll wake up?"

"His tummy is full. I expect him to sleep for quite a while. Naomi says that's mostly what babies do at this age as long as they're not hungry. Here, take him."

Joshua made no protest as I handed him over to Gaius, who held him out away from him at arm's length, as though he was holding a dangerous animal.

I suppressed a laugh. "Have you ever held a baby?"

"No, actually, I haven't. That's women's work. As Xenophon said in the Oeconomicus, the gods gave a greater share of concern for children to women than to men."

"But you don't believe in the gods," I said.

"Well, no—"

"Here. Hold him like this." I positioned Joshua against Gaius' chest and placed Gaius' hands under the baby and behind his head. Joshua's little hand reached up and came to rest on Gaius' chin.

"Don't you feel a kind of warmth between you and him?"

"I think that's because he just pissed on me." He handed the baby back to me.

I rearranged the cloth Joshua was wrapped in so that he settled in a dry spot. "I wonder if Merione was taking him so Regulus could pass him along to someone, or was she going to take him directly to someone else?"

Gaius reached over and patted Joshua's back and grew serious. "Regulus did show some concern about the baby's welfare, and the captain of the vigiles took Berenicianus' signet ring to him. Regulus clearly has some interest in this business, but I don't know what."

"Could Regulus have had Berenicianus killed? Maybe the captain took the ring as proof that the job had been done."

"I find that easy to believe," Gaius said with a snort. "But why? And where? Why would he have stuffed the coins in his mouth? None of this makes any sense."

"We need to start over," I said.

"What do you mean?"

"Let's go back to your warehouse, or what's left of it. We didn't have a chance to examine it as thoroughly as we should have. There was so much confusion."

Gaius nodded. "Berenicianus must have been killed somewhere in that area. No one would have carried a dead body any considerable distance in that weather. If we're going to start over, the first thing I want to know is where he was killed."

—◦◦◦—

I came out of my room wearing a clean, dry tunic and dropped the piss-stained one in a basket for the servants to launder. Across the garden, outside my mother's room, I saw Aurora handing Joshua over to Naomi and the Hebrew nurse. Even though it was her idea, I hadn't been sure if she would go with me back to the warehouse or if the lure of Joshua would keep her here. But she seemed to trust those women enough to leave the baby in their care. And her curiosity about an investigation can be as strong as my own.

"Are you going to send for Tacitus?" she asked as we left, with four slaves to accompany us. I had especially picked Archidamos, the largest and strongest of my servants, partly for protection and partly because we might need to move some of the debris from the building. Like most men of my class, I don't have a lot of male servants in my *familia urbana*, probably one male for every ten women. The men are needed to work on my rural estates, not to be sniffing around the women in the household. Some men of my class, I'm sorry to say, treat their household of female servants as a harem, like the ancient Persian kings one reads about in Herodotus.

"He and Julia are having guests for dinner," I said, switching to Greek since I knew none of these servants—not even the Greek-named Archidamos—could speak it. "Some friends of hers. I think he'll be too busy to poke around in ruins with us."

Aurora laughed and made the change to Greek, which would allow her to drop the "my lord" that she was sometimes careless about in Latin. "Oh, I suspect he would choose our company over Julia's friends any day."

"At one time you might have been right, but I think his attitude is different now." Julia is a year younger than Aurora. Tacitus married her when she was thirteen. When I first met him, on our way home from provincial service in Syria six years ago, he complained about her vapidness, even after a couple of years of marriage. Now she has grown up, and the miscarriage she suffered two years ago seems to have made her more thoughtful and mature. Aurora's injury and miscarriage last summer has created a bond between the two women that overcomes any distance their social status might otherwise impose.

"Besides," I said, "I don't think she'll give him any choice today. One of the guests, he told me, is another Julia."

"Oh, there are only a couple of thousand of those in Rome."

"Another...particular Julia."

Aurora considered that for a moment. "Titus' daughter?"

"None other. Domitian's niece. Oh, and by the way, his mistress."

"Well, I can't wait to hear Tacitus' account of *that* dinner."

"If he has any sense, it will be a very circumspect tale."

It was a relief to walk without rain drenching us. Because it was early afternoon, there weren't many people in the streets. Some probably were resting before going to the baths. Shops were closed. The streets of Rome are never quiet—not even at night—but at this time of day they can almost be called calm. We reached the river bank in about a quarter of an hour. The servants who were with me gasped when they saw the ruins of the warehouse.

"I had heard it was damaged, my lord," Archidamos said as we surveyed the exterior, "but 'destroyed' is a more accurate word. Are you going to try to rebuild?"

It was time to revert to Latin. "I don't think that will be possible. Even if I level what's left, the river bank has been eaten away so badly that I couldn't put up a building of any decent size. I hope I can sell the property to someone on either side of me. They'd be able to expand their buildings, and I could recoup a portion of what I've lost."

"That would mean selling to Regulus…my lord," Aurora said. She added the honorific with an extra breath, almost too late. I've told her often that, whatever our relationship, she *must* observe the proprieties in front of others. Maintaining discipline and respect among one's servants is crucial. If one servant violates a rule in front of the others and is not reprimanded, a man risks losing control of his entire household.

"Yes, I would hate to sell to Regulus, but he might be my only option."

"If he realizes that, my lord, I'm sure he'll insist on beating the price down."

"Whatever I lose will just have to be an investment in gaining my mother-in-law's good will."

As we talked I surveyed the small paved lane between my building and the one to the north of it. The lane was on my property.

"Are you looking for something in particular, my lord?" Archidamos asked from behind me.

"Yes, for blood."

Archidamos wrinkled his nose as though he smelled some. "Blood, my lord?"

"As I'm sure you know, there was a man found inside who had been stabbed."

"And had his mouth jammed full of coins, didn't he, my lord, and his lips sewed shut?"

I nodded and sighed. Those sensational details had probably been noised all over Rome by now. "Right now I'm concerned about the stab wounds. There was no bloodshed around his body. He must have been killed somewhere else, and I think not far away."

"Wouldn't the rain have washed away any blood by now, my lord?"

"You'd be surprised how stubborn blood can be," I said. "You think you've cleaned it up, but it gets into cracks and corners and you don't notice it unless you look very closely." I knelt near the base of the wall of my building. Even in daylight the shadows made it difficult to see every detail. "Someone bring me a lamp. There should be some right inside the door."

Aurora retrieved a lamp, lit it, and handed it to me. "You look like Diogenes," she said with a laugh.

To cover her omission of the honorific I quickly said to the other servants, "Diogenes was a Cynic philosopher from several hundred years ago. He once walked through the streets of Athens at midday holding a lamp. When someone asked him what he was looking for, he said, 'An honest man.'"

Archidamos furrowed his brow. His primary asset is his brawn, not his brain.

"He meant an honest man was so difficult to find," I said, "that you need extra light, even in the middle of the day."

"Oh, I see, my lord." He offered a perfunctory chuckle.

"And blood is hard enough to spot that you need some extra light." I pointed to a rusty brown spot right at the base of the wall. "But there it is."

Between the paving stones and the wall of my building ran a narrow strip of dirt and grass, the width of my thumb from the knuckle to the tip. The blood had soaked into the dirt but was still visible on the blades of grass.

"Is that blood, my lord?" Archidamos peered over my shoulder. "It's not red."

Unless they work in the kitchen, servants in an urban household don't see as much bloodshed as do those on a rural estate. If they see games in the arena—which I discourage in my household—the blood they see is fresh and red. "Blood turns brown when it dries," Aurora said as she knelt beside me. I hoped everyone assumed she was addressing Archidamos.

I moved the lamp along the base of the building. "There's a line of blood here. There must have been quite a bit for it to have left this much when the rain washed it off the paving stones." I surveyed the passageway, assuring myself. "This is where Julius Berenicianus was killed."

"And then someone carried him into the warehouse, my lord," Aurora said, "and stitched up his mouth?"

"I believe so. That must have taken a little time, so they would have needed a place where no one would see them." We stepped into the warehouse, with the other servants following us.

Aurora walked over to the spot where we had found Berenicianus. "And they must have brought the coins, the needle, and the thread with them, my lord."

I nodded. "That wasn't something they would decide to do on the spur of the moment."

"But why, my lord? It's so bizarre."

"The fact that it is so bizarre might be the best clue we have. It's not something that just anyone would do."

We spent over an hour sorting through the debris but found nothing except a sandal which might have belonged to one of the dead men. Archidamos moved the largest pieces of the beams that had fallen to the floor. The other servants helped him toss them into the river.

"My lord," Archidamos said as he took a moment to rest. "I believe somebody has already been in here."

"What makes you think that?"

"The way some of this stuff is stacked, my lord. It couldn't have fallen like that." He pointed to a pile of stones near the bank of the Tiber.

"This is pointless then," I finally said. "If there was anything here, someone has already taken it." I sighed and took one last look around the ruins. "Let's go home."

I had just stepped out the door when I met a woman coming toward me, accompanied by half a dozen men dressed in Eastern fashion, with embroidered robes and headgear. I couldn't tell at a glance whether they were slaves or retainers. "Are you Gaius Pliny?" she asked.

"Yes, I am."

"I inquired at your home and was told that I might find you here." She raised her head slightly. "I'm Julia Berenice."

VII

I HAD NO IDEA WHAT TO SAY, so I just sputtered, "Julia…
Ber…Berenice?"

"Yes."

"The mother of—"

"The mother of the man who, I understand, was found dead in
your warehouse."

The woman standing before me appeared to be about fifty and quite
impressive. She was above average height and wore a green *stola* and a
white cloak with a green fringe. Her hair and the lower half of her face
were covered by a light veil, but she countered that bit of modesty with
a gold necklace and several gold bracelets. The only thing amiss about
her was the small mole above the corner of her left eye, just below her
eyebrow. Her dress was not quite that of a grieving mother, but her
demeanor was subdued, in spite of an arrogance that seemed to be the
result of a long habit. Tacitus had called her striking instead of beautiful. Given how little of her face I could see, I could neither concur with
nor dispute his assessment.

"What can I do for you, my lady?" I asked when I recovered from
my surprise.

"My friend Sempronia tells me you have a knack for ferreting out
the truth."

My friend Sempronia? Those three words instantly put me on alert.
Anyone who counts Regulus' wife among her friends is someone to be
wary of. Just then Aurora stepped through the door and stood slightly
behind me. Berenice cocked her head but kept her eyes focused on me.

"What sort of truth do you want me to ferret out?" I asked.

Berenice wrapped her cloak more closely around her as a breeze picked up off the river. "I'm sure you can understand that I want to know who killed my son. Since he was found in your warehouse, I assume you have an interest in finding his killer as well before the blame falls on you."

I knew I was innocent, but in Rome that doesn't count for much. To prove my innocence I had to prove someone else guilty. "I certainly do want to find his killer, but I'm not sure how to go about it. We've just been through the building again, and we have no clues."

"What about the coins you found in his mouth?" She spoke matter-of-factly, without any break in her voice or other signs of the grief I would expect a mother to display when talking about the recent and violent death of her son. "They would seem to be a most salient clue."

"How do you know about the coins?"

Berenice reached out and patted my arm. "Why, Gaius Pliny, Sempronia's tentacles reach far and deep."

"And all this time I thought it was Regulus I needed to be concerned about."

Berenice laughed softly. "Sempronia's spies even spy on Regulus' spies. And, because they're women, you men never notice them." Her voice turned somber again. "Can you help me? *Will* you help me?"

"I hope we can help each other. Neither of us can solve this alone. Let's find a place where we can talk. Would you like to come to my house? We would be more comfortable there."

Berenice shook her head. "I would be seen by too many people and you would have to explain who I am." She adjusted the veil so that I could see only the bridge of her nose, her eyes and her forehead. "The Portico of Octavia isn't far from here. We have enough servants with us that we should be able to find a quiet corner."

Augustus built a portico to honor his sister, next to the theater named for her son Marcellus. During our short walk there Berenice told me that she was living on the Caelian Hill, in an *insula* owned by Sempronia. She and her household occupied the entire second floor. "It's no palace, but it's comfortable enough."

"I had the impression," I said, "that you…left Rome."

"You mean that Titus sent me away."

"Well, yes." I was trying to be diplomatic, but she was so forthright, almost brusque, that she made it difficult.

"He made a show of it, and I added buckets of tears, but 'away' wasn't very far. I moved into the quarters where I am now, behind the Temple of Juno Lucina, with a dozen servants so that we could remain close. Titus came to see me, at night and in disguise. Now I fill my time writing my memoirs. That seems to be what royal women do in their old age."

The Temple of Juno Lucina sits on the Esquiline, only a short walk from my house. "You must feel like an exile. How are your needs being met?"

"I've always had considerable means. Titus gave me even more before he died, a return on what I gave him and Vespasian when they were fighting for power. There is a small bath house on the ground floor of the building, and enough *taberna*s and shops of various kinds nearby. With Sempronia's help I'm able to remain out of public view. At this point in my life that's all I want."

We had reached the Portico of Octavia. Its colonnaded walls surround a generous open space with two modest temples—one to Jupiter Stator and one to Juno Regina—in the center. In the year after the eruption of Vesuvius the structure was damaged by a fire, another supposed omen of the gods' displeasure with Titus due to his relationship with Berenice. He who had been called "the darling of the gods" presided over more disasters in his short time in power than many long-lived rulers.

Titus died soon after that fire, and Domitian repaired the damage to the portico, rededicating it as though he was a descendant of Augustus. From the day they seized power, Vespasian and his sons have been keenly aware of their lack of a connection to our first *princeps*. They've added "Caesar" to their names but cannot infuse his blood into their veins. That hasn't stopped them from adopting various ruses to create the impression that they belong. Titus buried Vespasian in the mausoleum Augustus built for himself and his family. Domitian took his current wife, Domitia Longina, from another man because she is a fifth-generation direct descendant of Augustus. That will give his children at least a dollop of Augustus' blood.

The portico has two entrances, on its north and south sides, each featuring six columns in the Corinthian style. The interior walls are decorated with frescoes which my uncle described in some detail in his *Natural History*. As is always true of any space like this in the city, the portico sheltered knots of people here and there. For some of them, I knew, this was home. Food vendors and prostitutes moved from group to group, offering their various wares, some of which were being enjoyed right on the spot.

We found a bench in an unoccupied corner and our servants established a cordon around us. With the solid wall behind us, I felt reasonably secure from prying eyes and ears. Still, Berenice and I lowered our voices, and she kept her face veiled.

A particularly stubborn sausage seller was hawking his wares under my servants' noses. I motioned to Archidamos, who was carrying my money pouch. "Get everyone something to eat and then send that fellow packing."

While Archidamos took care of that task I resolved to establish some basic facts. It would have been helpful to have Tacitus here to make notes, as he often does, or help me remember what we heard. Even his sometimes sardonic questions could illuminate a point I might have missed. "Your son was wearing a tunic with an equestrian stripe on it when we found him." I decided not to mention that the killer had torn the stripe into shreds. "Was he an equestrian?"

Berenice nodded. "Titus gave him that honor, at my request. It's amazing what a man will grant you when you're...well, I'll leave that to your imagination."

I decided to ignore the provocation in her eyes. The mole, which might once have been considered a beauty mark, now served more as a distraction. "How old was your son?"

"Let's see. He was born when I was sixteen. That would make him thirty-five. And don't you dare do the sums in your head."

"I've never been good at mathematics." That made her eyes twinkle. "Did your son live with you?"

"Only recently." She adjusted the folds in her gown. "He had been living in Chalcis, where he was born and where his father's family live."

"Chalcis? That's north of Judaea, isn't it?" I vaguely recalled the name from the year I served as a tribune in Syria. It was a patch of sand, indistinguishable from all the other patches of sand in that desolate part of the empire.

"Yes. And, before you have to ask, his father is my late uncle, to whom I was married at the time." She looked down and then back up at me. "We haven't been the only ones, you know. Claudius married his niece, Agrippina, and Domitian is having an affair with his brother's daughter. It's a kind of royal prerogative, I guess."

"The *princeps* is not our king."

She patted my knee. "You just keep telling yourself that, dear. Besides, a king with his niece isn't the same as a man having an affair with one of his slaves."

She glanced at Aurora, who was standing next to the wall, at the end of our protective line of servants, finishing the sausage Archidamos had purchased and wiping her fingers on her gown. Even I had to admit she did not look her loveliest at that moment. I couldn't tell if Berenice was smiling behind her veil, but it sounded like she was, if one can hear a smile.

"Are you implying something?" I asked.

"I don't have to imply, do I? She's the only female in the group of servants you brought with you, your beautiful 'goddess of the dawn.' That implies that she has...some standing in your eyes."

The fact that she knew who Aurora was made me extremely uncomfortable. Someone was talking about us. Someone in my household? A spy of Regulus? Of Sempronia? I shifted in my seat to block her view. "Let's stick to the question of your son's murder. You said he had been living with you only recently."

"That's right. I hadn't seen him in five years and then he turned up here in Rome about a month ago."

"Do you know why he came to Rome at this time?"

"He said it wasn't safe for him to live in Chalcis any longer."

"Why not?"

"He wouldn't tell me. The more I knew, he said, the more dangerous it would be for me."

—◦◦◦—

We left through the south entrance of the portico and were skirting the south side of the Palatine on our way home. Domitian's construction project on the top of the hill loomed over us just as he himself threatens to overwhelm everything below and around him. He has already pushed everyone else off the top of the hill, but he just keeps building.

"Why didn't you ask her about Joshua?" I asked Gaius in Greek.

"I was waiting to see if she mentioned him," Gaius said. "When she didn't, I felt like something was off, the way you get that first whiff of what might be bad meat and you have to decide whether it's the meat or your nose. So I decided to keep it to myself, as a kind of test."

"But she must know about the baby. She knew about the coins in her son's mouth."

"If he was her son."

I looked at him in surprise. "What do you mean?"

"Are we certain that was Berenice I was talking to? She was veiled the entire time. All I saw were her eyes and the bridge of her nose."

"And that mole." I shuddered. "You couldn't miss that."

Gaius chuckled. "I think that was once considered a beauty spot. But when it's the only thing you can see, it doesn't have quite that effect, does it? I just wonder, do we really know who she was? Anybody in Rome that you've never seen before can walk up to you and say 'I'm So-and-So.' How do we prove it?"

"By a signet ring?"

"Pssht." Gaius waved a dismissive hand. "Anybody can buy a ring. Or steal one."

"Whoever she was, she knew about the coins. She must have heard that from someone in our house."

Gaius put his face close to my ear. "And she knows who you are, my goddess of the dawn."

I blushed. "I must admit I rather liked that."

"But did she hear it from someone in our house?"

"For all we know, she could have heard it from Livia, or someone that Livia talked to."

"Livia's not supposed to say anything about us or against you. That was our agreement."

I snorted. "Hah! Do you really expect Livia to—"

"I'll deal with Livia," Gaius snapped. "She's not the problem right now. What we need to figure out is why Berenice—and for now I'll assume that's who she was—did not say anything about that baby. You're right. If she knew about the coins, she has to have known about the baby."

Just talking about Joshua made me ache to get home and hold him again. I tried to walk a little faster, but the crowd was too heavy. "She said her son came to Rome about a month ago, didn't she? And Joshua was born about a month ago. That would mean Berenicianus and the boy's mother traveled a long distance just before he was born. That would have been dangerous for the mother and the baby."

Gaius nodded. "But what if she and Berenicianus came to Rome much earlier and he didn't reveal himself to his mother until a month ago?"

"Why wait?"

"So he could make arrangements for the child and his mother—insure their safety."

"But he couldn't insure his own safety. And we don't know what has happened to the mother."

Gaius fell silent as we started up the Esquiline. Halfway up the hill, as we passed the Iseum, he said, "We've been assuming he was Berenicianus' son, but that may not be the case."

"Then whose child could he be?" If he wasn't Berenice's grandson, there was a chance he might stay in Gaius' house, a chance that he might be mine. My heart leapt.

"I'm just trying to look at the question from all angles." Gaius gestured as though pointing to different places. "I suppose there has to be a connection to Berenicianus. A circumcised male infant is found a few feet away from a circumcised adult male—how could there not be a connection? I just don't know what it is."

"You mentioned how difficult it is to identify a person. It's even harder to know who a child belongs to. There might be some resemblance to a parent—big ears, hair color—but they're not irrefutable proof. People with brown eyes can have a child with blue ones."

"And circumcision is certainly not something a boy inherits from his parents," Gaius said.

"And there are so many other factors to consider," I said. "Stabbing some-one in the back—literally or metaphorically—isn't so unusual in Rome. But why the coins stuffed in his mouth? That took a lot of planning, and it must have some significance."

"But for whom?" Gaius slapped his hands on his knees in frustration. "Berenice said she didn't know what it means."

"Or she just doesn't want you to know what it means," I said.

"She asked for my help. I can't help her if she won't tell me what's going on."

I brushed Gaius' hand. It's so frustrating not to be able to touch him in public. "That woman frightens me. I wish you didn't have to get involved in this business. You heard her say she's a friend of Sempronia's."

Gaius squeezed my hand and quickly released it. "And knowing that makes me extremely cautious about dealing with her. But a dead man was found in my warehouse. Regulus could spin that single fact into a web of lies that might convict me in court."

Tacitus popped another grape into his mouth and swirled some well-watered wine in his cup. He was still a little bleary-eyed after his wife's dinner party the previous evening. Domitian's lover (and niece) enjoyed her wine, he said, and expected those dining with her to share her enthusiasm. Though not a queen or princess, she lorded it over everyone around her.

"I guess most of us would act like that," I said, "if our face had appeared on a coin, and on the front of the coin, no less."

We were sitting around a table in my library, with only a few lamps lit, at Tacitus' request, talking softly, also at Tacitus' request. He had promised to regale us with an account of the dinner when he felt bet-ter. I had related my conversation with Berenice to him almost word for word. Aurora, sitting beside me, had filled in at a couple of points.

"You say she was veiled? All you could see was her eyes?" Tacitus belched.

Aurora laughed. "And an ugly mole." I joined her.

"Just below her left eyebrow?"

We stopped laughing and nodded.

"That's Berenice, no doubt of it. When she was living with Titus, some women in Rome stuck fake moles in that spot. Damn things would fall off at the most inopportune times. You go to dip your wine cup in the mixing bowl at dinner and there's this little black blob floating in it. Do you remember that, Gaius Pliny?"

I shook my head. "I was living with my uncle and my mother at Misenum at the time. The fad didn't extend that far."

"Maybe this woman's mole was fake," Aurora said.

Tacitus shook his head, a gesture that made him wince. "It was a short-lived fad. When Titus sent Berenice away, all those fake moles dropped off overnight. If she's got one, it's the real thing."

So a couple of things were settled, because of a signet ring and a mole. "All we're certain of so far," I said, "is that the woman I talked to was Berenice and the dead man was Berenicianus. I have no idea how we're going to figure out who killed him."

Tacitus poured himself a little more wine and a good bit more water. "It seems to me that we're stumbling around in the dark if we start with the question of who killed Berenicianus. It could have been any man—or woman—in Rome. The coins in his mouth are the unique element in this case. If we can decipher the meaning of those coins in his mouth, we might be able to find someone who would have had a reason to put them there. That will be the killer."

I slapped the table, causing Tacitus to put his hand to his head. "You're brilliant," I said.

"How can I be when my head is throbbing like this?"

"Didn't Phineas say something the other day about a passage in the Jews' holy books that required thirty pieces of silver to be paid if an ox gores somebody's slave?"

"Yes, he did," Tacitus said. "But I still don't see how that can have anything to do with this murder. Was somebody paying the money to Berenicianus? Or is this some sort of allegory? If so, who's the slave? The Jews' holy books look like a dead end to me."

"Maybe not," Aurora said, "if we look in the right place. Naomi says there's another passage where a prophet asks to be paid what he's worth. He receives thirty pieces of silver, which he calls 'a handsome sum.' But it's all sarcasm."

Tacitus and I sat up straighter and turned toward Aurora, who drew back as though she was sorry she had said anything.

"Did Naomi say where that passage is found?" I asked.

"Just in the book of one of their prophets. I...I don't remember which one. Their names are so strange, you know."

"Would you go get her and ask her to come in here? I want to know more about this."

While Aurora was gone I poured myself some wine, not as diluted as what Tacitus was drinking, and broke off some bread from the loaf in the center of the table. "I take it the dinner last night was rowdier than yours usually are."

Tacitus sighed heavily. "I hope I can keep the story straight. I'm still hungover and both women are named Julia. By the gods, we need a better way to name our women. Titus' daughter calls herself Julia Flavia, so, for the sake of my convenience as well as yours, I'm going to call her that. She insists on Julia Flavia, but it's just too damn cumbersome."

"Very well, she's Flavia. That should clear up the confusion," I said.

"All right then. In the past Julia, my wife, has wanted to be part of the elite social set of Rome. It's difficult for her now because Domitian hates Julius Agricola so much. She has been cultivating Flavia as a friend for some time. She thought herself fortunate that Flavia seemed to like her. Last night she realized that the girl has been playing up to her, merely to annoy Domitian. 'He's not in love with me,' Flavia said. 'I know that. He hated my father, so coupling with me,' and she used a truly vulgar term for the act, 'is just a way to humiliate my father's memory.'"

I winced. "For her to say something like that in front of people, she must have been well into her cups."

"Oh, the girl could drink most men under the table. It was sad, really, to see how unhappy she is. Now this you will not believe"—he leaned toward me and I could smell the wine on his breath—"Flavia predicted that she would be dead within a year. 'And no matter what you hear,' she said, 'it won't be a natural or accidental death.'"

"By the gods! She's accusing Domitian of murdering her before the fact."

"My thoughts exactly. And in front of six other guests and several dozen servants. We were all terrified at what we were hearing. My wife couldn't wait for the dinner to end and for Flavia's servants to scrape her off the couch and carry her home. I'm sure Aurora will hear about this from my Julia. At least it has put an end to her social ambitions. She was even more disgusted than I was."

When I heard a soft tap on the door I expected Aurora and Naomi to enter the library. Tacitus and I both scrambled to our feet when my mother came in, followed by the other two women. Mother sat down and motioned for Naomi to sit beside her. Because of her age and her status as my mother's best friend, Naomi does not consider it disrespectful to sit in my presence. Except for Aurora, my other servants are uncomfortable doing that, and I don't think it's a bad thing. This time, though, Aurora remained standing behind them.

"Why did you ask to see Naomi?" Mother said.

From Aurora's expression and the few words she was mouthing, I gathered that she had found the two of them together—as was inevitable—and hadn't dared to tell my mother that her presence wasn't required or requested.

Tacitus and I sat down across the table from them. "I just wanted to clarify something she told me earlier," I began.

"About what?" Mother's tone was surprisingly adversarial. Some days lately she can snap without any warning, like a dog that has always been friendly in the past but has developed a nasty streak. I suspect it's because she's afraid of dying.

I turned to face Naomi. "You mentioned something in your holy books about a man being paid thirty pieces of silver because that was what he was worth. Where did you read that and what does it mean?"

Before Naomi could answer, Mother leaned toward her. "Does this have anything to do with that poor man who had the coins stuffed in his mouth?"

"That's what I'm trying to determine. Now, will you please let Naomi answer—"

"I can answer it."

"How—"

"I asked Phineas about it yesterday. He showed us the book. It's about a prophet named Zechariah."

"How many of my scrolls has Phineas used in copying—"

"I bought the scrolls from my own funds. We borrowed the books from Malachi, and I paid Phineas to copy them. He worked on them only at times when you had not given him anything to do."

I know I have no control over how she spends the money she inherited from my father and my uncle, but I had no idea she was compiling her own library. "Why, Mother?"

She sat up straight. "Because they're interesting and give me some comfort, like your books of philosophy and poetry."

"But you can't read Hebrew."

"The books have been translated into Greek."

"Where are they?"

"I keep them in my room."

From time to time I search my servants' rooms. Every master has to, and I'm always surprised at some of the things I find. It had never occurred to me that I might need to search my mother's room. "So this Zechariah"—I felt like I was spraying all over the table—"this Zechariah, what exactly does he say about the coins?"

"I don't really understand all of it." Mother squirmed in her seat. "But the prophet is told by his god to act as a shepherd to his people. He's given his payment—thirty silver coins. What are they called, Naomi?"

"In Hebrew they're *shekels*, my lady, something like a *denarius*. I think that what matters, though, is that they're silver and there are thirty of them."

"And it's considered an insulting wage," Mother added.

"Have someone bring that book to me," I said. As Mother and Naomi stood to leave, I asked, "How many of these books do you have?"

"About a dozen scrolls," Mother said. "Zechariah's book is on a scroll with some other short books."

"We call it the book of the twelve, my lord," Naomi said.

Tacitus cleared his throat. He'd been sitting so quietly, his head in his hands, that I wasn't sure he was awake. "I suspect their brevity will be their only virtue," he muttered.

—⟨⟨⟨⟩—

Tacitus called for his litter-bearers. The fact that he had ridden over here instead of walking was a sure sign of how hungover he was. Aurora and I walked with him to the street. He assured us that he and Julia would be back for dinner that evening.

"It will be a much calmer affair, I promise you," I said as he settled onto the cushions.

"Julia and I will both appreciate that. And she'll have a full report on our dinner last night."

Aurora and I returned to the library to find Phineas laying out scrolls on one of the tables and lighting a few more lamps. "Your mother said you wanted to see some of our holy books, my lord. This is the scroll containing the book of Zechariah. I've opened it to the passage about the thirty pieces of silver. This"—he pointed to the scroll next to it—"is a collection of songs and poems. Some of them were written by our King David, over a thousand years ago."

"That long ago? Are you sure? That would make them older than Rome."

"Yes, my lord. David lived in a palace in Jerusalem when Rome was a collection of mud huts."

I ignored the remark. As long as Phineas keeps his resentment of Rome within bounds, I don't object to every jibe. When we sat down and began looking over the scrolls, he rubbed his hands together nervously, like a woman watching someone touch her infant.

"You did a nice job," I said. "The letters seem a bit large, though."

"Your mother is beginning to have some trouble reading normal-sized script, my lord."

Now I remembered that.

"All right. We'll call you if we need for you to explain anything," I said.

Phineas stepped back from the table. "I was wondering, my lord, if I might go down to my synagogue. I need to return a couple of scrolls that I'm finished with and ask to borrow some more."

"Go ahead," I said.

When we were alone, Aurora and I moved closer together on

the bench. I took her right hand in my left. With our free hands we unrolled the scroll and she began reading at the point where the prophet demanded his payment for being a shepherd.

> *"I became shepherd of the flock marked to be slaughtered.... I tended the flock."*

"What on earth does that mean?" I said.

"Maybe we'll understand better if we read a little more," Aurora suggested.

> *"Three shepherds I destroyed in one month. But I became angry with them, and they hated me."*

After a few more lines I stopped her. "Does any of that make sense to you?"

She shook her head. "No more sense than the Sibylline Oracles. It could mean anything, or nothing. Who are the three shepherds?"

"Where does it mention the money?"

We looked further down the page and found the reference to the thirty silver coins, the "handsome sum."

"All I can make of it," Aurora said, "is that Berenicianus might have been in charge of some group—tending the flock—and someone became angry with him."

"But why?"

"I don't know. Because he didn't do a good enough job?"

"What about the other one, the collection of poems? While we've got them, let's have a look. I'd like to know what my mother finds so appealing about this stuff."

The first of the poems depicted the happy state of a man who obeyed the laws of the Jews' god compared to a man who refused to do so.

"Not all that different from some of our philosophers," I said.

We skimmed through the scroll. The poems celebrated victories, mourned defeats, and called upon the poet's god to rescue him. One compared the god to a shepherd who leads the poet beside quiet waters.

"I could see how that would have a certain appeal to my mother. That lump she found in her breast casts a shadow over the whole house."

"You can't talk to her and tell her you know?"

"How do you tell someone you know she's dying?"

"Well, just treasure the time you have with her. My mother's illness came on so quickly I had no time to get ready for it."

"And you were so young."

Aurora shook her head. "I don't want to go back to all that. Let's concentrate on this." After she had read another dozen or so of the poems, we stopped. "Not anything like Ovid or Horace, is it?" she said.

"No. I don't see how it gets us any closer to understanding what happened to Berenicianus. Like Tacitus said, these books seem to be a dead end." But I could have sat next to Aurora, holding her hand and listening to her warm, golden voice, for the rest of the day.

We heard a knock on the library door. I kissed her hand and we moved slightly apart as Phineas entered the room, carrying two more scrolls.

"Excuse me, my lord."

"It's all right. I think we've read enough. You may take these back to my mother."

"Yes, my lord." He placed the new scrolls on a shelf. "I have a message for you, from Malachi."

"From Malachi?"

"Yes, my lord. He's asking you to come to the synagogue. He's been thinking about Berenicianus' death and wants to discuss it further."

"Why can't he come here?" I did not like the idea of going into the Subura.

"He feels polluted when he goes into the house of a Gentile. He's not sure what he can touch or eat or sit on. He had to go through a ritual to purify himself after coming into contact with a dead body the last time he was here."

"He never touched the man."

"But he got too close to him. He felt…polluted."

"Do you feel polluted?"

Phineas began to stutter, as he does when he's nervous. "No, my... my lord. My mother and I ac...accept our situation, and our law allows us to accommodate ourselves to situations we can't control. With the lady Plinia's permission we're able to do what we need to do to stay within the limits of our law."

I wasn't going to pursue that topic at the moment, but I would certainly ask Mother what it meant for them to stay within the limits of their law. What were they doing or not doing that I should know about? "When does Malachi want me to come down there?"

"Your mother, my mother, and I will be going to the synagogue this evening, my lord, for a regular time of worship. Perhaps you could accompany us and talk with Malachi afterwards. All he asks is that you not bring a large group of servants or clients with you."

"Have you forgotten what happened the last time I got anywhere near that place?"

"The people who threatened you were not Jews, my lord. We're not the only ones who live in the Subura. You ran into danger because of the large *clientela* you had with you and the stripe on your toga."

"Are you about to suggest that I wear a toga without the stripe?"

"Yes, my lord, I am. In fact, if you were to dispense with the toga altogether, it would make you much safer. You would appear to be just another citizen, in a tunic without a stripe, not worth robbing."

"*Hmmph!* I'll have to think about that. When will you be leaving?"

"About half an hour before sunset, my lord."

When Tacitus and Julia arrived for dinner, we gathered in the *exhedra* and I told them about Malachi's invitation. Julia voiced strong objections to the plan. "It sounds like a trap. You're being asked to go into the most dangerous district of Rome without your *clientela* and to remove your stripe. Those are the two most important elements that protect you when you walk through the streets of this godforsaken city."

"They didn't do me much good the last time I ventured into the Subura."

"Yes. Tacitus told me about that."

"Malachi and his synagogue saved me on that occasion. I find the man honorable, if abrasive."

"You might be abrasive, too, Gaius," Aurora said, "if the situation were reversed and you were living in the land of your conquerors." Julia gasped softly. Even as good a friend as she is to Aurora, she is still sometimes shocked by her effrontery.

"You're determined to do this, aren't you?" Tacitus said.

"If someone wants to talk about Berenicianus' death but doesn't want to come here, then I'll go wherever I need to, even if I have to go alone."

"I'm going with you," Tacitus said. Aurora and Julia quickly agreed.

Aurora did not surprise me, but Julia did. "Are you sure?" I asked her.

"Well, your mother's not afraid to go down there. Besides, they may need someone to identify the bodies."

VIII

TACITUS AND I put on oversized, unmarked tunics, loose enough to conceal the short swords we would carry beneath our clothes. As we walked down to the synagogue Phineas explained that women sit on one side and men on the other. "I hope that doesn't make any of you uncomfortable, my lord."

I knew he was talking about Aurora and me.

"It doesn't matter," I said. "I'm not going in. There's a *taberna* across the street, isn't there? I've heard Mother mention it."

"Yes, my lord. I'll speak to the owner and ask him to take care of you."

"He's a very nice man," Mother said. "His name is Callicles. We've eaten there. He's not a Jew."

As we walked down the Esquiline, following the street called the Argiletum into the Subura, I tried to imagine my mother eating with slaves and Jews in a *taberna* in the worst section of Rome. It seems to me the natural order of things that children grow up and develop into adults who are different from their parents. But my mother was growing away from me.

Phineas did as he had promised when we arrived, and the owner of the *taberna* gave us a table where we could watch the entrance to the synagogue.

"Are there always squads of *vigiles* on patrol?" I asked as he seated the four of us and made a perfunctory swipe at the table. A unit of six watchmen was keeping an eye on the crowd.

Callicles, whose face was marked by the scars of a childhood disease, draped the rag over his shoulder. "They always have someone here when the Jews are worshipping in the synagogue like this. The group called Christians insists on coming when they're not welcome. When Claudius was *princeps* he drove all the Jews out of Rome because the Christians were creating such disturbances in the synagogues. Now the Jews are back, and so are the Christians."

"Are you one of them?" Tacitus asked. "One of either?"

"No, sir. I prefer to see what I'm worshipping."

I turned my attention to the street. Naomi and my mother chatted with other women on the steps of the synagogue. Several of them appeared to be Greek or Roman, judging from their blond or light brown hair. My mother apparently wasn't the only "god-fearer" among the women of Rome. None of these women was dressed lavishly. Phineas had told me that their tradition forbade excessive display of clothing or jewelry in the synagogue.

Watching Mother talk with the other women, I thought she seemed more...vibrant. She smiled more than I was accustomed to seeing. I seemed to learn something new about her every day, and I had no idea how much some things in her life meant to her. I watched her pull a veil up over her head as she went in with the group of women. A frightening feeling rushed over me, the feeling that I was losing her, that she was walking into some other world where I could not follow.

"It's certainly not an impressive temple," Julia said.

"It's not a temple," I corrected her. "As Phineas would be quick to tell you, the Jews had only one temple, which Titus destroyed at the end of the war, fifteen years ago."

"Then what is this?"

"As best I can understand, a synagogue is a kind of lecture hall or school. They read and discuss their holy books, sing and pray."

The synagogue was a two-story building, unadorned on the exterior, except for the plaster covering the stonework and some sconces for torches. People in the neighborhood must have respected the place, or had some superstitious fear of it. There were no graffiti on the walls and no evidence of frequent cleaning and repainting, which one finds on many buildings in Rome. Having been inside the synagogue once, I knew it must have originally been a market building, open on the first floor for merchants' stalls, with rooms on the second floor. Each upper room opened onto a small balcony.

Aurora nudged me. "Gaius, isn't that Berenice?"

I looked where she was pointing and spotted Berenice, dressed much more plainly than the last time I saw her, going into the synagogue with only two of her male attendants. As she approached the steps, her face was turned so that we could see the left side, with the identifying mole.

We ordered some food and settled down to wait. The food was surprisingly good—baked fish with leeks, a decent wine, and honeyed dates. As the time passed, though, I couldn't keep my mind off what was going on in the synagogue. Perhaps I should have gone in and observed their worship. It might help me understand what my mother was thinking.

Darkness, deepened by the narrowness of the street and the height of the surrounding buildings, had set in and torches were appearing here and there when the crowd emerged from the synagogue. Men and women begin mingling, regrouping in the narrow street.

"I didn't realize there were that many Jews in Rome," Julia said.

"They're not all Jews, my lady," Callicles said as he cleared our plates. "The beggars and hangers-on flock here. People seem to be in a generous mood when they come out."

"I believe I saw Berenice in that direction," I said. "Let's see if we can find her before the crowd gets too heavy. There are still some things I want to ask her about." I left money on the table and we started out the door.

"What about your mother?" Tacitus asked.

"I think Phineas and the servants with them can get her home safely. They always have before."

Tacitus, who is a head taller than I am and taller than many men in Rome, said, "You're right. I just saw them on the edge of the crowd. They're walking with some other women and their attendants. They turned onto the Argiletum."

I was relieved. That meant they had a large enough entourage to discourage thieves and they were out of the way, well on their way home.

People were stopping to chat, so the crowd wasn't moving much. With some difficulty we edged our way toward where I had seen Berenice. Everyone stopped moving when a woman screamed, somewhere in the direction we were trying to move.

"She's been stabbed!" a man shouted. "Call the guards!"

People panicked and started running in all directions, pushing and shoving. Several people fell to the ground and were in danger of being trampled.

"Get back in the *taberna*!" I told Aurora and Julia.

With the crowd dispersing from the place where the woman had screamed, Tacitus and I were able to make our way to her. We arrived at the same time as the *vigiles*, who were herding a small group of people along with them, and found Berenice lying on the pavement.

"Stand back, sir!" their captain ordered, with his sword drawn.

As Tacitus and I stepped away from Berenice, I was puzzled by something I *didn't* see—there was no blood on her clothing or on the street around her.

—∾∾∾—

Julia and I stood just inside the door of the taberna, *peeking out to see what was going on. "It looks like they've rounded up some suspects," I said. "We'd better get down there and tell them what we saw."*

Julia took my arm and held me back. "What did we see?"

"I saw a man running in that direction." I pointed toward the Argiletum. "He had dark hair and a black beard."

"There were lots of people running in that direction. Almost every one of them had dark hair and a black beard."

"But this man kept looking back. I think we ought to tell the vigiles, *before they arrest the wrong person."*

"You keep saying 'we.' I didn't see anything."

"Uh-oh, they're starting to search people."

Julia grabbed my arm again." Are you wearing your knife?"

"Yes, of course. That and the Tyche ring. I've always got them with me when Gaius and I go out."

"What if they search you?"

"Well—"

"*A slave carrying a knife, when somebody's just been stabbed? Aurora, you need to take that thing off.*"

"*And do what with it?*"

"*I don't know. Leave it here. Come back and get it later.*"

"*But it's got Gaius' dolphin symbol on it, just like on his signet ring. They'll know it's his.*"

Julia thought for a moment. "*Give it to me.*"

"*What?*"

"*If I'm carrying it, they can't do anything to me. They won't even search me. Hurry up. They're looking in this direction.*"

We stepped back from the door. I untied the knife in its sheath from my right thigh and handed it to Julia. Stepping out of sight, she strapped it on under her gown.

"*Put this in just the right place,*" *she said,* "*and it could produce a…well, a marvelous sensation.*"

I could feel my face reddening.

"*You've already done that, haven't you? You naughty girl!*"

—⟨∾∾⟩—

"Get those two women hiding in the *taberna*," the leader of this unit of the *vigiles* told a couple of his men.

"They're with us," I said. "They were sitting at a table with us when this woman was stabbed. They have no part in this." I couldn't let them search Aurora and find her knife.

"If you would bother to look down," Berenice said at my feet, "you would find that no one has been stabbed." She turned over so she was on her back. "Is that maniac gone? Is it safe for me to get up?"

I knelt beside her. "Are you all right?"

"I believe so. If one of you gentlemen would be kind enough to help me up, we'll find out."

Tacitus and I each gave her a hand and pulled her up. She dusted herself off and straightened her gown.

"I don't understand," I said in absolute amazement. "How did you—"

Berenice took my hand and placed it on her side. I felt something hard under her gown. "It's a linen cuirass," she said. "Alexander the

Macedonian and his men used them. Titus made me wear one whenever I went out in public. He knew how much people hated me. It's
more flexible than bronze and just as effective against a blade. But if I
get knocked down, it's difficult to get up without some help because
it's rather stiff."

The captain of the *vigiles* looked confused. "So no one was stabbed?"

"Oh, someone *tried* to stab me," Berenice said. She pulled at her
gown until we could see the hole the assailant's knife had made. "But,
as you can see, he did no damage."

Tacitus smoothed the gown out so we could see where the blade
had gone in and would have entered her back. "That's about where your
son was stabbed."

By now Aurora and Julia had joined us.

"Do you think it was the same person?" I asked.

"I would say so," Tacitus said, "or someone using the same
technique."

Malachi stepped out from the shadows cast by torches mounted
in the sconces on the front of the synagogue. "That's what I want to
talk to you about."

I turned to the captain of the *vigiles*. "I don't think we need your help
any longer. And you can release these people. They've done nothing.
Thank you for being so prompt."

Aurora cleared her throat. "My lord, I need to talk—"

"Just a moment," I said.

"May I have your name, sir," he said, "for my report?"

Tacitus, who prefers to carry his own money pouch, took it from
under his tunic and gave him enough coins to distribute among his
unit and an *aureus* for himself. "Nothing serious happened here. A
few people got knocked down, but no one was injured, so I don't think
you'll need to make a report,"

The captain touched his helmet in a salute. "No, sir, I guess not.
Makes it that much easier for me. All right, men, let's go."

When the *vigiles* were out of sight, I turned to Malachi. "Is there
somewhere in particular you'd like to talk?" Even though he welcomed
"god-fearers" into his synagogue, I suspected the presence of people he
considered outright atheists would offend him.

"Let's go to Callicles' place. He knows our law enough to make it all right for us to eat and drink there. He even learns Hebrew a little."

Malachi and Callicles exchanged greetings in Hebrew. It sounded like they were clearing their throats. Then they switched to Greek. We got a table in the back of the *taberna*. Berenice's two attendants stood by the door, surveying passersby and blocking access to the part of the *taberna* where our table was. The four servants Tacitus and I had brought with us were given places at a nearby table. As we sat down, Aurora pulled up a stool behind me, as befit a servant. Berenice scooted over to make a space. "Sit here, dear," she said in Greek.

Aurora looked at me for guidance. I didn't quite know what to say. I could see confusion on the faces of Tacitus and Julia as well, but I nodded to Aurora. When we were situated, Berenice said, "So you are the Aurora I've heard so much about."

"My name is Aurora, my lady." She kept her voice quiet, her head down.

"Excuse me," I said, "how have you heard about her?"

"Your wife is a friend of a friend of Sempronia's. Livia has been telling all sorts of tales about your 'goddess of the dawn.' Seeing her in the flesh, though, she's much prettier than I'd expected. And not nearly so much of a hulking Amazon as I'd been led to believe."

I was seething. Livia and I supposedly have an agreement. I will not flaunt my relationship with Aurora and she will not say anything derogatory about us. As much as I try to avoid contact and confrontation with my wife, this was something we would have to talk about.

Trying to calm myself, I directed my attention to Malachi. "What did you want to tell me?" I asked, with more of a snap in my voice than I intended.

Malachi gave Berenice a stern glance. "I believe the man who killed Berenicianus and who tried to kill this lady was part of a group called the *Sicarii*."

"The knife-men?" Berenice's face grew somber, as though she had put an actor's mask over it. "I thought they were all wiped out by the end of the war."

"Yes. Many of them die at Masada, at very end of war," Malachi said. "We thought all of them. No one hears of them since, but these two attacks fit how they worked."

"Who were they?" Tacitus asked.

I could see that Malachi's halting Greek was making Berenice nervous. Like a queen, she took over. "They were a group of fanatics dedicated to inspiring terror among the people of Jerusalem. They would skulk through the streets, stab someone, then melt back into the crowd with their weapons concealed beneath their cloaks."

"Whom did they kill?"

"It could be anyone at random. Or they would target Jewish leaders who they believed were collaborating with the Romans. And they killed a few Roman officials. They drove the Romans out of the city before the war began."

"Was your son involved with them?" I asked.

"I'm not sure," Berenice replied. "He hated the Romans, I know, but I wasn't aware that he was involved with the *Sicarii*."

Callicles brought us some more wine, bread, and a plate of dried apricots and dates. Berenice daintily bit off a small piece of an apricot.

"At the time of the war," she said, "my son was twenty years old and a hothead. At first he despised me because of my relationship with Titus, so I did not see him or have any contact with him for several years. He did come to see how that connection could be beneficial to both of us. After Titus died we exchanged a few letters—mostly his requests for money and my refusals—but when he appeared at my door a month ago, I couldn't have been more surprised if I'd found a god standing there."

"And he did not tell you why he sought you out after all those years?"

Berenice shook her head. "As I told you earlier, all he would say was that I would be in danger if he told me anything."

"Somebody must have thought he did tell you something," Tacitus said.

Callicles came to our table and said something to Malachi, who excused himself and went out to meet someone on the steps.

"Well, I can't tell you anything else, Gaius Pliny," Berenice said, "and

I must get home before the bandits and thugs take complete control of the streets." As she stood she seemed to lose her balance and put her hand on Aurora's thigh to steady herself. "Hmm, is it on the other leg then?"

"I beg your pardon, my lady?" Aurora said.

"Your infamous knife. Which leg do you wear it on?"

Before Aurora could say anything, I stood up. Berenice had touched her on the very spot where she wears the knife. "You must be referring to another malicious lie that my wife is spreading. I would never allow a servant of mine to go out armed. That's against the law."

Berenice chuckled. "All right. If that's your story, stay with it."

Without my asking, Aurora pulled her gown up to show her bare thighs.

Berenice shrugged and bade us good night. She and her two servants set out for home.

As soon as she was out of sight, I collapsed back onto my seat. "Where is it?"

"It's right here," Julia said, patting her leg and smiling. She explained why she and Aurora had made the switch. Concealing her movements under the table, she untied the knife and passed it to Aurora, who put it in place just as discreetly. "It felt really good," Julia said, "and it made me feel...powerful. I may start a new fashion. It might make you men respect us women a bit more to know that we could emasculate you in the blink of an eye."

"That thought is never far from our minds, my dear," Tacitus said.

"Let's get serious," I said. "One thing bothers me. Malachi and Berenice said these *Sicarii* assassinated people at random in crowds, but Berenicianus was obviously murdered in a way that took planning. We know he was killed outside my warehouse and then his mouth was filled with coins and sewed shut. That could not have been done spontaneously, in the middle of a crowd, by one person."

"And what was he doing at your warehouse?" Tacitus asked. "It's not exactly a place people gravitate to."

"The baby," Aurora said. "The baby was the bait that drew him there."

"You don't think he brought the baby with him?" Julia said.

Aurora took a dried apricot. "I really don't. Somebody wanted to

kill Berenicianus in a...spectacular way. No, a symbolic way. I think
it was one person, or a very small group. They had to lure him to a
secluded spot because there weren't enough of them to attack him in
the open. They had to get him in an isolated place and away from any
guards he might have."

"They had to make *him* come to *them*," Tacitus said.

"Exactly," I said. "And the only way to do that was to have something
he wanted very much. They must have told him where to come and to
come alone. But why choose my warehouse?"

"They must have known it was empty and unlocked," Tacitus said.
"Or did they break in?"

"The lock was broken," I said. "Since the place was empty, I hadn't
gotten around to having it fixed yet."

"If the baby was the bait," Aurora said, "Berenicianus must have
wanted him very badly to risk going anywhere in Rome by himself,
and especially down by the docks."

I pointed to the deepening gloom visible through the door of
the *taberna*. "It's going to be completely dark soon. We're going to
be in danger ourselves. Let's continue this conversation on our way
home."

I left money on the table and signaled to our servants at the other
table. We started out the door of the *taberna* into the bustling street. "I
wish we had a few more people with us," I said. "Keep an eye on anyone
who seems to be getting too close."

Aurora tugged my arm to hold me back. "I would recognize the
man, Gaius. I got a good look at him when he was glancing back over
his shoulder. And he was one of those the *vigiles* had rounded up
before you told them to let everybody go because Berenice hadn't been
hurt."

I gasped. "Are you serious?"

"I tried to tell you, but you cut me off. By the time you were ready
to listen to me, he was gone."

"That means he would recognize you."

"Or you."

———— ∞ ————

When we returned from the Subura Aurora held Joshua or watched while Miriam nursed him. Miriam showed her how to pat the baby on the back now and then during his feeding, in spite of his unhappiness at being taken from the breast. My mother, who was sitting with me beside the fish pond in the center of the garden, explained that the patting causes the baby to belch and helps him to feel better.

"Only as we grow up," she said, "are we taught that it's not polite to belch or make…other gaseous noises while we eat. They're really quite natural."

"When Claudius was *princeps*," I said, "he used to encourage people to do those things at dinner."

She gave me a sidelong glance. "An historical example! Did you learn that from Tacitus? Poor Claudius probably had some stomach disorder and wanted other people to help him cover it up. That's acceptable for babies and old men, I guess."

"Still, I would not have wanted to be a guest at his table."

Later, in the middle of the night, with a single lamp flickering on the table beside my bed, Aurora put her hand on my chest and sighed deeply. It was taking me a few moments to get my breath back. Our love-making, which she had initiated, had been the most intense we'd experienced since her miscarriage. Did the fact that she now had a baby—sleeping in the room on the other side of hers with his nurse—mean that she was able to move beyond that tragedy?

"Gaius, are you awake?" Her voice was low, even more sultry than usual.

"Yes." I ran my hand slowly down her bare back. If she was in the mood for—

"I think Berenice knows something that she's not telling us."

I sat up. "Is *that* what you're thinking about now?"

She propped herself on one elbow, her breasts brushing my chest, and kissed me on the cheek. "I know what *you're* thinking about." She slowly ran a hand down my chest and stomach and a bit farther.

"Well, it's difficult for a man to conceal—"

"I don't believe you men can think about this"—she began to move her hand rhythmically up and down—"and anything else at the same time."

I didn't want to get bogged down in a pointless discussion. "What do you think Berenice knows?" I managed to gasp as she straddled me.

"She knows who tried to kill her. I'm sure of it."

———◦◦◦———

I was almost asleep when someone outside my door made a noise, as though he had stubbed a toe against something. No matter how quiet a person is trying to be, that sudden bolt of pain will provoke a reaction. I slipped on my tunic and picked up the small sword lying on the table beside my bed. Aurora stirred when I got up.

"What is it?" she said, brushing her hair back.

"I think someone's prowling in the garden."

Aurora got into her gown and picked up her knife. I opened the door cautiously, just enough to get my head out. Aurora looked around me as best she could. The clouds were still heavy and low, so I didn't even have moonlight to help me see. But I could make out a figure skulking from one column of the peristyle to the next. He seemed to be examining the door of each room, as though looking for a sign or mark on the lower part of the door. Finally he stopped and opened one door.

"That's the room where Clymene is," Aurora whispered. "What on earth is he looking for in there?"

"Her, apparently," I said as the two of them emerged from the room. The man was holding Clymene's right hand in his left. In his right hand he held a knife with a blade about as long as the span of a large man's hand from thumb to little finger. "He's kidnapping her."

"He's not pulling her," Aurora said. "I think she wants to go with him."

As they drew closer to us I had the door open just enough for us to see but not be noticed in the dark. We could finally make out the man's face. "Is that the man who attacked Berenice?" I asked. Aurora nodded.

Now I could hear the man saying something…about a baby. Clymene replied, "In one of these rooms. I don't know which one. There'll be a nurse with him or that whore of Pliny's."

The man brandished his knife. "They'll be easy enough to deal with."

Aurora clutched my arm. "He's after Joshua, too. We've got to stop him."

Clymene and the man had been brought to a halt by a noise in front of the room where Miriam and Joshua were, two doors away from us. The baby was fretting.

"A very sign from God," the man muttered. He let go of Clymene's hand and reached for the door.

"I'll take him," I said. "You deal with her. Now!"

I flung the door open and Aurora and I rushed into the walkway in front of the intruders. "Get your hand off that door!" I barked, showing my sword. Aurora lunged at Clymene and knocked her up against one of the pillars.

The man feinted with his knife, but it was too short to be effective against my sword, even as short as it was. He couldn't strike without putting himself in range of my weapon. Instead he dodged behind the pillar where Clymene was pinned. She yelled as he passed her and ran toward the rear gate. I tried to cut him off, but he turned over a chair in my path and pushed it at me. I stumbled over it. By the time I regained my feet he was gone. I looked both ways out the gate, but there was no sign of him.

By this time Felix had come out of the room he shares with Aurora, and my mother and Naomi were running across the garden toward us, carrying torches.

"Gaius," Mother called. "What's going on?"

"Someone broke in," I said, "but he's gone."

"Was anyone hurt?" she asked.

"Clymene needs help," Aurora said.

The woman was sitting on the ground in front of the pillar, her hands on her side, blood darkening her gown. Eschewing modesty, my mother and Naomi lifted Clymene's gown and examined her wound in the flickering light. By now a crowd of servants had gathered.

"It's not bad," Mother said. "Let's get her back in her room and stitch her up."

Clymene was able to stand and walk. Turning to Aurora, she grimaced and said, "He was trying to kill *you*, you know. He loves me. He came to rescue *me*."

I closed and locked the rear gate and posted guards for the rest of the night. When Aurora and I were standing by ourselves in front of her and Felix's room, she said, "Clymene's wrong. He wasn't trying to kill me. He was definitely aiming for her."

When everyone was back in bed Aurora and I stood outside Clymene's door, where I now had a guard on duty.

"He obviously came over the wall," I said. "He's very agile, but how did he know which room she was in?"

Aurora held a torch close to the door. "Look, my lord, down here." She pointed to a mark scratched on the doorpost. "That's a Hebrew letter, isn't it?"

I nodded. "We certainly didn't put it there."

IX

THE NEXT MORNING the rain let up enough that Regulus sent word that Lucullus' funeral would be held as soon as we had finished with our clients' business at the *salutatio*. I informed mine that they would be expected to accompany me, for an extra donative, of course. The walk down to the Licinian Gardens, which sit on the southeast side of the Esquiline, was not arduous. The gardens themselves, like many of the open spaces in the city, are in danger of being smothered by the buildings that are encroaching on them from all sides.

The pyre had been erected on the eastern side of the gardens, the most open part. Since Regulus was responsible for it, it was enormous. I was glad to see there were no trees overhanging it or bushes nearby. Once it was fully engulfed in flames, it could spread to anything that would burn.

Lucullus' body was carried in by some of his servants and propped up in front of the pyre. I've always considered that practice an odd part of our funeral rituals. It's as though the dead man is going to watch the proceedings. Could he stop them if he wasn't satisfied? He was wrapped in embroidered linen. A wax mask had been placed over his face, painted to look as lifelike as possible.

Sempronia and her female *clientela* played the part of the mourners one reads about in Greek plays and sees depicted on Greek pottery. Some tore their garments, exposing their breasts, which they beat rhythmically. Others scratched their cheeks until they bled. None of this was typical of a Roman funeral. One might have thought Achilles or Agamemnon was going to be lying on top of the pyre.

Lucullus' wife showed more proper deportment, covering her head and holding her two small children by their hands, one on each side of her, one a girl, the other a younger boy. All three looked sad, but I saw no tears.

"I don't see anyone who looks like the older daughter by Lucullus' first wife," I said to Aurora.

"She may have suspected what this spectacle would look like if Regulus and Sempronia were staging it and had enough sense to stay away. The second wife looks like she'd just as soon be somewhere else."

Sacrifices were offered—ten sheep and five oxen—and Lucullus' body was lifted onto the top of the pyre. Regulus mounted a dais to deliver his eulogy. His toga was what any member of the senatorial class would wear, but the cloak wrapped around it was a deep blue with gold leaves sewn onto it. He looked down modestly and waited for the crowd to fall silent.

Since Lucullus had no career to brag of, Regulus stressed his glorious ancestors—a few consuls and some mediocre generals—and then launched into a lament over how tragic it was that Lucullus had been cut down before he was able to enjoy the greatest honor that Rome had to offer: a consulship with the *princeps* as his colleague.

Regulus didn't say it, but we all knew that Domitian would have done what he had done before. He would hold the office on the first day of the year, so that the year would forever be named "the year when Domitian and Lucullus were consuls," then he would resign and appoint some non-entity as a suffect consul. That man and Lucullus would hold the office for about six months, as long as they didn't annoy Domitian. Then they would have to step aside to allow the appointment of two more suffect consuls to finish out the year. Rome needs ex-consuls because holding a consulship is a requirement for filling certain provincial offices, and this is the only way to insure an adequate supply. Lucullus would at least have had the honor of being a *consul ordinarius*, one whose name was on the year, and alongside Domitian's at that. His family could boast of having a *vir consularis* in their ranks.

"I wonder why Regulus is making such a spectacle of this," Aurora said. "The man was Sempronia's cousin, not his. From what I've heard, Regulus doesn't do anything to gratify her."

"I've wondered about that, too. And how did he get Domitian to go along with this charade?"

Regulus actually shed a few tears at the end of his eulogy. I think he may have had something in his handkerchief to induce them. Then, mercifully, it was over. Torches were applied to the pyre, which had been soaking for a couple of days in olive oil and pitch, so that not even the misty rain which began falling was likely to dampen it.

"I wish I could have examined the body," I said.

"Why?" She looked at me like she smelled something unpleasant. "Sometimes I think you're becoming as ghoulish as Tacitus says you are."

"It's not a matter of ghoulish curiosity. Berenicianus was stabbed. Lucullus was stabbed. I'd just like to see if there were any similarities."

"My lord, I imagine there are dozens of people stabbed in Rome every day. It's the most common way people have of injuring or killing one another in this city."

Our conversation broke off when I realized that Regulus was walking toward us. Aurora moved back so that she was standing behind me.

Regulus extended his hand, which I clasped. "Gaius Pliny, thank you for being here today, and with a considerable number of your people. It made for an impressive turnout."

"I always honor my promises, Marcus Regulus. Very fine eulogy."

"Thank you. It's always a bit difficult when one doesn't really know the deceased very well. I had met him only a couple of times."

"I was wondering about that. Why did you promote him to Domitian then?"

Regulus looked at the ground, then glanced around before he said, "Since he's dead, I suppose there's no harm in saying this. He told me he knew a secret that would make me very rich. Of course, I'm already very rich, but there's no harm in being very much richer, is there?" He laughed in a way that turned my stomach.

"How was he going to do that, if I may ask?"

"You may ask, but I can't tell you because I don't know. He was murdered before he supplied any details."

We had to take a few steps away from the pyre as the heat grew more intense. Lucullus' body began to sizzle and pop.

"Are you sure there were details?"

"Very astute observation, Gaius Pliny. I've thought about that, about the possibility that he was merely leading me on. But, as one who has played that game many times, I thought I recognized a vein of truth in what he was saying. He did give me one hint: it concerns a hidden box, something the Jews have kept secret for centuries. He wanted a consulship in exchange for revealing the rest of what he knew. He was probably wise to withhold that until he had his prize. Now I guess I'll never know."

"Could his death have had anything to do with this hidden box?"

Regulus looked at me in surprise. "Do you mean could someone have killed him to prevent him from telling? I hadn't considered that. I thought he was killed by a disgruntled slave. The gods know that we all have a few of those in our households." He looked Aurora up and down. "But fortunately we have some very 'gruntled' ones, too, don't we?" He patted me on my shoulder. "Thanks again, Gaius Pliny."

"Certainly. Give my condolences to your wife." He could think I meant condolences on the death of her cousin. I meant condolences on being his wife.

I dismissed my clients with thanks and the money I had promised them. A few of them accompanied Aurora and me as we returned to my house in order to talk with me some more.

When I was finished with my clients' business, I told Aurora, "We need to go see Tacitus."

"Let's take Joshua with us," she said. "I'm sure Julia would enjoy seeing him."

"No, taking the baby would require taking Miriam with us, in case he got hungry. And taking her would require taking someone who could speak Hebrew, namely Naomi. And that would require an even larger entourage of servants for protection. It is simply too much trouble." I concluded my argument as forcefully as I might in a court case which I knew I could not lose.

We arrived as the last of Tacitus' clients was leaving. Joshua had slept in Aurora's arms during the whole trip to the Aventine Hill and Julia was delighted to see him.

"Aren't you just the most precious thing?" She took the baby from Aurora. "I was thinking about coming over to see you."

Joshua bestirred himself long enough to yawn and make a sucking motion with his mouth. Aurora gave me a look that said much more than it needed to.

"He looks good," Julia said.

"He's eating well." Aurora patted Miriam on the arm. She said two or three words in a language I assumed was Hebrew. Miriam nodded and smiled.

As the women made the little cooing and oohing noises that women always make over babies, Tacitus finished his conversation with his very last client. I sat on a bench and looked around the atrium. It had been several months since I'd been here. The decoration reflected more of Julia's taste than Tacitus', I suspected. It gave one the impression of being in a garden, with plants, birds, and trellises. Soft colors—mostly blues and greens—dominated. The house is smaller than mine, but Tacitus doesn't have his mother and her entourage living with him. Sadly, both of his parents are dead. Julia's parents have property in southern Gaul and a villa north of Rome, where Agricola can keep his veterans close enough to the city to give Domitian second thoughts about any rash moves.

Tacitus paid homage to Joshua because Julia practically shoved the child under his nose. Then he turned his attention to me. "This is a pleasure. May I offer you something to eat or drink?"

"No, thank you. I'm here because I think we should go talk to Berenice again."

"Why? She said she couldn't tell us any more."

"Aurora is convinced that she knows who tried to kill her. I think we should press her on that point."

Tacitus rubbed his chin. "You're probably right. Aurora has excellent instincts in such things. I need to give my steward some instructions. I'll be ready to go in just a few moments." He walked away to tend to those domestic matters and to gather a few servants and a cloak.

Aurora left Julia and the baby and stood in front of me like a servant, with her hands folded in front of her, waiting to be told what to do.

"We're going to see Berenice," I said.

"Shall I come with you, my lord?"

"You'll have to make a choice. You cannot bring that baby with you."

"I know, my lord." Aurora sighed and looked over her shoulder at Julia. "I think he'll be fine with Julia. Naomi and Miriam can bring him home later. He'll be all right." I knew she was reassuring herself, not me.

I leaned closer to her. "No matter how you feel about him or any other child, he will be an encumbrance."

Aurora lowered her voice to little more than a whisper. "Is that what I am, Gaius? An encumbrance? Were you secretly relieved that I lost the baby? *Our* precious baby?" She stepped back and raised her voice. "I'll be ready to go whenever you are, my lord." Turning quickly, she walked over and joined the women adoring Joshua. Several of Tacitus' female servants had been drawn to them. They looked like the paintings one sees of women fawning over the infant Dionysus. Aurora threw her head back and laughed at something.

Tacitus' arm settled around my shoulder as he chuckled in my ear. "That is the face of a man who is smelling what he just stepped in."

"I don't know what happened. I honestly don't know." I shook my head, genuinely befuddled. "I pointed out the simple fact that a baby makes things complicated, and she...took it as some kind of... accusation."

"Gaius, at some point we're going to sit down—just the two of us—and have a *long* talk. Perhaps I can make up for you losing your father at an early age and being raised by an uncle who never had a meaningful relationship with any woman but a slave."

"Aurora *is* my slave."

Tacitus clapped my shoulder heartily. "Oh, my friend, you didn't just step in something. Now you're rolling in it, like a dog in the street. You don't believe that she's merely a slave, do you?"

I pulled away from him. "Of course not. But this isn't the time to talk about such things. I want to get to Berenice before someone attacks her again. I want to find out what she knows."

—∽∾∽—

Berenice had told us that she lived in an *insula* behind the temple of Juno Lucina, on the west side of the Esquiline and near the Portico of Livia. It didn't take long to find it. The building was three stories high and reasonably well maintained. The plaster had recently been painted in an umber tone, so there was little graffiti visible. The building was large enough to have four or five apartments on each floor, but the stairways leading to some of them were blocked off. Workmen, moving rapidly, were installing bars on the windows on the second floor. An attendant stood on the street in front of one of the open stairways. As soon as he saw us, he put a hand on the hilt of his sword.

"We need to speak with Queen Berenice," I said.

"She's not receiving visitors, sir."

"Would you tell her that Gaius Pliny and Cornelius Tacitus are here?"

The man did not leave his post but called our names to someone higher up on the stairs. After a few moments a female attendant appeared on the landing where the stairs turned to the left and gestured for us to come up. The guards permitted only Tacitus, myself, and Aurora, at my request, to pass. The rest of our attendants had to wait on the street.

The walls of the lower part of the stairwell were undecorated, but as soon as we turned on the landing it was as though we had stepped into a different part of the empire. Frescoes in the heavy Eastern style showed scenes from the life of Dionysus. We didn't have time to study them before the servant opened the door at the head of the stairs and stood back for us to enter.

The first room we entered had an Oriental feel to it, not surprisingly since Berenice had lived most of her life in Syria and Alexandria. Such décor always feels decadent to a Roman. In addition to chairs and tables, it was furnished with large cushions strewn on the floor. I could see that what had originally been other apartments had been combined into one large residence by cutting doors from one room into the next. With the exterior doors sealed off and now with bars being installed on the windows, this entire floor of the *insula* was being transformed into a fortress.

"Welcome," Berenice said, emerging from the next room beyond us. She was wearing a loose, diaphanous gown, light blue with a red filigree, and a small tiara—the sort of outfit I suppose Cleopatra wore when entertaining Caesar or Marc Antony. But Cleopatra had been thirty years younger than Berenice. This queen would have done better to concentrate on hiding what charms she had left and letting those around her create their own details. Without her veil, one could see the wrinkles at the corners of her mouth and the sagging of her chin, not just the ugly mole over her eye. In full light, without her veil and makeup, she was one of those women who has passed the prime of her allure to men but has convinced herself that she's still attractive. That's always a sad sight.

"Gaius Pliny," she said, settling elegantly on a leather cushion. "To what do I owe this pleasure?"

"I'm going to be blunt, my lady. I believe you know who tried to kill you yesterday. I believe he was the same man who killed your son. He invaded my house last night, and I'm afraid he may come after us again. I need to know who he is."

"From what I've heard, your Amazon can defend herself. And perhaps you as well." She pointed to Aurora and patted a place on the cushion beside her. Glancing at me, Aurora took a seat there.

I waved a hand in the direction of a newly barred window. "You're obviously worried about defending yourself. You must know that the attack last night was not random. You're afraid he'll try again. I believe you know something about him, possibly who he is."

Berenice motioned for Tacitus and me to sit on a large cushion facing her. "No, I don't. I swear to you. There was something familiar about his voice, but I couldn't place it."

"You heard his voice?" Tacitus said. "What did he say?"

"Just one word. *Whore.*"

"Who would talk to a queen like that?"

"Oh, the list is long," Berenice said. "Many people think I gained power lying on my back." She lowered her head, looking at me from under her lashes, a coquettish gesture that might have been effective years ago. "I'm actually much better when I'm on top." Aurora blushed, and I may have as well. Tacitus just chuckled.

I recovered my composure enough to ask, "Are you sure you can't tell us any more?"

"Yes, I'm sure. I hope you can find this person. I won't feel safe, even with all these precautions, until you do."

The cushion we were sitting on wasn't all that comfortable. I shifted my weight and said, "We think we might find a clue to the killer if we could understand *why* he stuffed the coins in Berenicianus' mouth and sewed it shut."

"It may have something to do with the war," Berenice said, "but I don't know what really."

"How was your son involved?"

"At the very beginning of the war, my son, thinking the Jews might actually have a chance, joined the *Sicarii*. They operated in units of half a dozen. He was chosen the leader of a group."

"He was the shepherd," Tacitus said.

Berenice's face showed her lack of comprehension. "I suppose you could call him that."

"It's an allusion to a passage from one of your prophets," I said.

"Oh, all right. Those aren't among my favorite authors. Too much gloom and doom. I much prefer the Song of Solomon: 'Your two breasts are like two fawns'—that sort of thing." She arched her back. "But my son was never a man of strong convictions, a trait that runs in our family. He quickly saw the futility of it all and, like Josephus, surrendered to the Romans. I'm sure he was regarded as a traitor."

"But why would someone have waited this long to take vengeance?"

"In that part of the world, gentlemen, grievances are nursed like children or pets. Sometimes they span generations. Fifteen years would be no time at all."

"Didn't all the *Sicarii* die at Masada?" Tacitus asked. "Some sort of mass suicide?"

"A handful of them were still in Jerusalem when the city fell. They were captured and sold into slavery along with the inhabitants of the city who had not escaped."

Like Naomi and Phineas. "It would be terrifying to have one of those people in your household."

"But you couldn't tell them apart from anyone else," Berenice said. "That was what made them so frightening. You never knew who was a *Sicarius* until you felt the knife between your ribs."

"Well, that gives us something to think about." I stood, ready to leave. Tacitus and Aurora did the same. "Thank you for your time, my lady."

"I'm afraid I wasn't much help," Berenice said, still seated like a queen on her cushion throne. "If I think of anything else, I'll send you word." She stood. "Now, before you go, may I ask a favor of you?"

"Of course."

"I'd like to talk with Aurora in private for a few moments."

—⟿—

Berenice's request was so unexpected that I'm afraid I drew back too visibly.

She patted me on the arm. "Don't worry, dear. I don't bite—unless the man wants me to."

Gaius gave his consent and Berenice led me into the next room of her apartment. She motioned for a servant woman to draw a heavy drapery over the opening and then leave us. In unfamiliar surroundings I always try to take a quick survey of the place, but Berenice didn't give me time to do more than notice the bright mosaic floor with a theme of Venus and Adonis in the center.

"Now, it's just the two of us," she said, "and I want to see where you keep that knife."

"My lady, I—"

"Don't deny it." Her voice turned sharp. "I don't have time to waste. Someone is trying to kill me, and I want to have some way to protect myself. I'm not interested in getting you or Gaius Pliny in any trouble. Just show me where you wear the knife."

When I didn't move she grabbed my gown and began pulling it up. I wanted to slap her hands, but she was a queen and I was a slave. What choice did I have but to obey her?

"I'll...I'll do it, my lady." I pulled my gown away from her and lifted it on the right side until she could see the knife in its sheath strapped to my thigh.

"Hmm. So it's quite simple really," she said. "You keep the sheath on the inside of your leg and it's really not even noticeable. How do you get to it when you need it?"

"I've sewed a slit in my gowns with a flap over it and practiced drawing the knife." I showed her how I've learned to draw the knife in one smooth motion.

"Very effective. I wonder why other women haven't taken up the idea. May I see the blade?"

I handed her the knife.

"This seal on the handle, is that Gaius Pliny's mark?"

"Yes, my lady."

"And you've actually killed a man with this, I'm told." She ran a finger up and down the blade and traced the dolphin on the seal.

"My lady, please—"

She waved a hand and gave the knife back to me. "Don't worry, dear. Your secret is safe with me."

Why do I always worry when someone says that?

Berenice threw back the drapery covering the doorway and we re-entered the room where Gaius and Tacitus were waiting. "That was most enlightening," she said. "If you ever decide to sell her, Gaius Pliny, please let me make the first offer."

Gaius must have been too shocked to think. I've heard other people make a similar offer. Gaius has a standard reply, but maybe he thought it too indelicate to say to a woman. That didn't stop Tacitus, though. "My lady, with all due respect, Gaius Pliny would sell you one of his balls before he would part with Aurora. And he would cut it off himself."

"Well, I know where he could find a knife," Berenice said with a wink, "but balls—well, I have a large enough collection of those."

—◦◦◦—

Tacitus, Aurora, and I descended the stairs from Berenice's apartment in silence and rejoined our servants for the walk home. We did not speak until we were well away from the *insula*, and then we kept our voices low and switched to Greek. "What did she want?" I asked Aurora.

"She wanted to see where I wear my knife."

I gasped. "You're not even supposed to admit that you have it, much less show—"

"She was going to rip my clothes off," Aurora said. "She's frightened and wanted a way to protect herself. What choice did I have?"

Tacitus held up a hand to calm us. "It's done, Gaius. It's done. What I want to know is why you didn't ask her about the baby."

"Because I think most of what she told us was a lie. I didn't want to hear more lies about the baby. It would just confuse the issue."

"His name is Joshua," Aurora said. "And he's not an encumbrance. He may be the most important element in this whole puzzle. We need to find out who he belongs to."

We were approaching the Marketplace of Livia, which Augustus had dedicated to his wife. His Livia, I had read somewhere, was "the only woman he ever loved." Somehow I couldn't appreciate the irony. The late-morning crowd was growing heavier as people did their buying before the shops closed, so we were forced to slow our pace. Our servants were having a hard time keeping the press of the crowd off us.

Suddenly Aurora screamed, "Watch out!"

I felt myself being shoved to one side. A searing pain flashed across my lower back. I fell to one knee. Aurora knelt over me. "Gaius! My lord!" She stood up and began pushing against the crowd. "He's been stabbed. Get out of the way, damn you!"

In the general pandemonium that ensued after the attack my servants were able to pick me up and get me home. As we hurried through the streets Tacitus tore a piece off his cloak and pressed it against my wound to slow the bleeding. Once we were home he took a closer look at it.

"It's a slash, not a puncture," he said. "Aurora pushed you just as the man thrust his knife, so it slid along your skin instead of going into you. Think of it more as a scratch—a big, ugly scratch, granted—but not really serious. We'll get you sewed up and you should be all right. I would tell you to rest for a few days, but I know what a waste of words that would be."

"Where is Aurora?" I was afraid someone had stabbed her, too.

Tacitus patted my shoulder. "You thought she'd be standing over you, didn't you? She's fine. She was here until we were sure you were all right. Right now she's a bit encumbered. Julia and the others brought Joshua back. They're all out in the garden."

"I guess that tells me where I stand." I raised myself to a sitting position. Tacitus pressed a bandage over my wound. "Did anyone see who did it?"

"Aurora said it was the same man who attacked Berenice. She would have gone after him, but the crowd was too thick. Whoever he is, he has a real knack for melting into a crowd."

Someone knocked on the door and Tacitus opened it. My mother came in, carrying a basket of sewing materials. "How are you, Gaius?"

"I guess I'm all right," I assured her, although I was beginning to feel a little light-headed. Something wasn't quite right.

"I'm going to sew up your wound," Mother said. "I seem to be doing that a lot these days. It will hurt, but it has to be done. Let me see it."

I turned onto my left side. I wasn't wearing a tunic; the lower part of my body was covered by a blanket. On my estates outside of Rome one of the servants who handle the animals would have done this job because of his experience with tending to their injuries. Here we have no animals. The only sewing is done by the women. They keep thin strips of animal sinew handy for times such as this. My mother cleaned the wound with some wine, patted it dry, and inserted a needle. I moaned through my clenched teeth.

"This won't take long," Mother said. "And it's nothing like the pain I endured when I gave birth to you, dear boy." She worked quickly, tied off one last knot, and gave me a kiss on the cheek. "Now you get some rest." She packed up her gear and left us.

"You're not going to pay any more attention to her than you would to me, are you?" Tacitus said.

"I think I will. I don't feel good at all." I lay back on the bed, beginning to sweat. "Just until the pain subsides."

—◦◦◦—

It's the second day since Gaius was injured. He's been feverish, vomiting. I've stayed with him the entire time. I'm afraid we didn't get the wound cleaned out well enough. We've been trying to keep him cool, but nothing seems to help. His mother sent for a doctor this morning. I've been relegated to the garden. I swear, by any god who cares to listen, if Gaius dies, I will find the bastard who did this and...

The doctor and Plinia came out of Gaius' room. Naomi, who'd been sitting in the chair beside the door, stood up to join them. As they talked, Plinia put her hand to her mouth and Naomi began to cry.

I waited until the doctor was gone before I approached Plinia. "Excuse me, my lady. Can you tell me what the doctor said?"

Plinia sat in the chair Naomi had been using and put her face in her hands. She looked up at me and said, "He thinks Gaius has been poisoned."

"Poisoned? How?"

"It must have been on the blade of the knife."

I fell to my knees in front of her. "Is he going to die, my lady?"

Plinia shook her head and clasped my hands between hers. "The doctor thinks, because he was just scratched, he will survive, but he's going to be awfully sick, probably for another day or two, until that bit of poison passes out of his body."

"May I continue to tend to him, my lady?"

"Yes, dear. Please do. The whole time I was in there, the only thing he said that I could understand was your name."

"Shouldn't we notify his wife?" Naomi asked.

"If anyone does," Plinia said in her usual calm voice, "I'll cut their tongue out."

When I returned to the stool at Gaius' bedside, he was breathing more heavily and writhing from side to side.

"It's all right, Gaius. I'm here." I took his hand in mine but he was so hot I could hardly stand to touch him.

I completely lost track of time in the dimly lit room. People came and went, offering me food I could not eat and refilling the oil lamps. Julia spent a long time with me, hugging me and letting me cry on her shoulder.

Julia was sitting with me when Gaius died. I knew he was dead because he shuddered and expelled a heavy breath. The Greeks say that's the soul leaving the body. His head slumped to one side and he lay perfectly still.

"By the gods!" Julia cried. "Is he...dead?" She put her hand under his nose. "He's not breathing, Aurora. He's not breathing!"

I was sitting on the edge of his bed. "No! No! He can't be dead. I won't let him be dead." In frustration and disbelief I pounded on his chest with my *fists. Suddenly his eyes popped open and he took a gulp of air. He looked around like a madman waking from a bad dream.*

———ꞈᴍꞈ———

"Gaius, can you hear me?" At first the woman's voice seemed far away. Then she drew closer, or was I drawing closer to her? Her voice was so lovely. Was she the siren? Was I Odysseus?

"Gaius, it's me. Aurora. Can you hear me, darling?"

Something cool and moist swept over my face. I felt a hand that I knew was Aurora's. Then I fell into a deep sleep.

When I opened my eyes I recognized my room, and the ceiling wasn't swirling around. I didn't feel as hot as if I were roasting over a fire anymore. Then Aurora's face came into view as she leaned over me. I sighed deeply. "Is that really you?"

Aurora smiled. "Of course it's me, my love. Who else would it be?"

I rubbed my eyes. "I've been seeing such strange, awful things for… for how long?"

"It's been two days since you were knifed. There must have been poison on the blade, the doctor says. Enough of it got into you to make you very ill. It could have killed you."

"It did kill me, didn't it?"

Aurora nodded and gripped my hand more tightly. "I was so frightened."

"Julia was here with you when it happened, wasn't she?"

"Yes, but how—"

"I saw it all."

She sat up, her hand going to her mouth. "How could you, Gaius?"

"I think some part of me—and don't you dare call it my soul—left my body and was hovering over the bed. You and Julia were crying. You hugged one another. I saw a light and I was about to…to float away toward it when you pounded on my chest with your fist. Then I opened my eyes—the ones in my body."

"By the gods! That's exactly what happened. You started breathing again. You closed your eyes and I thought you had died again, but you kept breathing. You were just sleeping. I don't understand what happened."

"I don't either. If someone else told me that story, I would laugh in their face. I want to laugh in my own face, but I think it actually happened. Or I imagined it. I was seeing such strange things."

"What matters is that you're alive." She laid her head on my chest. "You've been so ill."

"And you've been taking care of me?"

"With help from your mother and some other servants. And Tacitus has checked on you frequently. Julia has also been here."

"Probably just as an excuse to see Joshua."

Aurora slapped me on the shoulder and laughed. "You must be getting better. There's that cynical wit that I love so much."

I squeezed her hand. "I would kiss you, but the inside of my mouth tastes like—"

"You don't have to say it. I've been cleaning you up more often than the other women have cleaned up Joshua. But today your eyes look clear and you've stopped sweating." She brushed my hair back. "When you feel like standing up, I'll bathe you and we'll change your bedding. We'll probably just burn what's here now."

I dimly realized that she was sounding like the mistress of the house. "I really do want a bath," I said.

"All right, see if you can stand up. Take it easy. Lean on me."

I sat on the edge of the bed until I felt able to get to my feet. Once I was standing steadily Aurora wrapped an old tunic around my waist and I held it to cover myself as we made our way to the bath. It was late afternoon, as far as I could tell. The sky was overcast, although it wasn't raining. My steward, Demetrius, crossed our path in the garden.

"My lord, it's wonderful to see you feeling better! I was just coming to check on you."

"Thank you. I gather a number of people have looked in on me from time to time."

"Yes, my lord. Except for Aurora. She hasn't left your room in three days. She slept on the floor beside your bed."

I put an arm around Aurora's shoulders. "No wonder you look— and smell—almost as bad as I do. Thank you."

"Someone had to do it, my lord. You needed someone there at all times. Demetrius, please tell the lady Plinia that her son is feeling much better and is going to take a bath. This would be a good time to change his bedding. And please bring him a clean tunic."

"And a clean gown for her," I said.

Demetrius nodded and left to carry out his instructions.

When we entered the bath Aurora took off her own gown and got into the water with me. We've bathed together on occasion, but this time there was nothing the least bit erotic about the experience as we scraped several layers of sweat and filth off one another.

"Have you learned anything about what we were working on?" I asked as we sat and soaked.

"I'm afraid not. Tacitus has had some of his men watching Berenice's *insula*. They say all the windows are barred now and they haven't seen anyone except her servants go in or out. They're not even sure whether she's there or not."

"As frightened as she seems to be, I doubt she would leave her fortress. Her solitude is her safety."

Aurora cupped water in her hands and rinsed my shoulder. "I think we need to concentrate on why someone would have killed or tried to kill in those two cases. For you there's a different motive. It's because you can identify the killer."

"Exactly. We need to leave me aside and focus on Berenice and her son. Someone resented her relationship with Titus and someone felt Berenicianus had betrayed the *Sicarii*. Could it be the same person?"

Aurora nodded. "I think so, and he must have had help in killing Berenicianus."

I put my head in my hands.

"Are you getting sick again?" Aurora asked.

"No. This case has me completely befuddled. And I'm exhausted."

"You should go back to bed. After a good night's sleep you'll be ready to start fresh in the morning. Now that you're better I'm going to go back to my room with Felix, but I'll be right next door if you need me."

"How's Joshua doing?"

"I'm about to find out. I haven't seen him for three days."

—⦅∞⦆—

After Aurora left I sat for a few moments longer in the bath. I was still uncertain about what I had experienced when I "died." Various writers have talked about what the soul is, but I've never found their opinions convincing. I don't believe that any part of us continues to exist after our bodies die. The soul is not the last breath that escapes our bodies and lives on some other plane of existence, as Homer and the early Greeks believed. What if a person drowns and can't expel that last breath? Is the soul trapped in the body?

Epicurus says that our bodies are made up of atoms. Our souls are likewise atoms, less densely packed. When we die, the atoms making up our bodies break apart and drift off to reconnect with other bits of matter, but they are no longer any part of us. That's what happens when any living thing dies and decomposes. In the same way, the atoms making up our souls disconnect from one another, so there is nothing of us left after death—physical or otherwise. That's why he teaches that we shouldn't fear death. There is no consciousness after death, so there can be no punishment by the gods because there is nothing left to punish. Or to reward, for that matter. There is no Hades or Elysian Fields. As his disciple Lucretius says, "Mind and body are born together, grow up together and together decay."

Then what happened to me? Why did I have that sensation of floating above my body on the bed, watching Aurora and Julia? The eyes of my body were closed, so I couldn't have seen what they were doing. I had no way of knowing that they hugged or that Aurora pounded on my chest three times. Then how did I know that was what happened? She didn't tell me. I saw it happen.

I took a breath and stretched out on the water, face down with my eyes open, letting myself float. The water in a bath is never entirely clear, but I could make out the mosaics on the bottom of the pool—the sea creatures surrounding Neptune being drawn in his chariot by the horses. How did a sea god ever become associated with horses?

Someone grabbed my shoulder and pulled me up.

"Gaius! Gaius! What's wrong?" Aurora cried.

I stood up, shaking water out of my face and pushing my hair back. "There's nothing wrong. I was just testing a theory."

Aurora sighed deeply. "I thought you were dead. I was afraid you were trying to kill yourself."

"Why on earth would I do that? I've just narrowly escaped being killed. Why are you back in here? I thought you were going to see the baby."

She gestured to the side of the bath, where Joshua was lying in a basket. "I thought you might want to see him, too."

"Well, yes, of course."

X

BECAUSE I STILL FELT somewhat drained, I let Demetrius handle my clients at the *salutatio* the next morning. Aurora and I were sitting in the *exhedra* about the third hour of a cool September morning. The rain had finally stopped and the sky was clear. Aurora was holding Joshua, who had just had a good meal and was making contented baby noises. If I could pick a moment in my life where I might live forever, this might very well be the one.

"Was I mistaken," I said, "or did you and Miriam have a few bits of conversation? You haven't learned Hebrew, have you?"

"No. Actually, what Jews speak today is a dialect called Aramaic. It's used all over the eastern end of the Mediterranean. I remember some Punic, my native language. I spoke it with my mother until she died. It's similar enough to Aramaic that I can communicate on a very basic level with Miriam, if we talk slowly."

"I'm confused. If they're speaking Aramaic, then what is Hebrew?"

Aurora shifted Joshua to her other shoulder and patted his back. "Phineas says it's the classical language in which their holy books were written. It's quite old-fashioned, like Homer's Greek compared to the Greek we speak and write. Very few Jews today understand the original Hebrew, especially those outside Judaea. They still call what they speak Hebrew, but the word today really means Aramaic. That's why they've translated their books into Greek."

"Can you understand what Naomi and Phineas say in this Aramaic?"

She shook her head. "Not at the speed of normal conversation. I might pick up a word or two. Miriam and I have found some terms we both understand if we speak slowly enough."

Demetrius appeared at the entrance to the *exhedra*. "My lord, excuse me. You have a visitor."

"Who is it?"

"The lady Sempronia, my lord. She's asking to see you in private."

"Regulus' wife wants to talk to me?" I sat up on the edge of my couch. "Did she say what it was about?"

"No, my lord, just that she would like to see you."

"All right. Bring her back here." I turned to tell Aurora that she would have to leave, but she was already on her feet. "I wish you could stay."

"I wish I could hide somewhere in here, but not with Joshua. And don't you dare say he's an encumbrance."

"Stay as close to the entrance as you can."

Demetrius returned in a few moments escorting Sempronia, a short, wiry woman with dark hair and what seemed to be a permanent scowl. I've never seen any other expression on her face. She was followed by four female servants. Everyone in Rome knows of her Sapphic predilections. She and Regulus have separate quarters in his house, where they each indulge their own passions. But they have somehow produced one son. At least Regulus acknowledges the boy as his, and he is enough of a little monster to validate that claim.

Sempronia's servants stopped outside the *exhedra* and I heard them admiring Joshua. Aurora must be within earshot.

I stood to greet her. "Good morning, my lady."

"Good morning, Gaius Pliny. And thank you for seeing me. I understand you've been ill for the past few days. I'm glad to see you looking well again."

I knew I was being snide, but I asked, "Did you learn about that from one of your spies or one of your husband's?"

She laughed without smiling. "No matter, as long as the information was accurate. Accuracy is what I pay for." She sat on the low couch and I resumed my seat on the high couch, facing her. "I've come to ask your help, Gaius Pliny."

"How could I possibly help you, my lady?" *More to the point*, why *would I possibly help you?*

"I'd like for you to find the man who killed my cousin, Lucius Lucullus."

"I thought one of his slaves killed him and escaped."

"That's what the *vigiles* and the Praetorians say, but they can't find him. Domitian has tortured several slaves to get information. He wants to execute all the slaves in the household, according to the ancient law, but Regulus has talked him out of that in order to show his clemency. We know which of his slaves are missing. We just can't find them."

"But I don't see what I can do, if the *vigiles* and Praetorians haven't had any luck."

Sempronia cocked her head, giving me the impression of a large bird about to peck at something. I hoped I didn't look like a worm. "I think you're already looking for him."

"What do you mean?"

"I believe his death may be linked to the death of Julius Berenicianus."

Now I was interested. "What makes you think that?"

"Lucullus and Berenicianus both recently came from Syria to Rome. Both were stabbed to death—in the back. Berenicianus was involved in the war against the Jews until he surrendered. Lucullus served under Titus in that war. He used to brag about being the first to put a torch to the temple after the city fell."

"That must have endeared him to the Jews."

"In that part of the world emotions do run high. People remember injuries for a long time. They will wait and wait for an opportunity to exact vengeance, into the next generation and even beyond."

"That's what I've heard. What can you tell me about the slave who killed Lucullus?"

"Nothing myself, but I can introduce you to his widow, Porcia. I'm sure she can give you more helpful information. I know you and my husband are not friends, in any sense of the word, but if you'll help me, Regulus will buy the site where your warehouse was destroyed. He'll pay you for whatever you have in it—the purchase price, renovations, damaged goods, anything. You won't even have to clear the site. Regulus will use the ruins of your building to reinforce the riverbank in front of his warehouse."

I've never expected compensation for helping people. It's what a man of my class does. And I hate being obligated to Regulus in any form, but 150,000 *sesterces* is a considerable sum to lose, and this way I would be able to pay back my mother-in-law without any difficulty. "All right, I'll see what I can do. When do you think I can talk to Lucullus' widow? Porcia, you say?"

"Yes. Would this afternoon suit you? About the ninth hour?"

"That will be fine." It would give me time to notify Tacitus. We stood and Sempronia took a step toward the garden. "While you're here," I said, "may I ask one more question?"

She did not nod or say no, but I forged ahead anyway. "Why is your husband so interested in the baby we found in the warehouse?"

"He was merely acting out of kindness."

I managed to keep from laughing out loud. "But the nurse he sent tried to steal the baby."

"And she admitted to us that she had her own motives for doing so. She was not acting on our orders or on our behalf."

"Can you tell me what those motives were?"

"No, since they had nothing to do with us, or with you. You needed a wet nurse and Merione was the one in our house who had given birth most recently. She was the obvious choice. Now, I will send word to Porcia to expect you at the ninth hour. I assume you'll have Tacitus with you, and that girl with the baby who's trying so hard to eavesdrop on our conversation."

I had noticed Aurora walking slowly back and forth in front of the entrance to the *exhedra*, as though comforting Joshua, but I had hoped Sempronia had not paid attention to her. I chuckled. "She's usually more subtle when she's trying to blend into the background."

"Well, the baby is an encumbrance."

"Children generally are," I said.

"The gods know my son is. Good day, Gaius Pliny, and thank you again."

———⁓∾⁓———

"What you're going to see," I told Aurora, "is going to horrify you, I'm sure. Just keep telling yourself that it's all an act. It will be hard for me to do, but I don't think we're going to get the truth out of her any other way."

"But why can't I be there with you?"

"I've told my mother to keep everyone else in the atrium and not to be frightened by what she might hear. You need to be with them and not receive special treatment. Now, go."

Looking back over her shoulder, Aurora finally did what I told her. With Archidamos following us, Tacitus and I crossed the garden to the room where Clymene was recovering. I wanted to question her again before we went to Lucullus' house. I was sure—and Tacitus agreed with me—that her story about coming from Spain was a pure fabrication. She must be one of the slaves who escaped when Lucullus was killed. She should know who killed her master, and probably Berenicianus as well.

No matter how many times I asked, though, Clymene's answer was the same. "My lord, please, I told you. I came from Spain with my father and some others, the ones who died in your warehouse."

I shook my head slowly. "I think every word you've said to me since we found you has been a lie. I'm not even sure your name is Clymene, but I don't guess that will matter when they throw you to the animals in the arena. The lions won't insist on formal introductions."

The woman began to tremble. "Oh, my lord, please, no. I didn't do anything."

"Then tell me who did. Who killed Lucullus? And who killed Berenicianus?"

"I can't, my lord. I can't."

I turned to Archidamos. "All right, then. String her up. We'll have to beat the truth out of her." This would be the hardest part of this little play for me to make convincing. My uncle had occasionally beaten a slave—for theft or some other serious offense, but I can't bring myself to do it. Usually the threat of being sent to do hard labor on another of my estates or being sold—and I have done both—is enough to improve their behavior.

Tacitus stepped between me and Clymene and put a hand on her shoulder, as though interceding for a client. "Gaius Pliny, is this really necessary?"

"She has exhausted my patience," I said and waved Archidamos into action.

Archidamos tied the struggling woman's hands in front of her and dragged her into the garden. We have a couple of posts there with hooks in them where the servants hang garments to dry or have the dust beaten out of them. Archidamos placed Clymene's tied hands over one of the hooks and ripped the top half of her gown so that it hung down around her waist, exposing her bony, unmarked back and her breasts. He uncoiled a whip and took up a position a few paces behind her.

—⁓—

I didn't care what Gaius said; I had to see what he was going to do. I ran up the stairs out of the atrium and found Miriam's room on the second floor. It overlooked the garden and had a window. The shutters were closed, but I opened one just enough to let me see and hear what was happening without being observed.

A Gaius I had never seen before—and hope never to see again—stepped up to Clymene, who was tied to a post. He grabbed her hair, yanking her head back. A wet spot spread over the lower part of her gown. She began to sob.

"This is your last chance," Gaius growled. He nodded and Archidamos cracked the whip right beside Clymene's head. She yelped as it caught her on the ear. I touched the spot on my earlobe that had been nicked when somebody tried to kill me. I couldn't believe that Gaius was going to use the whip on someone. I've known him for more than fifteen years and never seen him resort to it.

"The next one will land on your back," Gaius said, "and as many more after that as it takes. Tell me who killed Lucullus and Berenicianus."

Clymene shook her head.

The whip cracked again, landing between Clymene's shoulders, and she wailed. As soon as she could control her crying, she said, "I did, my lord. I killed both of them!"

—⁓—

"Not the confession you expected to wring out of her, was it?" Tacitus said. "Quite an impressive performance on your part, though, I must say."

"Thank you. That was an inspired bit of improvisation that you threw in. We could use that more in our interrogations—one of us heavy-handed, the other acting more like the friend of the person we're confronting."

We were on our way to the house of Lucullus—or of his widow, to be more precise. Sempronia had sent word of our arrival and an introduction. Porcia, we'd been told, was not a descendant of the illustrious Marcus Porcius Cato, but came from a less important branch of that family. Other than that I knew nothing about her. Clymene, in a new servant's gown and still weeping, was surrounded by Archidamos and several other servants walking far enough behind us that I didn't think she could overhear what we were talking about, especially with the buzz of conversation going on among passersby and the hawking of shopkeepers. We kept our voices down none the less.

"I still think she's lying," I said.

"But why would she confess to such horrendous crimes if she didn't do them?" Tacitus objected.

"She's covering up for someone, probably out of fear."

"Or out of love," said Aurora, who was walking between us.

"For whatever reason," I said, "she's lying. I'm sure of it. And I think Berenice is lying about not knowing who attacked her. And Sempronia is lying about Regulus' lack of interest in Joshua. If Joshua could talk, he'd probably lie to us. By the gods! I'm so desperate I might even have to…consult an oracle to clear all this up."

"And she would just give you an ambiguous answer," Aurora said, "that could mean anything and everything."

"What we need," Tacitus said, "is some infallible sign of when a person is lying. When a man is aroused by a woman—or anyone else—you get an unmistakable sign, the *mentula* sticking out in front of him for all the world to see. What if, when a person lied, his ears were to turn bright red? Or, even better, what if his nose started to grow longer?" He pulled on his nose. "Yes, that's it! On the analogy of the *mentula*, the more he lies, the longer his nose gets, and everybody can see it."

In spite of my desperation, I couldn't help but laugh. "That would be useful because it would apply to men and women alike. It sounds like the premise of a comedy by Aristophanes."

"The masks would be hilarious. Characters would have to change masks as their noses grew longer." Tacitus turned his head back and forth. "Whenever two characters conversed, they would look like gladiators hacking at one another."

Lucullus' house was a quarter of the way up the Viminal Hill, in a neighborhood of modest buildings. His steward answered our knock and escorted us into the atrium. When Porcia came out of one of the rooms on the side of the atrium, I was reminded that she was no older than I am. Lucullus had been about fifty, so I assumed this was a second marriage. She was accompanied by her two small children. She looked tired, as though bearing two children so close together had left her weak. On top of that, she had to deal with the murder of her husband. She handed the children over to an elderly nurse who took them away.

Before she said anything to us, Porcia glared at Clymene and said, "You wicked girl! Where have you been?"

Clymene drew herself up and snarled, "That's none of your business, *Mother*." The last word was coated in more venom than had been applied to the knife that wounded me.

———

"As you have probably guessed," Porcia said as we sat in some shade in the small garden of her house, "this woman you call Clymene is Licinia, the daughter of Lucius Licinius Lucullus by his first wife, Aemilia. I married Lucullus six years ago, after Aemilia's death in Antioch. Licinia has hated me from the first day. I'm only two years older than she is, and I've not been able to have any influence or control over her. You saw how rudely she refused to sit and talk with us. She has even hinted that I had something to do with Aemilia's death, but I was in Rome at the time."

"How did Aemilia die?" I asked.

"All I know is what I've been told, long after the fact. She was going to the games with some of her servants one day in Antioch and was stabbed to death, right in the midst of the crowd."

I tried not to show my surprise, but I felt my eyebrows go up. "Was the killer ever caught?"

Porcia shook her head. "I'm told he simply vanished into the crowd.

No one could identify him or even be certain what they had seen."

"Was she robbed?" Tacitus asked. "Any jewelry snatched off her?"

"No. There didn't seem to be any motive other than to kill her."

This was becoming an all-too-familiar refrain. Tacitus glanced at me, and I could see that he was thinking the same thing. "How was she stabbed?" I asked.

Porcia looked confused. "Well, with a knife, I suppose. I wasn't there."

"No, I mean, was she stabbed from the front or from the back?"

"Oh. From behind, I was told, in the middle part of her back. The blade was thrust upward so that it pierced her heart, Lucullus said. She bled profusely and died on the spot. As I mentioned, I wasn't there."

"And Lucullus was also stabbed, wasn't he?" I asked.

Porcia nodded.

"Where?"

"In the *latrina*." She pointed to the entrance, at the point where the garden joined the front of the house. "His body was stuffed into the drain. That's why he wasn't found for several hours."

I shook my head impatiently. "Again, I mean was he stabbed in the back or in some other part of his body?"

"Sorry. In the back, with a thrust that went between his ribs and pierced his heart, the doctor said. He died instantly."

My mind reeled. If what I was hearing was accurate, the person who killed Lucullus was the same as the person who killed his wife six years ago and Berenicianus a few days ago. "I've heard that one of your servants was suspected of killing your husband but was never caught. Is that true?"

"Yes, it is. The man's name is Simon. He disappeared along with several other servants and Licinia on the day when Lucullus was murdered."

"Had those people been in the household for long?"

"Since the war with the Jews. Lucullus bought a group of captives after that war."

"So, fifteen years or so."

"And he bragged about setting fire to the temple?" Tacitus asked.

"Yes, especially when he'd had too much to drink."

"Did any of your Jewish servants resent him for that?"

"I think they did. I could see it in their eyes, but Lucullus was oblivious. He also bragged that he knew a secret about the temple that no one else knew."

"Did he ever indicate what he meant by that?"

"I heard him say once that he knew where some special holy box was hidden. He never would say any more than that. When we came to Rome one of the first things we did was to go see the arch that Domitian put up in honor of Titus. Lucullus picked out one of the figures marching in front of Titus and said that was him. That was where he had marched in Titus' triumph."

"Those figures aren't meant to represent anyone in particular," Tacitus said. "They're just symbols."

"I realize that," Porcia said, "but I couldn't convince Lucullus."

"Had you had any trouble with Simon or any of the others in the time they've been here?" I asked. "Any reason to suspect that they might pose a danger to your household?"

"No. Simon was not a pleasant man, but he never threatened anyone in our house, that I know of. The others followed his lead. If he didn't make trouble, they didn't."

"When you say he's not a nice man, can you tell us more?"

Porcia folded her hands in her lap. "Lucullus wasn't a particularly nice man himself. He didn't hesitate to apply pressure on people in his business dealings—force might even be a better word. But Simon was the man he sent after people, like a hunter's dog after a deer that he's tracking. I wouldn't be surprised to learn that Simon killed some people along the way, on behalf of Lucullus, but I have no proof."

"Having someone like this Simon to turn loose on people would let Lucullus keep his hands clean," I said.

Porcia nodded. "In the long run, though, what it did was to give Simon power over Lucullus. He could expose him at any time, and he didn't hesitate to remind Lucullus of that power."

"What did Licinia have to do with Simon?" Tacitus asked.

"She's always been headstrong, a challenge to her father. She rejects our family's way of life. She dresses like a servant and won't eat meat. She developed a fascination for Simon. She claimed she was in love with him. I think she just wanted to spite her father. There was nothing Lucullus could do to keep them apart. He was that afraid of Simon."

"What do you know about Simon's life before he was enslaved?"

"Not much. Lucullus wasn't even sure his true name was Simon. But none of the other slaves Lucullus bought with him would tell us otherwise. He speaks excellent Greek. I think he was from one of the outlying areas, not from Jerusalem itself. But that's all I know."

"What did you think of him?" I asked.

Porcia shuddered and drew her arms around herself. "I was afraid of him from the first moment I met him. He's not a particularly large man—about as tall as you, Gaius Pliny—but broader in the shoulders. Something about him intimidates you, though, as soon as he comes into a room."

If he's not very tall, I thought, he could easily blend into a crowd. And he must be strong enough to inflict such a serious wound with one upward thrust of a knife. I turned to Aurora. "Does that sound like the man who attacked me?"

"Yes, my lord. And the man we saw at the synagogue."

"But you said he had a beard."

"Beards can be shaved, my lord."

"Simon often wore a beard," Porcia said, "but he would shave it at times. At other times he would let it grow."

"My lord," Aurora said, "Phineas says that Jewish men sometimes make a vow to their god not to shave their beards or cut their hair until they've carried out some important task."

"I hadn't thought about it," Porcia said, "but Simon could look very different at different times—the length of his hair, whether he had a beard or not. It was all quite unpredictable. Lucullus said not to ask him about it."

"So we can't even get a good description of the man we're looking for," I said.

Tacitus had fallen quiet. Now he said, "My lady, did your husband ever mention a man named Berenicianus?"

"No, I've never heard that name. What does he have to do with Lucullus?"

"We found him in a warehouse of Gaius Pliny's a few days ago. He had been killed by a knife wound in his back. And Licinia was also found there with several other people who had been killed when the warehouse collapsed."

"Who were those other people?"

"We don't know names," I said, "but they were three men and another woman."

"They must be the slaves who escaped with Simon when Lucullus was killed. There was a small group of them who were purchased when Lucullus bought Simon. They clung together, like a family. Their names were Reuben, who was the oldest, Gideon, Saul, and Deborah. We wanted to give them Greek or Latin names, but Simon refused and my husband didn't insist."

"So they were all Jews?"

"Yes."

"Did they have a particular craft or skill?"

"They were fullers. They had had a shop in Jerusalem and Lucullus let them open one for him in Antioch."

That explained the discoloration on their hands.

"How did they get along with others in the household?" Tacitus asked.

"Not well. They kept to themselves," Porcia said. "Licinia acted as though she was a friend of theirs, just to annoy her father, I'm sure. She treated them as practically her equals, like some Cynic philosopher. It was most disgraceful and kept the household in turmoil."

"Why did Lucullus let that go on?" I asked.

"He couldn't stop Simon from doing anything because of the dirty work Simon did for him. And no one can control Licinia. Simon would spend the night in her room, and they made no effort to hide what they were doing."

I wish I could be so bold, I thought.

"She sounds like one of those women who debase themselves with gladiators and chariot drivers," Tacitus said.

"Exactly. I don't know what I'm going to do with her now. How can I keep her in the house? Can I lock her up somewhere?"

"No, you can't, *Mother*," a woman's voice said. Licinia emerged from the house and stood in front of us with her arms crossed over her chest.

She had changed into one of her own gowns, which still looked like something a servant would wear. She had combed her hair and pinned it up but wore no makeup, emphasizing the boniness of her cheeks and neck. "I'm sure Simon will come to get me because he loves me, and there's not one single thing you can do about it."

"We could turn you over to the Praetorians and let them lock you up," I said. "You confessed to killing two men of equestrian rank."

Licinia snarled. "You forced that confession out of me. I would have said anything to avoid a beating. I should have let you lay the whip on me a few more times. You know it's a violation of the law to beat someone of the citizen class without a trial."

I stood up and turned to face her. "I had no way of knowing who you were. You passed yourself off as a plebeian or lower. You never indicated who your family was. And you confessed after only one light blow from the whip."

"Yes, I'm ashamed of myself for that." She straightened her bony shoulders. "I thought I could hold out and let you hit me a few times, for the sake of all the other unfortunates who've suffered like that. Then I could bring a charge against you. But the pain was too great."

"You're nothing but a posturing hypocrite," Porcia said.

Licinia hung her head and looked away. "For the first time in your life, *Mother*, you're right. I can't deny that."

"Why did you want to cause trouble for me?" I asked. "You don't know me."

"I know that damn stripe. You, my father—every one of you who wears that thing—you lord it over people. You think you can own them, like cattle. You think you own that girl, sitting there so meekly behind you." She threw her hand out in Aurora's direction.

—◦◦◦—

I was surprised to suddenly find myself the focus of everyone's attention. "Yes, Gaius does own me," I wanted to say, "in the eyes of the law. But it's not that simple. I can't imagine not being his slave. Or maybe I just don't want to imagine it."

Licinia would probably say that was because I was too stupid to think in any other terms. There have been philosophers who have taught against slavery, she would say.

"And I've read them," I would reply. "*They never advocate doing away with it. They just want masters to treat their slaves more humanely. Seneca wanted everyone—slave or free—to treat those beneath them as they wished to be treated by those above them. Our world would collapse without slavery. If my father hadn't sold my mother and me, we would all have died of starvation on the edge of the desert in North Africa. That would have been worse than slavery in the house of Gaius and his uncle, wouldn't it?… Wouldn't it?*"

——⁓——

"You were the one who tore up Berenicianus' stripe, weren't you?" Tacitus said.

"Yes." Licinia lifted her chin proudly. "And I would rip yours off you right now, if I could."

I didn't want to get into a debate about the morality of slavery or social classes. Some things just are. "If you didn't kill Lucullus or Berenicianus, then who did?"

"If you give me time, I'll tell you, Gaius Pliny, and you won't have to beat it out of me."

I sat back down and motioned for her to do the same. "Take all the time you need. Tell us what you know. Maybe you can be the oracle I need to make sense out of this."

Licinia looked at me in consternation, sat down, and took a breath to compose herself. "I was in my room a few nights ago, when it was raining so badly. Simon came to the door. I thought he was going to… spend the night, but he said he was leaving—he and the others who had come here with him. I asked him why. If they ran away and were caught, they would be severely punished. That's what happens to slaves. He had never been mistreated by my father."

"Your father was too afraid of him to do anything," Porcia said.

"Had Simon been letting his hair and his beard grow?" I asked.

"Yes, but he just did that sometimes," Licinia said, "whenever the mood struck him."

Or whenever he was planning to kill someone? "Did you tell you why he had chosen that moment to run away?"

"He said something had happened to my father and he had to leave. He was sure he would be blamed."

"What had happened?"

"He didn't say, just that he had to leave. I told him I wanted to go with him."

"So he didn't force you to go?" Porcia asked.

"No, *Mother*. He would have had to force me to stay."

"Did you see your father's body before you left?" I asked.

"No. I heard later that he was stabbed in the back."

"Do you know who did it?"

"No, I don't. I swear it."

"We believe it was Simon."

Licinia shook her head vigorously. "The Simon I know couldn't have done that. He could be provoked, I admit, but at heart he was a tender man. When he took me in his arms—"

"That's not the issue here," I said quickly. "You're saying that you led this group of escaping slaves out of the house."

"It was easy." She looked proud, smug. "I guess my father's body hadn't been found yet. No one had raised an alarm and no one thought there was anything unusual about his daughter leaving the house with a few slaves to accompany her, even in the rain."

"How did you end up in my warehouse? Of all the warehouses—"

"Simon didn't seem to have much of a plan after we left here. I'm not sure he intended for anyone to go with him. He had a bag of supplies, but I didn't learn until later what was in it. I could see that we needed shelter. I thought we might find a place in a warehouse along the river. That would put us close to boats and a way out of Rome. We could also find something to eat. We chose yours because it wasn't locked. Unfortunately, it was also empty."

"Can you swear that Simon did or did not kill your father?"

"He never told me, one way or the other. But he did kill Berenicianus."

"How can you be so sure of that?"

"I saw him do it."

XI

YOU *SAW* SIMON kill Berenicianus?" I leaned forward in disbelief. "Did you try to stop him?"

Licinia shook her head slowly. "There was nothing I could do."

I needed to test her reliability, which I certainly had good reason to doubt. "Where was Berenicianus killed?"

"In the alleyway beside your warehouse."

"How did he come to be there? And, I presume, by himself?"

"Simon lured him there. He sent a message telling Berenicianus to come to the warehouse alone or he would kill Berenice. 'You know I can do it,' he said in the message. 'I can get to that whore any time I want.'"

"How do you know what was in this message?"

"I wrote down what he dictated. I was the only one in our group who could write. Reuben and I delivered it. We gave it to the guard at the door of Berenice's *insula* and did not wait for an answer."

"How did you know where Berenice lived?"

"Reuben knew. But Simon had been following you since the first time you came to your warehouse. You were a good piece of bait, Gaius Pliny."

Of course I should have realized I'd made it easy for him.

"He saw where you lived and he saw you talking to Berenice later, that day she came to you," Licinia continued. "He followed her home from there."

Her smirk taunted me as much as her words.

"Berenicianus was a fool," Tacitus said, "to meet anyone under those circumstances—alone in a dangerous part of the city."

"He had to do it to protect his mother," I said. "Wouldn't you? I would have done it." I turned back to Licinia. "What happened when Berenicianus arrived?"

"Simon met him in the alleyway beside the building," she said. "I hid around the corner so I could see and hear what was going on. Because of the rain I couldn't hear every word, but they were both very angry. Simon said something and Berenicianus said, 'You would kill your own mother?'"

I jumped up. "Wait! He called Berenice Simon's mother?"

"Yes. It surprised me, too. Simon didn't deny it. He said, 'My mother? Is that what she is? Let's see. My father was her uncle, so that makes her my cousin. But, if she was married to my uncle, she's also my aunt, isn't she?' He put his head in his hands, as though he was hopelessly confused. 'Mother? Cousin? Aunt? How…how do I know what to call her? And then she spreads her legs for her own brother. I guess "whore" covers all the possibilities, so that's what I call her.'

"And Berenicianus said, 'Hyrcanus, you can't—'

"'Don't call me Hyrcanus!' he shouted. 'That's the name that whore gave me. I'm Simon ben-Hur. I can call myself that because I have heard what the Lord says. You and your Roman friends, with your stripes on your clothes, you think you've won, but you haven't listened to the Lord like I have.'"

Licinia took a deep breath. "Berenicianus asked him what he had heard. Simon said, 'We have to live by the rules, by the law. Our family breeds like a flock of sheep. The rams mount any ewe they want. Sister, cousin, mother—it makes no difference. And you and I, dear brother, are their offspring. They're disgusting. *We're* disgusting. They call themselves Jews, but they pay no attention to the rules. Isn't that what Jews are supposed to do—live by the rules, by God's laws?'

"Berenicianus shook his head. 'We did that for a long time—for centuries—and what good did it do us? How many times has Jerusalem been sacked? If a god fails to protect those who live by his laws, what good is he?'"

Licinia clenched her hands together and drew them to her mouth. "Simon became furious. 'He hasn't failed us,' he said. 'He imposes trials on us because *we* fail *him*. We don't live by his laws. When we return to him and his laws, he will restore us.'

"'And you think running around in the streets stabbing people will restore us to him?'

"'If we scare enough people badly enough, we'll make the point. They will return to him. That's what I was trying to do, what all the *Sicarii* were trying to do—sort the wheat from the chaff. But you weren't faithful. Your Roman stomach was too weak for the hard work.'

"'You're on a fool's errand, Hyrcanus, and you're the perfect fool for it.'

"'I told you, don't call me Hyrcanus! My name is Simon.'

"'Call yourself whatever you like,' Berenicianus said. 'I'm finished with this conversation, and with you. I'm going to be sure I can protect my mother.' He turned to leave. Simon grabbed him around the throat and plunged a knife into his back.

"'Are you sure you don't mean your *cousin?*' he said. Then he stabbed him again. 'Or maybe you're talking about your *aunt?*' The second time he thrust it so hard I thought the whole knife, handle and all, was going to go in. There was blood all over the place. Then Simon told me to get the bag he had brought with him."

"You stuffed coins in Berenicianus' mouth and sewed it shut," I said.

She nodded. "Simon put the coins in his mouth. I had to sew it up, though. Berenicianus wasn't quite dead. He knew what I was doing." She was amazingly calm. "Simon's hands were shaking too badly, from excitement, I think. He kept muttering something about a king who had to watch his sons get killed and then had his eyes gouged out. Simon propped him up against the wall in the warehouse and told the others to keep quiet. Then I cut up as much of Berenicianus' stripe as I could."

"Why did Simon want you to do that?"

"He didn't. That was my idea," she said proudly. "I hate those things and everything they stand for."

"Part of what they stand for is the luxurious life you've enjoyed for years."

———— ∞ ————

"I don't know what to do, Gaius Pliny," Porcia said. She had sent Licinia to her room and we retired to the *exhedra* to get out of the sun. Porcia ordered a servant to bring wine and fruit. "I can't control her. She'll run away again or Simon will come to get her."

"If he comes to get her, I believe it will be to kill her. He tried to do that at my house. You saw the wound on her side."

"Why would he want to kill her? I thought they were in love."

"Licinia may be in love with the idea of a dangerous romance. Simon is in love with himself and obsessed with revenge."

"I think he was also having an affair with Deborah, the girl who escaped with him."

"You said these people were captured after the war, but Deborah would have been quite young then, wouldn't she?"

Porcia nodded. "I understand that she was ten when Lucullus bought her, along with her father, Reuben." She paused, gathering enough courage to say something difficult, even painful. "Lucullus had…an interest in girls…of that age, I'm afraid. He lost interest when they began their monthlies. The main reason he married me, I believe, is because I looked so young. I was only twelve and looked even younger. I've never had the sort of voluptuous body some women have." She glanced at Aurora. "I didn't want Lucullus dead, but I wasn't sure how I was going to protect my daughter in a few more years."

Aurora whispered something in my ear and I turned back to Porcia. "This is not easy to ask, but do you think he might have…?"

"To Licinia? I've no doubt of it. She's never admitted it, mind you, but I think it's why she has never wanted to make herself pretty. And why she threw herself at Simon, the one thing that would cause her father the most distress. Simon was her way of punishing Lucullus, I believe."

"We found a baby in the warehouse," I said.

"A living baby?" Porcia said in surprise.

"Yes. Could the father have been Lucullus?"

Porcia shook her head. "As I said, Lucullus preferred girls who weren't nubile. Any coupling he did with a woman like me or his first wife was just an obligation. Roman men are supposed to produce children. The law requires it. I don't have to tell you gentlemen that."

No, she didn't. Roman law does require that a man have three legitimate children to hold the upper offices in the state and to be allowed to inherit property. Neither Tacitus nor I has fulfilled that obligation.

Many men of our class have failed to do so. Rather, they don't inquire too closely about the paternity of their children or they ask for an exemption, the *ius trium liberorum*, that gives them the legal status of having three children. Tacitus has it. I guess I'll have to ask for it at some point, given Livia's adamant refusal to do that part of her wifely duty.

I wanted to turn the conversation away from our lack of children. I hear enough about that from my mother. "Could the child have belonged to someone in your household, perhaps the slave woman who escaped with Simon?"

Porcia pursed her lips in thought. "I suspect the baby you found was Deborah's."

"You suspect?" Tacitus said. "You don't know if one of your servants had a baby?"

"Deborah worked in the kitchen by her choice. I didn't see much of her in other parts of the house. Her room was back here, next to the kitchen. It was her responsibility to get up early and start the fire and that sort of thing. She kept to herself, had very little to say to anyone. Another of our servants had a child recently, one of the women with whom I work more closely. I guess I was more aware of her than of Deborah. I did notice at some point that Deborah seemed to be gaining weight, but these gowns conceal a lot." She pulled at her own garment.

I had to agree. Deceiving a husband about a pregnancy was a frequent theme in comedies. "Do you have any idea whose child he might be?" I didn't really need an answer to that question. The child was circumcised and Simon had invaded my house looking for him.

Porcia didn't have time to answer before her two children came out of the room where the nurse had been tending to them. "I'm sorry, my lady," the nurse said. "They wanted to see you and your visitors."

"It's all right," Porcia said with a smile. "I think we're finished here." The children ran to her and she embraced them. Seeing them up close, as opposed to the distance from which I'd seen them at their father's funeral, I could see that they were both quite handsome, the girl resembling her mother already and the boy sporting dark hair and round features, which the mask of Licinius had displayed. "Is there anything else I can tell you, Gaius Pliny?" their mother asked.

We all stood. "You've been most helpful, my lady. I would advise you to keep a close eye on Licinia. Post a guard on her at all times, if possible."

"Do you really think there is any further danger?"

I nodded. "I do think Simon will come after her, but not to take her away, as she believes. He disposes of people after he's finished with them. That's what he did when he killed Lucullus. He manipulated Licinia. Now he has no further use for her. I think he wanted to kill her before she could tell us what we just heard. That's why he came to get her at my house."

"But why would he kill her now?"

"Either he doesn't know if she has talked to us, or he does know and will want revenge. Revenge is the fuel that stokes whatever fire is burning in the man. He's consumed by it."

"He's far more dangerous than Licinia realizes," Tacitus said. "She can't see the real man because of her childish, romantic notions."

Porcia's face showed her indecisiveness. "I really don't have enough servants here to watch her. And we couldn't defend ourselves if Simon came after her. He and Reuben were the two most able-bodied men in the household."

"Let me take her to my house," Tacitus offered.

"You're not going to lock her up in some dark hole, are you?" Porcia asked. Recalcitrant slaves are sometimes confined under harsh conditions. "As little as I care for her, I wouldn't want her subjected to that."

"Not at all," Tacitus assured her. "She'll be treated as a guest, but I can call on some of Agricola's veterans who live in an *insula* nearby to stand guard over her."

"But Simon may think she's still here," Porcia objected, holding her children closer to her. It struck me that the little boy clinging to his mother's gown was actually the owner of this property now. If something happened to me—if I died again and did not awaken—there would be no one to inherit all that I own.

"I doubt it," I said. "He has an uncanny knack for following us without being seen. I'm sure he knows we're here, and he will know where we take Licinia. Once we leave with her, I don't think you and your household will be in any further danger." I knelt in front of her and put my hand on the boy's head. "You take good care of your mother."

—◦◦◦—

Licinia, of course, did not want to go with us. "This is always what happens to the child of the first wife!" she screamed. "The second wife has a couple of brats and I'm thrown out."

"We're just taking you to a safe place," Gaius said. He motioned for me to walk beside her.

I slipped my arm through hers. She accepted the gesture, still in her pose as sympathizing with a servant, I guess. From what I had heard at Porcia's house, I knew what had happened to Licinia when she was a child. That made me look at her very differently. Her father had taken advantage of her when she was ten or eleven. My father might have sold me, but he had never hurt me that way. Licinia's mother had been killed when she was twelve—

I stopped myself right there as a string of questions came into my mind. What if her mother had found out what Lucullus was doing and tried to stop him? What if she threatened to expose him? Roman men do marry very young girls, but coupling with children is considered abnormal, something embarrassing if it's made public. It would have disqualified him from public offices. Would Lucullus have had his wife killed to prevent that? He had an assassin in his household, and his wife was killed by the method that assassin liked to use.

"You know, I was perfectly safe back there," Licinia said, speaking rapidly, the way I've seen crazy women in the streets yammering to themselves. "Simon wouldn't hurt me. He loves me. And I love him."

I didn't say anything, just held her arm a little more tightly and patted her hand.

"We could have been very happy if it hadn't been for that Deborah." She sneered as she pronounced the name.

I leaned into her, as though we were two friends chatting, like the women in the Tanagra figures Gaius' mother likes to collect. "What did Deborah do?"

"She seduced Simon, back in that little private room of hers, off the kitchen. She thought no one knew, but I knew."

Or maybe Simon took advantage of the seclusion and forced himself on Deborah.

I wasn't sure how to get to the topic of Joshua. Clearly he was Simon's child by Deborah. Did Licinia know, or suspect, that?

"Can I tell you something?" Licinia dropped her voice to a whisper.

"Of course."

"I wasn't entirely honest about when I left the house with Simon and the others. He showed me my father's body in the latrina and I helped him shove the bastard into the drain. I really enjoyed doing that, after what he did."

"Did Simon tell you who killed him?"

Licinia shook her head, which also twitched now and then.

"He's very handy with his knife, isn't he?"

Licinia laughed. "He even used it to circumcise Deborah's baby. That was a sight to see. That big knife and that tiny mentula."

"He didn't take the child to a rabbi?"

"He said the rabbis here are all lackeys of the Romans."

"So Deborah had Josh—the baby with her when you left the house?"

"Yes. I didn't want to take him, but Simon insisted."

It was his son, I thought. Of course he would insist. I was beginning to appreciate how deluded—almost deranged—Licinia was.

We were passing the Flavian Amphitheatre, or the Colosseum as people were already calling it. "What happened when you got to Gaius Pliny's warehouse?"

She seemed to be relaxing, taking me more into her confidence. "We spent a couple of days planning and finding enough to eat. It's hard to keep track of time, with all the rain and the warehouse being so dark. Reuben and I took that message to Berenicianus. I told you what happened after that."

"Yes, I'm glad you were so honest with us. How long did you stay there after Simon killed him?"

"I'm just not sure. We hoped the rain would let up and that maybe we could find a boat to take us down the Tiber, but then the building collapsed."

"Why was the baby hidden, away from the rest of you?"

Licinia waved a hand dismissively. "That Deborah was pretending the baby was Simon's. He held it a few times, but you could see he wasn't interested. So, while everyone was sleeping I took the baby away from her and stashed him under a pile of junk with a rag stuffed in his mouth to keep him quiet. When the building started to collapse, Deborah woke up and couldn't find the little bastard. I wouldn't tell her where he was. I told

*her I'd thrown him in the river, but she didn't believe me. She kept crying
and looking for him. Reuben said we had to get out, but Deborah wouldn't
leave without her damn baby. She was screaming for everybody to look for
him, so everybody was still in there when the roof fell on us."*

"Why didn't you leave?"

"It was too much fun to watch Deborah going crazy." She cackled.

I had told Gaius that the dead woman—Deborah—was trying to help
me save her baby. Now I knew I was right. Gaius could scoff all he wanted.

"Simon wasn't in the building when it collapsed. Where was he?"

*"He had gone out to find food for us. That's all I remember until you
people found us."*

———❦———

By the time we got Licinia settled in Tacitus' house and Aurora and I
returned to my house, it was dinner time. During our walk she told
me all she had learned from Licinia. "From her voice and some of her
mannerisms," she concluded, "I believe the poor girl is going mad, and
I can't say I blame her. She's been treated horribly and lost her mother
at a time when she most needed her."

"And you really think Lucullus had Simon kill his first wife? What
was her name?"

"Aemilia. Yes, I do. The time when it occurred, the method—it all
points to Simon."

"Well, no Roman man would want to be revealed as a despoiler
of girls that age. The practice is considered aberrant. And his own
daughter! By the gods, the man was vile."

"Perhaps your whole system of arranging marriages is at fault here."

"It has worked for us for hundreds of years."

"Maybe something else would work better, if you would only try
it. The Spartans used to make their girls wait until they were twenty
or so before they married them off," Aurora said. "You Romans might
do well to emulate them. Children should be children."

"But the highly esteemed Athenians and other Greeks married
their girls off as soon as they started their monthlies," I countered.
"And they still do. As soon as a girl is able to have children, she should
get started. At least, that's always been our philosophy."

We had reached the front door of my house and were waiting for Demetrius to let us in. "The less said about this, the better," I said.

Aurora bowed her head. "Of course, my lord."

"Tomorrow we need to talk to a few people, including Berenice and Merione. I think in both cases it would be helpful for me to have a woman with me. Can you tear yourself away from Joshua long enough to accompany me?"

Aurora chuckled. "Miriam, Naomi, and your mother can take excellent care of him."

"But can they protect him if Simon comes for his son again?"

—◦◦◦—

Of the three women I needed to talk to, Sempronia lived closest to me, so I would start with her. At midmorning the next day we were at Regulus' door. Because there was so little distance between our two houses, Aurora and I made the trip unaccompanied by the usual gaggle of servants or clients. Walking by ourselves felt liberating but also induced a degree of fear as we edged our way through the crowd. We knew all too well that Simon could be anywhere in that throng.

Regulus' *ianitor* informed us that the great man was not in. That suited me fine, since I wanted to talk to Merione and figured that would go just as well if Sempronia were with us. The doorman, his eyebrows arched in surprise when I asked to see his mistress, escorted us to Sempronia's wing of the gigantic house. It must have originally been someone else's house that Regulus had purchased—or seized in some nefarious scheme—and incorporated into his own by breaking through walls in appropriate places. Like Domitian taking over the top of the Palatine, Regulus seemed to be oozing all over the top of the Esquiline.

The doorman stopped before a large bronze door decorated with a scene of Sappho reading her poetry to two of her devotees. When he knocked, the door was opened by a woman I guess I could call the *ianitrix*.

"Gaius Pliny asks to see the lady Sempronia," he said.

The young woman, blond and wearing a short tunic, stepped

back and motioned for us to enter. We followed her through a short passageway into an atrium about half the size of mine. Some young women were engaged in wool-working and other tasks one expects to see women doing in a household; others were reading. They all stopped and looked up, their attention focused not on me but on Aurora.

The frescoes around the atrium glorified Amazons and showed scenes of women—known as *hetairai*—entertaining at dinner parties. There was one significant difference: the guests reclining on the couches were women, embracing and kissing as men are shown doing on Greek pottery used at the parties known as *symposia*. I had the impression I was in an all-female brothel, or rather, one with female customers.

"My lady Sempronia is in the garden," our guide said. "Please follow me."

We could hear voices coming from the garden, making the sort of noises one usually associates with people watching a fight of some sort. When we emerged into the full daylight of the garden, I was stunned to see Sempronia and another woman wrestling—oiled and clad only in loincloths, such as women wear when having their monthlies. We stopped and waited until Sempronia tripped the other woman and pinned her to the ground with a knobby knee on her chest. The vanquished woman raised her hand with the index finger extended to indicate her surrender. A cheer went up from the circle of women who were watching. I doubted that Sempronia lost many matches.

Aurora leaned toward me and asked, "Are these slaves or free women?"

Looking at the women exercising or reading in various spots in the garden—most of them only partially clad—I recognized the wives and daughters of several prominent families. "I believe there are some of both," I said.

One woman began wiping the oil, dirt, and sweat off Sempronia, dipping a towel in a bowl of water. She was followed by a second woman who dried her mistress with another towel. While they were tending to her, Sempronia turned to face me so that I could see her small breasts and almost nonexistent hips. She untied her loincloth and dropped it to the ground. When her servant handed her a gown, she hesitated a moment before slipping it over her head and pinning it at her shoulders. She did not take her eyes off of me the whole time, nor did the languid expression on her face ever change as she approached me. A servant gave her a cup and she took a long drink.

"Well, Gaius Pliny," she said, wiping her mouth on the back of her hand, "to what do I owe this intrusion, or pleasure, or whatever it may be."

I finally managed to find my voice. "Thank you for seeing me, my lady. I have some information on that matter you asked me to look into. I thought I might discuss it with you...in private. And I'd like to talk to your woman Merione, the nurse that Regulus sent to my house."

Sempronia gave an order to one of the woman close to her, who left the garden. "Merione will be here shortly. Meanwhile let's adjourn to this room here."

We followed Sempronia to one of the rooms off the garden, containing a table and three chairs. She looked surprised when Aurora came in with me.

"Are you sure you want her here?"

I nodded quickly. "She gives me a reliable witness to conversations, in case I can't remember exactly what was said."

"Hmm. I'm sure some of my girls would enjoy wrestling with her."

I didn't think she was talking only about the kind of sport we had just witnessed.

"Your girls seem to be in excellent physical condition," I said. "As do you yourself, if I may say so."

"I'd be disappointed if you didn't, Gaius Pliny. Now, what information do you have for me?" She sat down in one chair and I took another, one with arms. She waved a hand at Aurora. "Oh, sit down, girl. You're making me nervous." Aurora sat on the arm of my chair.

"I have learned, beyond any doubt, that your cousin, Licinius Lucullus, was murdered by one of his servants, a man named Simon."

"That's what I suspected. Do you know where this Simon is? Nobody seems to be able to find him."

"He is quite elusive, but he is still in Rome, and I don't think he will leave any time soon."

She crossed her legs and propped her arms on her knee. "Why not?"

"He wants to retrieve his son and kill his mother."

I expected her face to register shock, but all I could see was indifference. "That's an ambitious agenda. Who is his mother?"

"Berenice."

Sempronia sat bolt upright. "*Our* Berenice? But her son was killed a few days ago, in a most gruesome fashion."

"It seems there is a second son. His name is, or was, Hyrcanus. He was taken captive after the destruction of Jerusalem and was sold to your cousin Lucullus. He now calls himself Simon ben-Hur."

"By the gods! Berenice has never so much as hinted—"

"There was bad blood between them. He hates all things Roman, including his brother and his mother. He sees her mainly as a woman who was involved with Titus, the man who destroyed Jerusalem."

"Does Berenice know that he's here and the danger he poses to her?"

"I sent her a message this morning, and I'll go there and talk to her when I leave here."

"She must have suspected something. She asked for the bars on her windows and made it sound urgent. As her landlord and friend, I was glad to comply."

"I hope they will protect her, but the man got into my house two nights ago. I'm not sure anything will ultimately stop him."

A knock sounded on the door and Sempronia called, "Enter." The door opened and Merione stepped into the room.

"You wanted to see me, my lady?"

"Yes. Close the door." Sempronia changed her position in the chair so she could easily look from Merione to me and back. "Gaius Pliny would like to ask you some questions. I want you to answer him forthrightly, as you would if you were talking to me or Regulus."

"Yes, my lady." Merione clasped her hands in front of her, rubbing them together nervously.

I decided to attack directly, as I would in court, to try to throw someone I didn't trust off-balance. "Merione, you tried to steal a baby from my house. You said you weren't doing it for Marcus Regulus or your lady Sempronia. Tell me what you intended to do then. For whom were you going to take that baby?"

Her voice quivered. "For a man, my lord. I don't know who he was."
Aurora gave a muted gasp.

"You expect me to believe that you would give a baby to a man you
didn't know? Why would you do such a thing?"

"He offered me money, my lord," Merione blurted. "An *aureus*."

"An entire gold coin? Is that what a baby's worth?" I sat back in my
chair, as though settling in for a long conversation. "Maybe you'd better
start from the beginning."

"Yes, my lord." She took a deep breath. "You see, my lord Marcus
Regulus told me to go to your house to be wet nurse for a baby. As I
was on my way there a man fell into step beside me."

"Did you know this man? Had you ever seen him before?"

"No, my lord."

"Where did he come from?"

"I'm not sure, my lord. He just seemed to appear—out of an alley,
from behind a door. I don't know."

"What did he look like?"

"About your height, my lord. He had dark hair and a beard."

That had to be Simon, both from his appearance and his sudden
presence out of nowhere.

"What did he say to you?"

"He said he knew I was going to be wet nurse to a baby, my lord."

Now it was my turn to gasp. Simon had been somewhere near us
when we were bringing people out of the warehouse. Near enough to
hear what was being said and to know who we were. The man was
ubiquitous.

"Did he say why he was interested in you or the baby?"

"He said the baby was his, my lord. It had been taken away from
him."

I crossed my arms over my chest. "How could he prove that?"

"That's what I asked him, my lord. He said I would see that the baby
was circumcised. Well, that's something he couldn't exactly be guessing
about, isn't it? I mean, first of all, just knowing it was a boy and then
knowing it was circumcised."

I held out a hand to prevent Aurora from saying that Joshua wasn't
an "it."

"No, I suppose he couldn't be guessing. What else did he say? Did he threaten you?"

"Not at all, my lord. He seemed very nice, sort of sad. He said he would give me an *aureus* if I helped him get the child."

"Where would he get that kind of money?" Sempronia put in.

"I don't know, my lady, but he showed it to me."

I didn't want Sempronia distracting Merione, but I couldn't very well protest. The woman was her slave and this was her house. "I'm sure this man was Simon, the man who killed Lucullus. Porcia said that Lucullus shared some of his profits with Simon because of the… type of work Simon did for him."

Sempronia's lowered eyelids let me know that she understood that Simon was a paid assassin. That would also explain where he got thirty *denarii* to cram into his brother's mouth. "How were you supposed to get this baby to him?" she asked.

"He said we should wait a full day, to let people in Gaius Pliny's house start to trust me." She turned to me. "I'm sorry, my lord. I'm not usually a devious person."

I waved a hand. "It's all right. Go on."

"Well, then, in the middle of the second night, I was supposed to be by the back gate. He would tap on it. I would open it and give him the baby. He would give me the *aureus* and would make it look like I'd been knocked out and the baby stolen."

"But you were knocked out, weren't you?" Sempronia asked.

"Yes, my lady. By *that* one." She pointed to Aurora. "She gave me a blow on the head and took the baby and left before Simon got there. As far as I'm concerned, she owes me an *aureus*."

I laughed in disbelief. "For giving away a baby that wasn't yours?"

"With all due respect, my lord, he wasn't yours either. He was just something you found, entirely by accident. This man did know he was circumcised."

"I assure you, Merione, all you would have gotten from Simon would have been a knife between your ribs. You owe Aurora your life. Being knocked out is not nearly as bad as being dead."

And that I know because I have been both knocked out and dead.

XII

SEMPRONIA'S SERVANT showed us out by a door that led directly from the women's part of the house onto the street. "I'm going to need a bath when we get home," Aurora said with a shudder.

"What? You don't like being the object of everyone's desire?"

"Only yours, dear Gaius. Only yours."

"I must admit it felt odd to be completely ignored by all those women. I know I'm no Adonis, but still…"

Aurora shivered. "Let's talk about something else."

A stray dog crossed our path and trotted into an alley. "Agreed. It worries me to learn how freely this Simon moves among us. He could just as easily have been that dog. We pay no attention to him. That first day when we were at the warehouse, did you see anyone that could have been him?"

Aurora shook her head. "It was raining, and we had so much else to deal with. I know there were people standing around, but I couldn't tell you how many or what they looked like. It was all so confusing. Simon obviously saw and heard everything that was going on. He could be ten feet away from us right now, and I don't think we would know, just as we didn't see him until he stabbed you."

"And we've left ourselves very vulnerable right now without a *clientela*. That was reckless on my part." I glanced around as I took Aurora's arm. "Let's get home quickly."

"Are you afraid, Gaius?"

"In all honesty, yes, thoroughly afraid."

I hated myself for being afraid. That was what Simon wanted to inspire in me—fear not only of what he did but of what he might do.

We picked up our pace, like children being chased by imaginary monsters on a dark night. But there was nothing imaginary about Simon, only monstrous.

I felt great relief to see the front of my house and even greater relief to see Tacitus emerging from it. He turned to his left, away from us and summoned his men to start down the hill, but I called out to him. "Cornelius Tacitus, wait!"

He paused and turned back to us. "Well, this is fortunate," he said. "Your man Demetrius told me he didn't know when you would return."

"Do you have time to go with us? We're going to see Berenice."

"You're quite the peripatetic today. Yes, I'd be glad to go with you."

"Let me gather a few men to add to yours."

Feeling much more comfortable surrounded by my servants and Tacitus', but still glancing around me for any sign of Simon as we walked, I told him what we had learned from Merione.

"That explains the thirty *denarii* we found in Berenicianus' mouth," he said. "Simon was blackmailing his own master, Lucullus. That gave him his own funds."

"A lot of us are fortunate that our slaves don't take advantage of what they know about us," I said.

Tacitus drew himself up and looked down at me, which is easy enough for him to do, given the difference in our heights. "I know what you're insinuating, Gaius Pliny. Coupling with young men might not suit your tastes, but it's by no means the most disgraceful activity a Roman man might engage in. If one of my servants tried to blackmail me over it, I would laugh in his face."

"And then sell him?"

"Precisely. And to someone who would take him far from Rome."

———ɷɷɷ———

Berenice greeted us with some reserve. "I hadn't expected to see you again so soon. Do you have news about my son's murderer?"

"Yes, we do," I said as we settled on the cushions in the main room of her apartment. Several of her servants stood behind her. "And we have news about your other son."

"My other son? You mean…Hyrcanus?"

"I suppose so. He calls himself Simon ben-Hur now. I think the 'Hur' is a shortened form of Hyrcanus."

"I'm surprised he kept any part of his original name. He hated everything Greek or Roman."

One of her servants, an older man, bent over and whispered something in her ear. "This is Benjamin, my scribe," Berenice said when she turned her attention back to me. "Please, tell Gaius Pliny what you just told me."

Benjamin bowed his head. "My lord, in Hebrew the word 'hur' can have several meanings. Perhaps the most common is 'to burn' or 'to set ablaze.'"

"Appropriate for someone who wants to spread terror in a city," Tacitus said.

"Yes, my lord, all too appropriate," Benjamin said.

I turned back to Berenice. "So you do have two sons."

"Yes, I have two sons, Gaius Pliny, although I've never been much of a mother to either of them."

"They're your children by your uncle Herod, king of Calchis."

"Who was my husband at the time, remember that." She said that as if the marriage justified the incest.

"And Hyrcanus was the one who tried to kill you outside the synagogue, wasn't he?"

Berenice nodded. She held her head high, when I was expecting to see her bow it in shame.

"How can you be sure?"

"Because I heard his voice. No matter how long it's been, a mother—even as poor a mother as I am—knows her child's voice."

"What did he say?"

"He called me a whore. That was the last word he said to me, the last time I saw him."

"And when was that?"

"Just after the fall of Jerusalem, fifteen years ago. Most of the *Sicarii* left in the city escaped to Masada, but a handful were captured and sold into slavery, along with other survivors."

Berenice shifted on her cushion and adjusted her gown. "I did not know where Hyrcanus ended up. Berenicianus tracked him down. He was sold to a man named Lucullus and taken to Antioch. Lucullus brought his household to Rome late this past summer to be ready to take up a consulship in January."

"But Hyrcanus killed him and escaped."

"That seems to be the case. Berenicianus came to Rome when Hyrcanus did to warn me because he knew, if Hyrcanus was in Rome, he would come after me."

"Why?"

"Because of my relationship with Titus. And he wanted to take vengeance on Berenicianus as well, because he had cooperated with the Romans. I can't emphasize too strongly how much Hyrcanus hated everything Roman. I should say 'hates,' since he's still alive. I'm sure he hasn't changed."

"Did you come to the synagogue that evening in hopes of drawing Hyrcanus out?" I asked.

Berenice nodded. "I thought a synagogue was the one place in Rome that might attract him."

"What did you hope to accomplish, other than getting yourself killed?"

She sighed and seemed to feel as old as she looked. Her shoulders slumped. "That would not have been the worst outcome I could imagine. I thought I knew how he would try to kill me. I hoped, with my cuirass and my guards, that I might be safe enough."

"Did you think you could talk to him, change his mind?"

"No, I had no hope of that. I thought it might be my one chance of having him arrested, if there were guards around and he tried to kill me. I knew the *vigiles* patrol that area when people gather in the synagogue. There have been arguments between Jews and Christians. Sometimes they go beyond words and spill over into the streets."

"The *vigiles* actually had Simon in a group of suspects until I told them to release everyone. I regret that, of course, but at the time it seemed reasonable, since you hadn't been hurt."

"Do you have any idea where Simon might be?" Tacitus asked.

"None whatsoever. He's a stranger to this city, with little knowledge of where things are. Your visits here, however, have led him to me, I'm sure. You said you found a baby in your warehouse."

"Yes. We now know that it's Simon's baby."

"Then you can be sure he was watching you when you left the warehouse. He knows where you live. He must have been watching your house, if that's where his child was, and he must have followed you here. You would never see him. The *Sicarii* prided themselves on being able to move around without being detected. They were like the shadows that move all around you, but shadows that carry knives."

We stood to go. "At least we now know who killed Berenicianus and Lucullus," Tacitus said.

"But you haven't caught him yet," Berenice said, "and I doubt you will."

"Even if we did," I put in, "we have no proof against him. The only witness we have won't testify. She'll probably deny everything she told us earlier. She's too much in love with him."

"You'll have one more chance," Berenice said.

"What do you mean?" I asked.

"He won't leave Rome until he's killed me. If you can witness that, you'll be able to make your case against him."

"My lady," I said, "we're not going to just sit around and wait for him to do that. We'll do everything we can to prevent him from hurting you."

—⁂—

I sent word to Josephus that I wanted to see him but did not tell him why. When he arrived at my house we met him in the atrium and I asked if he would accompany Tacitus and me to the Arch of Titus.

The lines in his brow deepened. "May I ask why? Have you not seen it?"

"Yes, we have, but I'm not sure I've really seen all I need to see. I would appreciate having someone with me who could interpret it for me."

"As would I," Tacitus put in.

Josephus bowed his head. "I will tell you what I can, but I hope you understand that my view of it is not entirely objective."

"It might be helpful if your view isn't entirely Roman," I said.

We were almost out the door when my mother hailed me from the other end of the atrium. We stopped and waited while she, Naomi, and Phineas caught up with us.

"Is it true?" Mother asked. "Are you going to see the Arch of Titus?" I couldn't believe how fast the news had traveled through the house.

"Yes."

"We'd like to go with you. I mean, Naomi and Phineas would like to, and I'd like to accompany them."

I motioned for Naomi and Phineas to step out from behind my mother. I wanted to talk with them directly, not through my mother as an intermediary. "Have you not seen the arch?" I asked.

"No, my lord," Naomi said. Phineas shook his head.

"It's been there for three years and you haven't seen it? I would think Jews would have a particular interest in it."

"We haven't seen it, my lord, because it symbolizes so much pain for us," Naomi said. Her voice broke.

My mother stepped in front of her. "They were forced to march in Titus' parade, Gaius. Did you know that? Forced to march in chains!"

I looked at Naomi and Phineas as though seeing them for the first time. "No, I didn't know that, Mother. I was only nine years old at the time."

I had been just a child, but my uncle had brought some of his family up from Laurentum to witness the triumph. Everyone knew it was going to be a splendid show. Well in advance rumors were spreading about the wooden displays that were being constructed to be carried in the parade—huge replicas of buildings and entire villages that had been destroyed in the war. And they had lived up to the predictions. Aurora and I had stood together and I had explained to her, as best I could, what we were seeing. Some years later, when I read Ovid's advice about meeting women, I had to laugh. I had done exactly what he recommended, making things up if I didn't know what we were seeing.

"I'm sorry," I said to Naomi and Phineas, "for all you've suffered. This must be painful. Perhaps it would be better if you stayed here."

"You needn't apologize, my lord," Naomi said. "You did nothing to us, and you've been as kind and humane as anyone could be."

I nodded to acknowledge what she said, although I knew Phineas bore much resentment against Rome and Romans, resentment which he sometimes had trouble suppressing.

"Now, my lord," Naomi continued, "we think it's time that we do see the arch, when we can be with others who can give us comfort. Your mother has seen it. Malachi says he saw it, but only once."

"Was he in Jerusalem?"

"No, my lord. He lived in one of the villages north of there. He left before the war began, but he had seen the temple numerous times. Those of us who did not live in Jerusalem went there once a year for a feast."

I turned to Josephus. "I gather that Naomi and Phineas do not think highly of you. Do you mind if they accompany us?"

Instead of answering me directly, Josephus took a step toward Naomi and Phineas and said something in Hebrew or, I corrected myself, in Aramaic. Phineas answered him in the same language. Their conversation went back and forth for several moments, with Naomi adding a comment here and there. At times they sounded friendly, at other times more hostile. Josephus finally turned back to me.

"I think your servants and I understand one another. I have no objection if they accompany us."

"What did you say to them?"

"I prefer not to discuss that. If they wish to tell you, or if you, as their master, compel them to, that is not my concern."

Given the disgust in his voice when he said "master" and "compel," I knew I wasn't ever going to know the gist of that conversation. "Very well, let's go."

—◈◈◈—

As we walked down the Esquiline I studied Naomi and Phineas, trying to imagine them in chains, but I couldn't do it. I've seen slaves in chains, of course. Everyone has, but not in our household. I know slaves in many houses are treated brutally, but I've never seen Gaius or his uncle do that. When a woman who helped raise Gaius was too old to work anymore, he gave her a small farm near his house on Lake Comum.

Gaius is convinced there are no gods. What if he's wrong? People all over the empire worship gods, and they always have. Can all those people be wrong? The Jews' god seems most peculiar. There was only one place in the entire world where they were allowed to sacrifice to him. But sacrifices are a way of feeding a god. How is their god fed if they don't sacrifice to him? Or is Jerusalem the only place where he exists or has any power? Gods are supposed to protect the people who worship them. But the Jews have been conquered several times and carried off into slavery. Will they get back to their holy land after this defeat? Domitian hates them, so he's not likely to be sympathetic to them returning. Naomi and Phineas say there was nothing left of Jerusalem after Titus and his soldiers finished with it, anyway. Phineas says some of their prophets predicted this would happen if the people didn't change their way of doing things. Why didn't people listen to them?

Other people have worshiped gods or goddesses and yet have been conquered. Just look at Athens. Once it was one of the most powerful cities in the world. Now it's part of a Roman province. Egypt, with its ancient gods and incredible temples in their honor, is just another Roman province. My own ancestors, the Carthaginians, once rivaled Rome. Over two hundred years ago their city was reduced to rubble. Does that mean the gods who are defeated aren't as strong as the ones who vanquish them? Or does it mean they're displeased with their people and turn their backs on them?

Naomi and Phineas talk about their god loving them. He has a strange way of showing it. Do gods love people? Athena was fond of Odysseus, she says in the Odyssey, *because he was so much like her—tricky, devious. But is that love? The only other examples I can recall of gods loving people were actually just lust, and the outcome for the people was always disastrous.*

⌐∿∿∿⌐

Since we were going into the heart of the city at a busy time of day, I gathered a dozen servants to accompany us and we set off down the Esquiline. At the bottom of the hill we turned onto the Via Sacra, which runs slightly northwest, and passed the *Ludus Magnus*, the gladiatorial school Domitian had just finished building, and the Amphitheatre. Even though it has been in use for five years now, it still seems new and strange to me, perhaps because I've not yet been in it.

Titus' arch stands on the Via Sacra, next to the temple of Jupiter Stator, at the far southeastern end of the Forum. It was one of the first—and last—things Domitian did to honor his brother, after probably killing him. It's not nearly as large as the Arch of Augustus, which stands farther into the Forum, next to the temple of the Deified Julius. Augustus' arch has three openings, while Titus' has just the one. I suspect Domitian did not want his brother to rival Augustus in any way but felt he had to honor him in some fashion because he was so popular with the people of Rome. They called him "the darling of the gods."

The arch is about ten times the height of a man and two-thirds that wide. It has a dedicatory inscription at the top, with a gilded chariot sitting above that. Fluted columns flank the opening. The keystones are decorated, with a male figure on one side and a female figure on the other. The overhead relief shows the apotheosis of Titus. The north panel shows him marching in a triumphal procession, along with his father, Vespasian. The south panel shows some of the items taken from the temple in Jerusalem.

"These are only the most important items," Josephus said, "the Menorah—the candlestick—the Table of Shewbread and the horns used to signal the Sabbath."

"My mother gave Naomi a small menorah as a Saturnalia gift several years ago," I said. That festival occurs at the same time as some Jewish celebration.

"That was thoughtful of her," Josephus replied.

The south panel was the one that interested me today. The panels are in color, with the Menorah and the Table painted yellow to symbolize gold. The horns used to signal the Sabbath are silver. The background of the panel is blue. Soldiers carry placards describing what is being displayed. To see it at best advantage one would need a ladder. All I could do was stand against the north side and tilt my head back.

"Why didn't Domitian use real gold and silver leaf?" Naomi asked.

"I suspect he didn't want to glorify his brother that much," Josephus said. "And, even though the objects are high off the ground, gold and silver leaf would attract thieves."

We all fell silent until Tacitus said, "I thought there was much more. At least from reading your description in your book about the war, that's the impression I got."

"I remember seeing the Menorah," I said, "but there was so much loot, the parade seemed to go on for hours." Aurora nodded.

"There was *so* much more," Josephus said. "These are only the most important items. In addition there were representations of buildings, some of them three or four stories high. I wondered how the men carrying them did not collapse under the weight. The men carrying objects in the procession wore purple, decorated with gold and gems. It was like watching a river of purple flow through the streets of Rome. People had been giving gifts of gold and silver and other precious items to the temple for generations. The building of that temple, our second, began when Cyrus the Persian allowed us to return from exile."

Tacitus let out a low whistle. "Cyrus was king just before the Roman Republic was established. That's almost six hundred years ago."

"That's how long treasures had been piling up in the temple." A trace of pride crept into Josephus' voice. "I doubt that anybody knows—or could know—how much had accumulated. And then Herod rebuilt it, in the days of Augustus whom you call deified, and made it even more magnificent, and more treasure poured in. I could hardly contain my grief that day as I watched it all pass before those laughing and jeering crowds." His voice broke and he looked down.

"Remember," Naomi said, "you only *watched* the parade. My son and I walked in it, in chains. We were forced to carry silver bowls, *heavy* silver bowls." My mother put an arm around Naomi's shoulder as servant and friend began to cry.

Josephus looked at Phineas in awe. "I believe I do remember seeing a boy with red hair carrying something that day."

"You should have been walking beside us," Phineas said angrily. He moved toward Josephus. I stepped between them and pushed Phineas back.

"I shouldn't have come here," Naomi said. "It's too painful." She pulled away from my mother and began to run along the Via Sacra, back toward my house.

"Go after your mother," I told Phineas. "See that she gets home safely."

Phineas glared at me, then at Josephus. For a moment I wasn't sure whether he was going to obey me. Then he spat out, "Yes, my lord." Naomi was already out of sight as Phineas pushed his way through the crowd to catch up with her.

"She needs me," my mother said, turning to go after Naomi.

"You can't go alone." I made a grab for her arm but failed to catch her.

Mother shook her head. "I'm just a pathetic old woman. No one is going to bother me."

Watching her disappear into the crowd, I turned to Aurora. "I don't like this. My people are getting strung out, in single file."

"I'll go," Aurora said. Before I could pick out a few men to go with her, she was gone. I chose two men and told them to gather up my mother, Naomi, Phineas, and Aurora and escort them home.

"I'm sorry this has been so difficult for you," Josephus said. "Perhaps another time…"

I shook my head. "I think everything's under control. I just want to ask you about one more thing."

"And what would that be?"

"A box. I don't see a box depicted on the arch."

"Why should there be?" Josephus asked.

"Lucullus claimed to know something about a special box—some kind of treasure, I think—that was buried under the temple. He was going to tell Regulus what he knew, once he had his consulship."

Josephus shook his head. "Then he knew something that no Jew knows."

"You don't know where this box is buried?"

"It's called the Ark of the Covenant and, no, we don't know where it is."

Or won't admit to knowing, I thought.

"It was last seen before the Babylonians destroyed our first temple. That was almost a hundred years before your Republic was founded. There is no mention of it among the loot that Nebuchadnezzar took to Babylon. It may have been hidden at that time or carried off, but no one knows where it is now."

"What's so special about it?" Tacitus asked.

"It is the place where God meets his people. It sat in the Holy of Holies in the temple. The high priest entered there only on one day of the year. No one else was ever allowed in there."

"Does it have any magical powers?" I asked. "Lucullus seemed to think it does."

"Our sacred texts say that it granted us victory when we carried it into battle. On the other hand, anyone who touched it would be killed."

"How could you carry something without touching it?" Tacitus asked.

"Special gold-plated poles ran through rings on the sides."

"So your god would be carried around like someone riding in a litter?"

"I wouldn't put it exactly like that, but that's not entirely inaccurate. It wasn't God himself, though—he has no physical existence—but the sense of his presence, his glory."

Sounds like Epicurus' less densely packed atoms, I thought, *something that might just float away.*

"What did this box look like?" I asked. "Are you allowed to describe it to non-Jews?"

"Its appearance is no secret. It's described in our texts as being two and a half cubits long, one and a half cubits high and the same width. On the top of it were two angelic figures facing one another with their wings covering the lid. It was coated in gold, inside and out. Phineas can show you the passage when you get home."

"Was there anything in this Ark?" Tacitus asked. "Gold? Treasure?"

"Nothing like that," Josephus said. "It contained two stone tablets on which were inscribed the ten basic rules of our faith, which God gave to Moses on Mount Sinai. There was also a rod which had sprouted buds, and a jar holding samples of the special bread with which we were fed during our wandering in the desert."

"So Lucullus had no idea what he was talking about?"

Josephus stroked his beard. "Over the centuries legends have grown up about the Ark, mostly among people who don't understand what it is. It would be a treasure beyond any price for Jews if we could find it, but I suspect it would bring disaster down on anyone who tried to use it for their own purposes."

Maybe I should hope that Regulus finds it then. Perhaps Titus had found it. That could explain why his short time in power had been filled with disasters—the eruption of Vesuvius, a plague and a fire in Rome. Of course, the destruction of a god's temple might be enough to bring down his wrath, without touching his magic box.

XIII

*B*LAST! WHICH WAY *did they go?" I muttered, as I came to the place where the* Via Sacra *crossed the* Vicus Piscinae Publicae *in front of the Amphitheatre. The crowd was heaviest if I bore to my right and went along the southern face of the colossal building. Thinking that a couple of older women might not want to fight that mob, I turned left.*

Just past the Amphitheatre I came into a district of insulas, *most three to five stories high. Straining to see above the crowd, I thought I spotted a woman's gray hair above a familiar blue cloak. That must be Plinia. I pushed my way through the crowd, ignoring protests, lewd suggestions, and threats, until I was almost close enough to touch her. Suddenly someone reached out from the narrow, dark street between two buildings and grabbed her arm.*

"Hey! Let her go!" I shouted as Plinia was pulled into the alley. "Help! Somebody, help!"

I turned into the alley and saw Plinia being dragged farther into it by a dark-haired man. She was too frail to put up any resistance. "Let her go!" I yelled.

Because the man was holding Plinia so close to his chest, with an arm around her throat, I didn't want to pull my knife. If I tried to stab him, I could easily injure her. He surprised me when he stopped and threw Plinia to the ground. I hoped she would get up and run, but then I realized that the alley ran into the back of another building. There was no way out that I could see.

The man—and it was Simon—turned to face me. I was expecting him to draw his knife and I was about to reach for mine, but he lunged at me and knocked me up against the wall of one of the buildings. As I slid to the ground I had difficulty drawing a breath.

Simon kicked me in the stomach. "I could kill you, but I need you to take a message to Gaius Pliny. He has my son. Now I have his mother. I'll be in touch with him soon. Can you tell him that?"

I nodded and Simon kicked me again, causing me to vomit. "Good girl." He bent down close to my ear. "I'll bet your master Gaius Pliny says that a lot."

I fell unconscious.

I was awakened by hands on my body and an awful smell. A hand started moving up between my legs.

"Oh, she's awake," an unshaven...thing chortled. At first I wasn't sure if it was a man or a large rat. Maybe I was dreaming. Since it could speak, I decided it was a man. "This'll be even more fun."

I landed a solid blow to his mouth and felt some of his few remaining teeth crumble. I got to my feet, still unable to stand up straight, and hobbled toward home.

Tacitus and I did not stay at the arch much longer. If Josephus knew anything more about the Ark of the Covenant, he wasn't going to tell me. He urged me again to visit the Temple of the Caesars, near the arch, to see the actual Menorah and other objects depicted on the arch, as well as other booty from Jerusalem, but I was too worried about my mother. If Aurora had caught up with her, and if the men I sent after Aurora had caught up with *her*, everything must be all right. But those were two big "ifs."

We parted company when we came to the Amphitheatre. Tacitus and Josephus turned right toward their homes on the Aventine and Palatine hills respectively and my servants and I retraced the route we had followed on our way down here. When we arrived home I walked into a scene of turmoil. Demetrius met me at the door with the news.

"My lord, I'm so sorry to tell you, but your mother has been abducted."

"What on earth are you talking about?"

"Aurora is in here, my lord. She can tell you herself."

He led me to a room off the atrium, where I found Aurora lying on a couch with two servant women tending to her.

I dismissed the other two women and knelt down beside the couch. "What happened?"

"Gaius, I'm so sorry." She sobbed and told me how Simon had taken my mother.

"Are you badly hurt?"

She shook her head. "Just some bruises where he kicked me. He was wearing something like *caligae*, not regular sandals."

"Can you walk?"

"I think so. I'm not bleeding."

I stood up. "Then get up. You have to show me where this happened. I've got to find my mother."

She put a hand on her ribs. "Gaius, I can tell you—"

"I'm sorry to be so insistent when you've been hurt. Finding some dark alley with just your description might be impossible. You have to *show* me the place. Now, get up." I gave her my hand and she pulled herself off the couch.

I knew Aurora was in a great deal of pain, but she was the only one who could show me exactly where this incident had happened. Even though it would slow us down a bit, I ordered a litter brought to the door for her to ride in. Following her directions, we made our way slowly down the Esquiline, accompanied by Archidamos and two other servants.

"In here," she finally said, pointing to an opening off to our left, between two *insulas*. She stayed in the litter while I entered the alley. My servants blocked the entrance.

I walked to the end of the alley and back. It was strewn with barrels and amphoras and garbage. "There's no other way out," I said. "Did he step over you as he left?"

"I don't think so, but I was unconscious part of the time."

"Surely someone on the street would have noticed him manhandling an older woman. She wouldn't have gone with him willingly."

"Noticing doesn't mean helping, my lord. I called for help when I saw someone grab your mother. No one paid any attention. I doubt many people would try to stop Simon from doing anything. Evil hangs over him like a cloud."

"All right. If he didn't come past you to get out of here, there must be some other way out. That's the only logical conclusion."

"Let's look more closely then, my lord." With a groan she pushed herself out of the litter and walked into the alley. "I was attacked later by a man who smelled like he had crawled out of a sewer."

"But I don't see any grates or openings into the sewer," I said.

"Someone must have covered it up." We were far enough away from the other servants now that she could be more casual. "Can you move some of these barrels? I think they're empty."

I shoved a couple of barrels out of the way but found nothing.

"How about the one back in the corner?"

One barrel in a corner had been partially crushed. I tried to push it to one side, but it was stuck to something.

Aurora examined the barrel and said, "Try lifting up."

When I pushed up, the barrel moved and brought something solid with it. "It's nailed to the sewer cover," I said. The stench rising from the hole verified what I had said. We also heard voices and rustling sounds and saw moving lights, as though people were walking around, carrying torches.

Aurora looked closely at the results of my work. "There's a handle on the bottom of the cover. Someone could close it behind them."

I sat on the edge of the hole, with my feet on the top rung of a wobbly ladder. I shuddered to think that Simon forced my mother to climb down that thing, or, more likely, climbed down it himself with her slung over his shoulder. As best I could tell in the dim light filtering into the hole, it was about twice the height of a man.

"Are you going down there?" Aurora asked.

"I think I have to. This is where Simon took my mother."

"But the sewers are as vast as Rome itself. They lead everywhere. How do you expect to find her?"

She was right, of course. People have driven wagons and sailed boats in Rome's sewers. Their layout is as complicated as the streets of the city. "I don't know, but I have to try, don't I?" I took a step down the ladder. "You've heard Martial tell about his exploits in the sewers to rescue his baby daughter."

"But he knew where she was going to be. He went in and got out quickly. If you go down there and wander around trying to find your mother, you might never come back."

I couldn't stop the tears. "But what else can I do? Tell me, what else can I do?"

Aurora put her arms around me. I didn't care if the servants at the other end of the alley could see or hear us. "Let's think this through, Gaius. Simon isn't waiting at the bottom of that ladder. We know that. He went down it, but he had a plan—some place to go."

That started me thinking. "Simon can't possibly know his way around the sewers. Lucullus moved his household here less than a month ago."

"You're right," Aurora said. "The man has learned a lot about the city in the time he's been here, but he's been above ground." She was making sense.

"What if he went down here," I said, "made his way to the next opening and came up there? Or maybe he waited down here until he was sure you were gone, then came back out. Then he could find his way to wherever he's hiding. And he must have some hiding place, in a deserted building perhaps."

"So we need to be thinking about where that might be. Instead of trying to follow him, let's try to get ahead of him."

Encouraged by Aurora's suggestion, I was ready to climb back up out of the hole when a hand grabbed my ankle and pulled hard.

—◦∾◦—

Before I could do anything to help him, Gaius disappeared into the sewer. I heard a splash. A dirty, bearded man rose far enough out of the hole to pull the cover down. I tried frantically to open it again, but someone was holding it or had barred it in some way. I could hear splashing and yelling from more than one voice. Gaius was being attacked. I was sure of it. I ran to get our three servants who were blocking the entrance to the alley.

—◦∾◦—

I landed in shit. I could smell it and feel it all over me. Flailing around just made it worse. I tried to get my feet under me, but I kept slipping. Rats were squeaking and scrambling over me. People were running toward me. There was barely enough light from the torches they were carrying for me to get some sense of where I was. I made it to my feet but uncertainly. "He's a narrow-striper!" someone cried. "Get his money bag!" Then someone landed on top of me from behind, knocked me to my knees, and tried to force my head underwater. I reached over my shoulder, grabbed a fistful of hair and flipped him over my head. Only it wasn't a "him."

Getting to my feet again, I blew water and filth from my mouth and nose and drew my sword from under my tunic. I wanted to take a position with my back to the ladder but half a dozen inhabitants of this literal Underworld were creeping toward me, threatening to get between me and the ladder. Two had knives; the rest were armed with sticks and clubs.

"Aurora! Help!" I cried. What was taking her so long to lift the grate?

Our minds do funny things at the oddest moments. Here I faced the possibility of dying alone in a sewer, but my mind wasn't frantically planning how to get out. Instead, I was thinking of how, when we were children, Aurora and I used to thrill at reading the passages in the *Odyssey* and the *Aeneid* where the heroes went into the Underworld. They both drew their swords to fight off what Virgil called "bodiless, airy lives flitting about with a hollow semblance of form." Aeneas wanted to rush at them and hack at the shadows uselessly with his sword. The creatures that I faced looked like such ghostly apparitions, but they had very solid bodies.

They started moving slowly toward me. I took a step toward the ladder and called out, "Who wants to be the first to die?" I hoped my voice wasn't quavering as much as I felt it was. The threat was enough to stop them for a moment.

The man with the longest stick stepped forward. His weapon had a sharpened point. He could reach me with it before my short sword could do any damage to him. Above my head I could hear Aurora urging my other servants to break through the grate. The thing splintered and dim light filtered into the tunnel.

"Come on, my lord!" Archidamos reached his strong arm down into the hole. My attackers drew back, like monsters from myths who are afraid of the light.

I scrambled up the ladder. "You don't want to touch me," I told Archidamos. "Do you have my money pouch?"

"Of course, my lord."

"Throw it down there." One man was already on the bottom rung of the ladder. I hesitated to kick at him for fear that he would grab my foot.

"All of it, my lord? There's nearly—"

"Yes, all of it, damn you!"

When Archidamos was still slow to move, Aurora reached into the top of his tunic and pulled out the money bag. She yanked so hard the strap holding it around his neck broke. She opened the bag and poured the coins down the shaft. "That will distract them," she said. The man below me on the ladder dropped off.

When the coins began plopping into the water, the wretches beneath me plunged in after them. Others came running and fights broke out. People fell beneath the blows of clubs. Even as desperate as I was to get out, I couldn't help but watch the uproar for a moment. I've heard that Caligula used to throw gold coins from the balcony of his house on the Palatine to crowds in the street below. Everyone thought he was being generous, but he actually just enjoyed watching people fight over the money.

"Are you all right, my lord?" Archidamos asked as I emerged from Hades, smelling a lot worse than any mythical hero I'd ever read about.

"I will be as soon as I can get a bath. Pile some of those barrels over this opening and let's get out of here."

———◆———

Even with only a small contingent of servants to escort Gaius, we had little trouble cutting through the crowds in the streets. People laughed and covered their noses as they got out of our way. The men bearing my litter even made good time. Gaius would have had us running if he could. I knew he was eager to get cleaned up and start the search for his mother, but I've always known that he's sensitive to ridicule.

When we were children he didn't like it if I outdid him in our lessons.

One of our tutors—a man I never liked—was particularly insensitive about Gaius being outshone by "a mere girl." I tried not to best him regularly, but I couldn't be too obvious about it or he would spot my deception at once.

In the last year there has been one occasion—and one only—when he was unable to couple with me. He couldn't "rise to the occasion," as Ovid says. I didn't laugh at him, of course, but he heaped enough scorn on himself for both of us.

Whatever the future holds for us, I know I'll have to treat Gaius delicately at times. If we don't find his mother, I'm afraid he may fall apart completely. Sometimes I think neither of us appreciates how deeply attached he became to her because he lost his father so early and moved around so much as a child. But then, the same could be said about me.

Gaius was walking as close to me as my nose would allow. "My lord," I said, *"I'm sorry I acted so rashly with the money. I have some saved up. You can take it, and I'll accept whatever punishment you decide on."*

"Nonsense," Gaius snorted. "You did exactly the right thing. You deserve a reward, not a punishment." The way he glared at Archidamos made me uncomfortable.

———⁂———

When we got home I did not stop to explain anything to Naomi and the other women who came running up to me, then backed away. Aurora helped me wash off thoroughly before I got into the bath so I wouldn't befoul the water for everyone else. When I was clean enough, I got into the pool, rubbed olive oil on myself vigorously, and scraped myself with a *strigl* as I had never scraped before. I wished the water could be even hotter.

I emerged from the *caldarium* with a rosy glow to my skin. I still didn't feel clean, but, as Aurora rubbed me with scented oil and helped me don a clean tunic, she assured me that she could not detect any hint of the odor of the sewer. Since we were alone, she kissed me on the neck and shoulder. "Would I do that," she said, "if you still smelled like *merda?*"

I sent a message to Tacitus asking him to meet me at the ruins of my warehouse. "I think that's where he'll go," I wrote, "because it's the one place in the city with which he is most familiar."

It was almost evening when Tacitus arrived at the warehouse, shortly after I got there with my servants. My mother was nowhere to be seen. I could not find any evidence that she and Simon had been there. I picked up a broken piece of timber and slammed it against a collapsed part of the wall. It splintered in my hands.

"Where is he?" I yelled. "He took my mother down into the sewer. I've seen what's down there. What if somebody—"

Tacitus held up his hands to calm me. "We know how vicious Simon is. I doubt if a few starving sewer rats could overpower him and that knife of his. He won't let anything happen to your mother because he has to have her to get his son back. Don't let yourself go crazy, Gaius. We have to keep our wits about us."

I picked up another piece of wood and shattered it against the wall. "*That's* what I want to do to Simon when I find him."

Aurora put a hand on my shoulder. "It's getting dark, Gaius. Why don't we get some rest and start again in the morning?"

"Start where? Where in the whole city of Rome could I hope to find this bastard?"

"Aurora's right," Tacitus said. "We can't do any more than we've done today. It is almost dark. We all need to get home while the streets are still safe. We'll be able to think more clearly after we've had some sleep."

"Sleep? Do you think I'm going to get any sleep tonight?"

Aurora and Joshua spent the night in my room. Neither of us was willing to let the child—or our weapons—out of our sight. Contrary to my expectations, I did fall asleep at some time during the night. Aurora had Joshua in her arms the whole night, except when Miriam came in to feed him, which I was only barely aware of.

When I awoke the next morning I found a piece of papyrus under my door. It was a note—written as a formal letter—from Simon to me:

Simon ben-Hur to Gaius Plinius, greetings.
    Did you really expect to find me in that broken-down warehouse of yours? That would be the first place anyone would look.

I'm not that stupid. If you want to see your mother again, bring
my son to the Esquiline Gate at noon on the day you receive this.

I am sorry to have caused your mother any distress. She is a
fine woman, unlike that whore who calls herself my mother. I have
not harmed her and I will not, as long as I get my son back.

"How did he get in and out of the house again?" I said in a rage. "There
were people on watch!"

But watchmen, it turns out, need to relieve themselves or can't stay
awake for an entire night. And they think "it's just for a few minutes."
On top of my displeasure with Archidamos, I felt my resolve not to
whip my servants weakening. Aurora tried to soften my anger as we
stood by the fishpond. I had to remind myself that no one had been
harmed. But what about the next time, a voice in my head argued.

I hadn't answered that question when Tacitus burst into the garden.
"Gaius! Gaius!" He gasped as though he had run all the way from his
house. "It's Simon. He came...after Licinia."

"So you've got him?" My spirits brightened instantly.

"No, he's got her."

"What? How—"

Tacitus took a deep breath. "Maybe half an hour ago...he came over
the roof...dropped into the garden...these damn gaping holes." He
pointed upward. "We might as well leave the front door open."

"Never mind that. What happened?"

"Agricola's veterans confronted him. I was just waking up when I
heard the noise and came out of my room. I gave them orders to grab
him and lock him up, but he said, 'If you do *anything* to me, Gaius Pliny
will never see his mother again.' I asked him what he wanted and he
said, 'Licinia.' What could I do? I let him have her. They walked out
of my house as free as guests leaving after dinner. I'm surprised they
didn't ask for some leftover food to take with them."

"You did what you had to," I said. "As long as he has my mother,
we don't have any alternative but to do what he says." I showed him
Simon's note. "This means that he left her alone somewhere. Is she tied
up? What has he done to her?"

Tacitus pointed at the letter. "He says he hasn't harmed her."

I scoffed. "Do you trust the word of a cold-blooded killer?"

Tacitus patted my shoulder and shook his head. "Noon it is, at the Esquiline Gate. I'll be there. Shall I bring some of Agricola's men?"

"I'll have to think about that. After the exchange we could grab him."

"But," Aurora said, "he might bolt if he sees any kind of force."

"I'll get there them early and conceal them," Tacitus said. "There are plenty of places around that gate where they could hide."

"He seems to have an extraordinary sense of what's going on around him," Aurora said. "It's like he has eyes all over his head, like Argus."

"We have to try something," I said. "I want to get my mother back, but we can't let a killer escape."

"If he has Joshua," Aurora said, "he will still have a hostage."

I put a hand on her shoulder. "I don't think he'll hurt his own child. Frankly, though, a threat to the child won't be a strong incentive to leave him alone."

Aurora's eyes widened in horror.

"I promise you, we'll make every effort to capture him without anyone getting hurt. But you know what he's capable of, and his technique."

"That will be the plan then." Tacitus gave me a soldier's salute. "I'll see you at noon."

When Tacitus was gone I retreated to my bench in the arbor. Aurora, with Joshua in her arms, stood in front of me. "Sit down," I said.

She sat beside me and patted the baby. "You have to give him back, don't you? I know you do."

"Of course I do. I know how you feel about him, about some destiny that brought the two of you together. But what else can I do?" I turned sideways on the bench so I could look directly at her. "You're not seriously suggesting—"

"No! No! Nothing of the sort. Your mother comes first." She hesitated and took a breath. "It did occur to me, though, that we might substitute a baby. Like you've told me, it's easy to find unwanted children in Rome."

"Could you do something that callous to a child?"

"A child who's likely to starve to death in an alley, if he's not eaten by rats first? Is a death like that better than a life with someone like

Simon? I've heard you say that life is always better than death. Lorcis and Martial have told you their story...."

"This baby has been circumcised. I'm sure Simon will check that. And I can't do anything that would put my mother at risk. As hard as it will be for you, I have to give *this* baby back to his father. I'm sorry."

A tear started down Aurora's cheek and she put Joshua on her shoulder, close to her face. He snuggled into her neck and sighed.

—⁓—

I was assembling a group of servants in the atrium to go to the Esquiline Gate. Miriam would be included, in case Joshua needed to be fed while we were waiting for Simon. A crying baby could attract unwanted attention. Archidamos had pleaded to go along, to redeem himself for his failure at the sewer yesterday. I decided on him and five others. That seemed an adequate number without being unwieldy.

"You must remember," I told them, "this man is ruthless and clever. He has been in this house twice without anyone seeing him. That's how clever he is. Because he has my mother we can't just rush in and attack him. Everyone, please watch me and do what I tell you. And do it immediately, with no hesitation." I glared at Archidamos, who nodded.

I thought we were ready to leave, but Naomi approached me. "My lord, I want to go with you. I want to be there to comfort your mother when we get her back."

I hadn't thought in those terms, but it seemed like a good idea to have someone who meant so much to my mother with us. I appreciated that she had said *when*, not *if*. "All right. But stay back until we're sure the exchange is complete."

The exchange would also involve Aurora. She would not let anyone else carry Joshua. I had to let her hold onto him until the last possible moment. Miriam had fed him, what I assumed was for the last time, and now Aurora was clutching him to her, cooing to him and rocking him.

We arrived at the Esquiline Gate ahead of time, as I had planned. Because it's close to the Market of Livia, it's a busy spot. We call it a gate, but it's really just an archway. Rome long ago outgrew the need for actual gates. No one is going to attack us. One road leads out of Rome at that point and then splits into the Via Labicana, running southeast, and the Via Tiburtina, which takes a sharp turn to the northeast. I did not see any sign of Simon, but I couldn't see anyone I suspected might be one of Agricola's veterans either. That I took as a good sign. Tacitus, sitting at a table in front of a *taberna*, waved when he saw me. I went over and joined him and ordered a cup of wine, which was served promptly.

"Agricola's men did a good job of concealing themselves," I said.

"There are eight of them, but I don't think anyone other than Agricola could spot them."

A man, coming from behind me, sat down at the table with us. "Eight, eh? That's good to know. I had counted only six," Simon said.

I jumped up, knocking over my wine. "By the gods! How—"

"I could have easily killed a couple of them," he said with a smirk, "but I didn't want to damage my chances of getting my son back."

"Where did you come from?"

"What if I told you I can walk through walls?"

In spite of his appearances in my house, I didn't believe that. He had shaved and, with a dark green cloak and a traveler's broad-brimmed hat and a patch over one eye, had changed his overall appearance enough that I would not have recognized him if I'd walked past him on the street.

"Where is my mother, you bastard?" I looked around wildly.

"An aptly chosen epithet," he said, removing the eye patch. "Where is my son?"

"He's right over there." I pointed to Aurora. "But you don't get him until my mother is standing in front of me."

"No, Gaius Pliny, you don't make the rules. If I were to hand her over to you right here, you would give me my son—I believe you are an honorable man—but then you would set those veterans on me before I could walk through that gate. Oh, wait, the two I missed must be on the other side of the gate."

I felt absolutely helpless. All I could do was threaten him. "I will not give you your son until—"

"Calm down! You're going to get your mother back." He placed a piece of papyrus and a key on the table. "Here are the directions to the apartment where your mother is and a key to the room."

"You left her alone, locked up somewhere?"

"She's not alone. Licinia is with her. She's being fed and cared for. But I told Licinia that, if I'm not back with my son in two hours, she is to kill your mother. And you know she's mad enough to do it, if she thinks you've done anything to me. When we escaped from Lucullus she wanted to kill Deborah and the baby." He looked up at the sun. "Now, you don't have a lot of time left."

"I see what you're doing," Tacitus said. "You're going to take the child and leave. You're not going back to the room where Plinia and Licinia are. And you know we can't follow you because if Pliny doesn't get there in time—"

"Then why are we still talking?" Simon said. "I'm not sure how accurately Licinia keeps track of time. It's hard to see the sun out the small window in that apartment."

I motioned for Aurora to come to the table. Naomi came with her. I pried Joshua out of Aurora's arms and gave him to Simon, who immediately checked to see if the baby was circumcised. Joshua began to cry as Simon walked away from the table. Naomi followed him, with a stream of Aramaic spewing out of her mouth and her arms flailing. It was enough to stop Simon for a moment. She slapped him on the arm.

At that point I felt I had to intervene before she provoked Simon and his knife came flying out from under his tunic. "Calm down, Naomi," I said, pulling her away from him. "What did you say to him?"

Naomi blushed. "I would be ashamed to repeat it, my lord, but I had to say it."

Simon hoisted Joshua on his shoulder and mocked Naomi. "'My lord, my lord.' Doesn't that phrase just stick in your craw? I've said it for the last time. And my son never will say it." He said something to Naomi in their language, then added in Greek, "You're probably right, though, you old hag. And I deserve every curse you've put on me." He gave Naomi a shove which sent her stumbling back into Aurora's arms. The two of them joined Miriam on the edge of my group of retainers.

Simon turned to me. "Your time is running out, Gaius Pliny, so I'll let you get to it. By the way, your mother is a very nice lady. She's very maternal, not a self-serving whore, like my mother. I truly am sorry for any discomfort I've caused her. I assure you, I have not harmed her."

I shook my fist in his face. "Maybe I can't do anything right now, but once I have her back, I will not rest until I've tracked you down. You deserve to be punished for two murders—"

"Two that you know of."

"You also killed Licinia's mother, didn't you?"

"Lucullus told me to. She had found out what he was doing to Licinia."

"Does Licinia know what you did?"

"I'm sure she will as soon as you find her."

"Well, it doesn't matter how many you've killed. I'll be coming after you for abducting my mother."

Simon threw back his head and laughed. "Do you see how I'm trembling?"

He had taken only a couple of steps toward the gate when Aurora called out, "Simon! How do you plan to feed Joshua?"

"Who?"

"Your son."

"You've named him?"

"Yes."

Simon held the baby up and looked him over. "Joshua, eh? That's not bad. At least you didn't call him Lucius or Marcus or some other slave name. But you're right. I'll have to think about how I'm going to feed him."

"Miriam here can do it." Aurora put her hand on Miriam's back and prodded her toward Simon, who said something to her in Aramaic. Miriam replied and the two of them walked away together.

"What just happened?" I asked Naomi and Aurora.

Naomi spoke first. "We devised a plan while we were walking over here, my lord. It was Miriam's idea, in fact. She said she would go with the baby."

"We can't follow Simon, my lord," Aurora said, "but Miriam will know where he is and what he's planning. She'll let us know when she can. She'll be our spy."

"Can she just run away like that? Isn't she a servant?"

"No, my lord," Naomi said. "She's a free person."

"Isn't she married?"

"Yes, my lord, but her husband treats her badly. Very badly. And her baby died."

"Does she understand what it will mean to be with Simon?"

"I doubt it, my lord. But when a woman loses a child and then is given the chance to be the mother of another one who needs her, it can feel like a gift from God."

I knew better than to look back at Aurora at that moment.

XIV

SIMON'S NOTE named a street that no one in my group had ever heard of. We asked the owner of the *taberna*, and all we got in reply was a shake of the head. We were on our way out the door when one of the serving girls called after us.

"Sirs, wait, please."

"What do you want?" Tacitus asked. "We're in a hurry. A woman's life depends on it. We paid our bill, didn't we?"

"Yes, sir. It's just that the street you want—"

"Shut up, girl!" the owner barked.

"No, I won't. Somebody's in trouble."

"He paid us to keep quiet, and you heard what he'll do if we talk."

"He's not coming back," I said. "Where is this street? Quickly, please."

"It's the one at the next corner." She pointed to the right. "That fella had been sittin' in here for almost a hour, watchin' people."

I shook my head. Simon did not have magic powers after all. He had watched Tacitus and his men arrive and had seen exactly where they stationed themselves.

"Is there an *insula* belonging to the freedman Lachyses on that street?"

The girl nodded vigorously. "It's the first one after you turn the corner."

We ran out of the *taberna*, picking up the rest of our entourage, and turned where the girl had indicated. There were three *insula*s on the street, each one three stories high. Being this far from the center of the city, they were not desirable places to live and the owner had not spent

207

any money recently on upkeep. Simon must have used money he got from blackmailing Lucullus to rent a place. Tacitus started up one set of stairs, but I pulled him back.

"We have no idea which apartment she's in," I said.

"We have a key," he said.

"But Licinia's in there. If we frighten her, she might harm my mother. Like Simon said, she's mad enough to do anything. Let's see if we can figure out where she might be."

Several shops occupied the ground floor of the building. Tacitus and I stepped into one—a sandal-maker's—and I asked a man who was bent over his workbench, "Do you know Lachyses? I believe he's the owner of this building."

"Yes, sir, he is."

"Where would I find him?"

The man peered closely at his work for a moment, then looked up at me. "He doesn't come around here much. You know how owners are."

I grabbed the front of the man's tunic and pulled him up off his bench. "A life is at stake here, man. I need to find someone before it's too late. Is there a manager of this building that I can talk to?"

"You're pulling on his very tunic, sir." I let go and he stepped away from me. "There's no need to get violent. Who are you looking for?"

"A man named Simon. He has dark hair, possibly a beard. He's Jewish. I believe he rented a room or an apartment here recently. He may have had an older woman with him."

The sandal-maker scratched his chin. "Let me think. We've got so many people living here."

Tacitus, who likes to carry his own money pouch, pulled out a couple of *denarii* and pressed them into the man's hand. "Does that jog your memory?"

The man smiled. "It's not exactly a kick in the rear, but it is a helpful nudge. Yes, the man you're looking for rented an apartment three days ago. It's on the second floor, in the back. The door will be to your left at the top of the stairs. I haven't seen an older woman with him. He left early this morning and hasn't come back, as far as I know."

We thanked the man and Tacitus gave him a couple more coins.

"I doubt you'll be seeing him again," I said.

"He paid a month's rent. I don't need to see him until the next month's is due."

With our people following us quietly, we made our way to the staircase on the back of the building. I motioned for everyone else to wait on the sidewalk while Tacitus and I climbed the stairs, but Naomi and Aurora stayed a few steps behind us. I couldn't say anything to them for fear of Licinia hearing my voice.

I put the key in the lock and turned it. From inside, Licinia's voice came toward us, "Simon! I've been getting anxious. Is everything—" She stood stock-still when I entered the room. "You again! What have you done with Simon?"

She turned suddenly toward the room behind her. I lunged at her and knocked her to the floor. She kicked and swung her arms at me, cursing me the whole time, but I kept her down. Tacitus grabbed the belt off a tunic that was draped over a chair and we tied her hands.

Naomi brushed past us and into the next room. "My lady, my dear lady!" she cried.

I left Tacitus to deal with Licinia and bolted into the next room, dreading what horror I might see. But my mother was sitting in a chair, unharmed as far as I could tell, and Naomi was untying her hands and removing a gag from her mouth.

"Oh, Gaius! Naomi! Thank the gods!" She threw her arms around Naomi and they embraced tightly, both weeping. Naomi looked up and said something, obviously a prayer, in Aramaic. I looked up, but all I saw was the ceiling. Mother released Naomi and grabbed me, kissing my cheeks.

—⁓—

Gaius, Tacitus, and the men with them set out in search of Simon. They knew the direction he had taken when he passed through the Esquiline Gate—one of Agricola's men stationed on the other side of the gate had spotted him before he got lost in the crowd—but after that the search would be largely guesswork. Now that Gaius' mother was safe, there was no reason not to try to find Simon. Gaius was also concerned that the man might still plan to attack his own mother.

Plinia, Naomi, and I took Licinia back to our house. With her hands still tied, we led her into Plinia's room and locked the door. Naomi pushed her down on the bed, none too gently.

"This isn't fair!" Licinia squawked. "You're ganging up on me. You can't keep me prisoner. Untie me! I haven't done anything. I didn't hurt anybody."

"Not me, you didn't," Plinia said, "and I'm grateful for that. Now calm down. We're not going to hurt you. We just want to talk to you."

"About what? I don't want to talk to you." Licinia struggled against the belt tying her hands. "Simon's going to come get me, you know, and you'll be sorry when he does."

"That's what we need to talk about," Plinia said. "Simon's not going to come get you."

"He came here to get me. He got me from Tacitus' house." She laughed. "You should have seen the look on their faces when we walked right out the door. There was nothing they could do."

"When he came here," Plinia said, "he intended to kill you—"

"What? You're insane. Why would he want to kill me? He loves me."

"No, he doesn't, you silly child," Naomi said. "He wanted to kill you so you couldn't tell anyone what he had done and what he was planning to do."

Shock and disbelief showed in Licinia's eyes. "No! He was trying to kill her"—she jerked her head in my direction—"but he missed because of the struggle. He needed me. He told me so."

"Oh, he needed you," Plinia said. "He needed you to get him out of Lucullus' house after he killed the poor man. And he needed you to watch me."

Licinia shook her head vigorously. "You don't understand. We planned it together. I was the one who lured my father into the latrina where Simon was waiting for him. It was my idea to stuff his body into the drain."

"Did you plan for him to kill your mother?" I asked.

"What? He didn't—"

"I heard him tell Gaius Pliny. Your father told him to do it."

"He couldn't have.... He wouldn't—"

Plinia took Licinia's face firmly between her hands and tilted it upward. "Listen to me. He doesn't need you anymore. He's got his son and a wet nurse. He used you, and now he's finished with you. You'll never see him again."

Licinia began to cry. Since she couldn't wipe her eyes, I sat down beside her and used the sleeve of my gown to dry her tears. I hugged her and felt a piece of cloth wrapped around her body under her gown, a strophium, *I assumed. She didn't seem so well-endowed that she needed a breast band, but some women are just more comfortable with everything held in place. And men consider overly large breasts more comic than erotic.*

"Can we untie her, my lady?" I asked.

"I suppose so," Plinia said. "We do outnumber her."

"Thank you," Licinia said as I loosened the belt on her hands. She stood up and flexed her arms, then said calmly, "Now I can kill all three of you."

She reached into the top of her gown and drew out a knife. She must have had it tucked into the strophium. *Plinia and Naomi screamed as Licinia lunged toward Plinia. I grabbed the girl's hand and twisted it so that the knife turned back toward her. The force of her attack carried her right onto the blade.*

—⁓—

I returned from a fruitless search for Simon to find my household in an uproar. My mother and Naomi kept interrupting one another as they tried to explain what had happened to Licinia, who lay seriously wounded in my mother's bed, with Aurora standing guard over her.

"That girl is out of her mind," Mother snapped. "It would be just as well if she died."

Naomi patted Mother's shoulder. "Now, my lady, we should never wish misfortune on others. It may rebound onto us."

"I'm only wishing her what she tried to do to us. She was going to kill us, Naomi. Both of us. And Aurora."

"Have you notified her stepmother?" I asked.

"We sent a message," Mother said. "There has been no reply except to thank us for letting her know. I hoped she would say we could take Licinia over there."

"Well, someone needs to take responsibility for her. I'll not have her on my hands any longer. Sempronia is her father's cousin. Doesn't that give Licinia some claim on her and Regulus? They're the ones who brought the family to Rome in the first place."

Voices at the front door of the house drew my attention in that direction. Demetrius was escorting Regulus and Sempronia into the atrium, with Jacob and several other servants accompanying them. One of the servants I recognized as Regulus' doctor. They paraded over to where I was standing with my mother and Naomi.

"I see your spies have saved me the trouble of sending a messenger," I said.

Regulus kept a stern demeanor. "Let's forgo our usual exchange of insults, Gaius Pliny. I understand that the daughter of my wife's cousin has been seriously injured in your house. I'm here to inquire about the incident and to see if we'll need to bring charges."

"The young woman tried to kill me," my mother said.

"I may be the one bringing a charge," I added.

That stopped Regulus, but Sempronia said, "Where is Licinia? I'd like our physician to examine her."

I pointed to the room where we were keeping Licinia. "She was stabbed with her own knife when one of my servants was defending my mother."

Sempronia and her doctor went into the room and Aurora came out and stood beside the door. I motioned for her to come to me.

"I hoped you would stay in there with them," I said quietly.

"Sempronia insisted that I leave, my lord."

"Has Licinia said anything?" I asked.

"No, my lord. She's bleeding badly and is very weak."

"Let's hope Regulus' doctor can do something for her."

I offered Regulus something to drink. He has never been known to turn down a cup of wine. We sat on a bench by the *impluvium*. I was trying to think of some way I could speak to Jacob—whom I respect and regard as a friend—without making Regulus more suspicious of him as my spy when Sempronia and her doctor came out of the bedroom where Licinia was.

"She's dead," Sempronia said without emotion. "We'll have her body taken to our house and will see to arrangements for her funeral. I'll notify her stepmother."

I was sorry to hear that she was dead and yet relieved. I would not have any more responsibility for a tormented woman, but I had hoped to ask her a few more questions.

"When you prepare her," I told Sempronia, "you'll notice that she is quite thin. Her stepmother says she ate very little and never any meat. I believe Lucullus probably…mistreated her when she was a child."

Regulus snorted, "Oh, come, a swat on the behind isn't mistreatment."

I could tell that Sempronia grasped my meaning. "At any rate, that experience and the death of her mother may have disordered her mind more than anyone—herself included—realized."

"Why, Gaius Pliny," Regulus chuckled, "I thought you were a student of crime, not of the *psyché*, as the Greeks say."

I drew myself up and straightened my shoulders to face Regulus. His bulk makes him an intimidating figure. "To understand why people commit crimes, Marcus Regulus, it is essential to understand how they think. That's something our courts should take into consideration more than they do."

"Would that be your defense," Regulus asked, "if I brought a charge of murder against you?"

Behind me I heard my mother gasp.

"Murder? I didn't touch Licinia."

"Oh, not her. The equestrian Julius Berenicianus was found stabbed to death in your warehouse. He and his family have been close allies of Rome for a long time. We can't let his killer go unpunished."

"I had nothing to do with his death. His brother, Julius Hyrcanus or Simon, killed him."

"Can you prove that?"

"Licinia saw it happen. She told me about it in great detail."

Regulus feigned a look of confusion. "Licinia? Do you mean the girl who's lying dead in that room right now?"

—◈◈◈—

Tacitus and I walked in the garden as I tried to quell my rage. I had notified him of what happened to Licinia after we got her back to my house and he and Julia had come over immediately. Julia, sitting with Aurora on the bench in my arbor, was comforting Aurora about the loss of Joshua. I could hear Aurora crying.

"The *nerve* of those two!" I fumed. "They come down here like concerned relatives of Licinia's. But all the time they're planning to make sure she was dead, even kill her themselves if necessary."

"Now, Gaius, you said the girl was seriously injured. She may have simply died as a result of her wound."

"Granted, but I saw scratches on Sempronia's arms when she came out of the room."

Tacitus stopped and looked at me. "Scratches? I don't understand."

"My uncle made note of this in his unpublished work. If someone tries to smother or choke a person, the victim will instinctively fight back." Without any warning I put my hands tightly on Tacitus' throat for a moment and he raised his hands to grab my arms. "He or she will grab the hands or arms of the attacker, as you just did, and leave scratch marks if the struggle is violent enough. That's exactly what I saw on Sempronia's arms, right above her wrists. She killed that girl herself. She didn't even leave it to her doctor. That's why they insisted Aurora leave the room."

"But why? She barely knew Licinia, and the girl was her cousin's daughter. That's hardly motive for murdering her."

"They wanted to remove any witness who might testify that I did not kill Berenicianus. Regulus is planning to bring a charge against me for Berenicianus' death."

Tacitus rolled his eyes. He thinks I'm overly suspicious of Regulus. Even as my friend for several years now, he still doesn't appreciate how deep the enmity between Regulus and my family has run, first toward my uncle and now toward me. Regulus and my uncle were bitter enemies back in Nero's day, twenty-five years ago. Regulus had the upper hand then, because Nero was as big a scoundrel as Regulus and listened to his lies eagerly. Vespasian and Titus were sane enough to listen to my uncle and keep Regulus at a distance. But now Domitian relishes every bit of scandal Regulus whispers in his ear.

"How do you think Regulus plans to accuse you?" Tacitus asked. "What could he know about Berenicianus' death? How could he know anything?"

"He must have a spy in my house." I tried to remember which of my men had actually carried Berenicianus into the house. And Felix had seen us remove the coins from the man's mouth. But, if I couldn't trust Felix, whom could I trust?

"That goes without saying. He has at least one in my house. I believe I know who it is, so I'm always careful about what I say around him. Sometimes I say things that aren't true, just to mislead Regulus."

"That may not be enough. Sempronia says she has her own spies. Nobody notices them because they're women. I now suspect every woman in this house except Aurora, Naomi, and my mother. My mother is careless enough about what she says that she may aid a spy without meaning to do so."

—*∽∽*—

I snuggled up close to Gaius as we finished our love-making. Ovid says that a woman should pretend she has reached the point of satisfaction, even if she hasn't, but tonight I just couldn't reach it or pretend. I could still feel Gaius ripping Joshua out of my arms to give him to Simon.

"Are you angry at me?" he asked softly.

"No, of course not." I laid a hand on his chest, which was still rising and falling as though he had been running hard. "It was the only way to save your mother." I knew that, and really believed it, but it didn't make me feel any better.

"I wish we could figure out what Simon is going to do and when."

"Don't you think he's going to try to kill his mother?"

Gaius brushed my hair off my face and kissed me lightly. "I believe so, but her apartment is well protected, with only one entrance, and she doesn't go out. I don't see how he can attack her."

"Up to this point he has managed to get into any place he wanted— including this house—whenever he wanted. I suspect he'll find a way when he's ready."

Gaius sighed. "I wish we would hear something from Miriam. That might give us a clue about what to expect."

"If she hadn't agreed to our plan, I think I would have gone crazy by now. At least I know there's somebody with Joshua who will protect him and feed him."

Gaius raised himself up on one elbow. "Do you think she might try to get the baby away from Simon?"

"That wasn't part of the plan we discussed. I think it would be extremely dangerous to try to do that."

"But she lost a child, and she has been nursing this one."

Suddenly I wondered if Miriam had come up with this plan in order to steal Joshua. She could get a baby, a Jewish baby who was already circumcised.

—◦◦◦—

Tacitus was at my front door with the first of my clients the next morning. He rushed right past Demetrius and didn't even knock on my bedroom door.

"We've been fools," he said without greeting me.

Aurora let out a squeal and grabbed her gown.

"Good morning, Aurora. I hope you slept well."

"Come in and close the door," I said. "What on earth is the meaning of this?"

"Just what I said. We've been fools."

"I have no idea what you're talking about."

"We have to find Simon, don't we?"

"Of course."

"Where is the most obvious place to look?"

I got up and slipped a tunic over my head.

"Well, I would say some place that he's familiar with. He can't know too many hiding places in Rome. He hasn't been here long enough to be familiar with the city. He rented the apartment where he held my mother."

"That's where he is now. I'll guarantee it."

Aurora had recovered enough of her composure to light a lamp. She sat on the bed and ran her fingers through her hair. "But in that note he said he wasn't stupid enough to go back to the most obvious place. Of course, he was referring to Gaius' warehouse then—"

"But it could apply just as easily to that apartment."

My head was still thick with sleep. "I don't follow you."

"He's told us, 'Oh, I'm much too smart to go back to the one place you know about.' And, like fools, we've been looking everywhere else. He's not that smart. He has to go to a place that he knows."

"And that's either Lucullus' house," Aurora said, "or the apartment. You're right, Cornelius Tacitus."

"Then why are we just sitting here?" Tacitus said.

—◦◦◦—

We must have looked bizarre, a group of nine men and one woman rushing through the streets in the first light of morning, half-awake. Some were still pulling garments and sandals on. I had brought Phineas with us, to translate for Miriam. When we arrived at Simon's apartment we rushed up the stairs. Archidamos threw his broad shoulder into the door and it splintered.

Miriam was lying in the middle of the floor, tied hand and foot and with a gag in her mouth. We freed her and helped her sit in a chair. She began to babble as soon as we got the gag out of her mouth. I held up a hand to slow her down.

"Where is Simon?" I asked through Phineas.

"Where's Joshua?" Aurora cried, looking around the two rooms.

"Joshua is with Simon," Miriam said. "Simon is on his way to his mother's place."

"Did he say—"

"He plans to kill her," Phineas translated. "Then he says he's going to come back and get me and we'll leave Rome. I know he's not interested in me, just in my breasts and my milk. I could be a cow or a goat, for all he cares."

Her face showed signs of the blows Simon had inflicted on her.

Aurora grabbed Miriam's hands. "Is Joshua all right?" she pleaded.

Miriam nodded. "I've been taking good care of him. Simon hasn't hurt him. I think the boy is the one person in the world that he actually loves."

XV

WE RAN UP TO THE entrance to Berenice's *insula*. Some of her servants were standing on the steps, frightened—most of them trembling, even the men. At the head of the steps stood Simon, holding Joshua on his left arm and in his right hand a long knife. He looked as if he hadn't slept or changed his clothes in several days.

"I said, open the door," he ordered. None of the servants moved. Simon placed his knife at Joshua's throat. "None of you want to see that, do you?" I had to grab Aurora's arm. "Abraham wasn't afraid to sacrifice his son," Simon snarled. "Don't think for an instant that I'll hesitate."

"But God stopped him," a woman's voice said from the top of the stairs. We all looked up to see Berenice standing in the open doorway. Simon lowered his knife and Aurora took a step back. Her right hand still rested on her leg, over the spot where she wore her knife.

Berenice stepped away from the entrance. "Simon, Pliny, Tacitus, Aurora—the four of you please come in," she said.

"No!" Simon barked. "No one else comes in."

"Then you'll have to do whatever you're going to do out here," Berenice said, "in front of the world."

Simon grimaced but waved his knife to direct us inside. "Everyone else has to leave," he ordered.

Another dozen of Berenice's servants scrambled down the stairs.

"They're going to get the *vigiles*, aren't they?" Simon said. "Then I'd better move fast." Holding Joshua and the knife in the same hand, he patted down Tacitus and me and discovered our swords. "Leave them outside." We complied and started to go in. Simon stopped Aurora. "I

218

know it's unlikely, but it could be fun." He patted her up and down, lingering longer than necessary at certain places. When he put his hand between her legs and he felt her knife, his eyes widened. "What the…" Aurora tried to fight off his hands, but he reached up under her gown and pulled out her knife. "Where did you come up with that idea?"

Aurora glanced at me apologetically as Simon dropped her knife beside the swords. Then he barred the door and directed us into the main room of the apartment.

"Now, isn't this cozy?" he said. "I hadn't figured out how I was going to get in here, with all those bars on the windows and the doors barricaded. I never dreamed the front door would just be opened for me, and by the queen herself. You three, get over there. I want you all close together so I can keep an eye on you."

We gathered in a corner of the room. Simon and Berenice were on the other side, well out of our reach. Simon could harm Joshua long before any of us could get to him. He stood directly in front of his mother, hardly more than an arm's length away from her. "Hello, whore."

Berenice flinched but managed to say, "Hello, son."

Simon sneered and his face twisted in rage. "That's what you choose to call me? Not cousin? Not nephew? Those titles would fit just as well."

"You are my son, the fruit of my womb. It doesn't matter who put the seed in here." She placed a hand on her belly.

"That's where you're wrong, whore. It's the only thing that does matter."

"Then why is it that our law says a man is a Jew if his *mother* is a Jew?"

"But his mother isn't supposed to be coupling with her male relatives! Our law is very clear about that. You can't just pick and choose which parts you want to obey." Simon took a step closer to Berenice, shaking the fist clenching his knife at her. Joshua began to cry.

Berenice seemed to sense that she needed to change tactics. Her voice softened. "Is that my grandson? May I hold him?" She held out her arms. "Please?"

"No! I won't have filth like you touching him."

"Are you going to kill him?" Berenice sounded genuinely concerned.

Aurora tensed, and her hand went to the spot on her leg where her knife would have been strapped, if Simon hadn't taken advantage of her.

"Don't worry, I'm not going to hurt him. He's my son and my insurance against those three." He jerked his head toward us but did not take his eyes off Berenice. "I wanted you to see him. I had hoped you could see the body of your other son—your favorite son—before you died, just like faithless king Zedekiah had to watch his sons being executed before the Babylonians gouged out his eyes, so that was the sight that would remain with him for the rest of his life." He was talking faster and faster. "But at least you know he's dead and you know how he died. I hope you take that memory with you as you descend into Sheol."

"Yes, I understand you did yourself proud in the way you killed him."

"It was even better than you know. He wasn't quite dead when we sewed up his lips. I could see in his eyes and from the way he twitched that he felt everything we were doing."

Berenice was breathing more deeply. Her hands rested on her thighs.

"He got what he deserved," Simon snarled, "a fitting payment for a shepherd who did not tend his sheep. That's what the prophet said."

"And what do you think I deserve?"

"The law says a whore should be stoned to death, but we obviously can't do that here."

An incongruous thought flashed through my mind. *Who among us is morally superior enough to throw the first stone?*

"We'll have to improvise." Simon pointed his knife directly at his mother.

Berenice held out her hands, to show they were empty. "You'll have to look me in the eye if you're going to kill me, you coward. I won't let you sneak up behind me." She backed up against a wall.

"I can gladly do that, *Mother*." Simon took two steps toward her and tapped the blade of his knife against her chest, like a man looking for the best place to split a log. Berenice was wearing her linen cuirass.

"You're still wearing your shell, eh? Like a damn turtle. Well, even a turtle has a vulnerable spot or two." He stabbed her between her legs, with a violent upward thrust of the knife. Joshua's crying grew more insistent. I had to put a hand on Aurora's arm to hold her back.

As her son stood over her, gloating, Berenice doubled up, then from somewhere pulled out a knife and stabbed him in the stomach with an upward thrust as hard as the one he had given her. It happened so fast I wasn't sure what I was seeing. Simon looked at the knife sticking out of his stomach, as though in disbelief. He grabbed the handle as he slowly sank to his knees but could not pull it out.

Aurora lunged across the room and grabbed Joshua in spite of Simon's efforts to cling to him. The baby was wailing loudly now. Aurora kicked Simon in the face and stepped away from him, cooing to Joshua and holding him tightly. Simon made one effort to crawl toward her before he fell completely still. Tacitus stood over him, his foot on Simon's back. A pool of blood began to collect under the man's body.

I stepped over Simon and knelt beside Berenice, putting my hand under her head. She grasped my arm weakly with both of her hands. She was still alive but barely breathing. The lower part of her garment was turning red.

"Please take care of...my grandson, Gaius Pliny. And thank Aurora...for showing me...her trick." She lifted the flap she had sewn into her gown over a slit so I could see the strap and the sheath that had held her knife. Then she shuddered and expelled one last breath.

XVI

JOSHUA LAY ON HIS BACK in my lap. I was sitting on the bench in the arbor at the back of my garden. The rain was done and an autumn-like chill had settled on the city, so the baby was wrapped in several blankets. They kept him warm and kept my tunic dry.

That morning Regulus had sent the 150,000 *sesterces* to buy the property occupied by the ruins of my warehouse. He had paid it in *aurei*. The box wasn't the gold-lined Ark of the Covenant, but it looked that good to me. I could pay off what I owed my mother-in-law, as well as the interest I had promised her, and break even on my first and likely last foray into purchasing real estate in the city. In future, I resolved, I would be content with the properties my uncle had left me.

Regulus also told me that he had decided not to proceed with a murder charge against me. He was quite blunt. He didn't want to initiate a case unless he was sure he could win, so he would wait for a better opportunity. For the first time in several days I felt at ease.

Joshua stirred and fretted. I bounced my legs gently, the way Aurora had showed me, and rubbed his stomach until he settled down. Aurora was supposed to be getting us something to eat but she was taking an inordinate amount of time to do so.

"Well, young man," I said, "here we are. But where are we? Aurora says you need a father, and I'm the most logical candidate, or the most available. She wants me to get comfortable with you and you with me. She's determined to be your mother, and she'll be a good one. Don't you worry. She's convinced that some divine power has brought you two together. I don't believe that, unless Fortune is a divine power." I touched the Tyche ring on its leather strap around my neck. Was there more to that image than I suspected?

"I find it harder and harder to refute her arguments." For some reason I didn't feel inane talking to the baby. Naomi and my mother had told me he was still too young to direct his attention to us, even if he looked as if that was what he was doing. "Was it merely chance that she and her mother joined my uncle's household?"

Out of the corner of my eye I saw Aurora emerge from the kitchen and start across the garden toward me. She carried a tray with wine, bread, and fruit on it. I lifted my head to watch her. The morning sun was still low behind her, just appearing over the roof. It showed the outline of her body through her gown. Her hair was down, the way she prefers to wear it, although that's not considered fashionable. Her exquisite face had a glow to it that wasn't just the effect of the sunlight.

"By the gods, Joshua," I muttered. "By the gods." It was all I could say or think.

She placed the tray on the table in front of the bench and sat down next to me. As she picked Joshua up she laughed lightly and asked, "What were you two talking about?"

CAST OF CHARACTERS

HISTORICAL PERSONS

All dates are A.D. unless otherwise noted.

Agricola Gnaeus Julius Agricola (40–93), Roman general and father-in-law of Tacitus. He was responsible for much of the conquest of Britain. In his biography of Agricola, Tacitus suggests there was something suspicious about his death. There was a "rumor that he had been poisoned," he says. "We have no definite evidence. That is all I can say for certain."

Berenice Daughter of Herod Agrippa and great-granddaughter of Herod the Great. She was born in 28 and died sometime after 81. She was married several times, including once to her uncle Herod of Chalcis, by whom she had several children (see below). She and Titus, who was younger than she, had an on-again, off-again relationship, which ended when he sent her away from Rome as a result of popular resentment. She is not mentioned in any source after that, except that Juvenal (ca. 120) derides her (and other "notorious" women) in his sixth *Satire*. She lived with her brother, Agrippa II, in what was almost certainly an incestuous relationship. They appear in Acts 25–26 at the trial of Paul, where Agrippa delivers the famous line: "You almost persuade me to be a Christian."

Berenicianus We know that Berenice had a son named Julius Berenicianus, born in the mid-40s to Berenice and her uncle, but we know nothing else about him. I'm sorry I had to use such a tongue-twister, but it was his name. In my writers' group we called him Bernie.

Caninius Rufus A friend of Pliny's from Comum. He apparently eschewed politics and remained in Comum, writing poetry. Pliny chides him a bit for not being more engaged in politics but also envies him his freedom to write.

Hyrcanus Julius Hyrcanus, another son of Berenice and her uncle, about whom nothing is known, except that he was also born in the mid-40s. I've given him the name Simon in this book. Many Jews in this era had both Jewish and Greco-Roman names, such as John Mark, the author of the Gospel of Mark.

Josephus Jewish historian who lived and wrote in the last third of the first century A.D. When the Jewish revolt broke out in 66, he led a contingent of troops, but he surrendered to the Flavians early in the war, rather than commit suicide with his men, and took the name Flavius as part of his own. He is our main source of information about the war, although he contradicts himself between his two main works, the earlier *Jewish War* and the later *Antiquities of the Jews*, and then he adds a few more contradictions in his autobiography.

Julia Wife of Tacitus and daughter of Julius Agricola. We know she lived at least until the late 90s because Tacitus mentions her in his biography of her father.

Julia Flavia (64–91) daughter of the emperor Titus. Her image appears on several coins issued by her father and we have numerous busts and other portrayals of her. Titus proposed a marriage between her and his brother Domitian, which Domitian refused. However, Domitian later had an affair with his niece. She supposedly died from an abortion that he insisted she have. Her ashes were mixed with Domitian's after his death in 96. We don't know how Domitian's wife—who remained proud of her status as his widow—felt about that.

Livia A very common name in ancient Rome. I have given it to Pliny's wife. He had two, possibly three, wives, depending on how one interprets his letter to Trajan (*Ep.* 10.2), in which he says he has married twice. The only wife he mentions by name was the teenaged Calpurnia, whom he married late in life. We don't know if *Ep.* 10.2 was written before or after his marriage to Calpurnia, so we don't know if she was his second or third wife. In any case, we don't know the name of the wife who was the daughter of Pompeia Celerina, so I have taken the liberty of calling her Livia.

Martial Roman poet G. Valerius Martial, author of witty and salacious epigrams. Pliny mentions him in a couple of letters and was a benefactor of his. He plays a major role, along with Lorcis (see below) in my novel *The Flute Player.*

Plinia Pliny's mother and the sister of the elder Pliny. She is mentioned only in Pliny's letters about the eruption of Vesuvius. We do not know the dates of her birth or death. Pliny was born in 62. If his mother married and had a child in the normal timing of things for that day, she would have been about 15 at that time, putting her birth ca. 47. She was alive when Vesuvius erupted in 79, but seems to have been somewhat frail by then. Pliny says that she wanted him to leave her behind when they were trying to escape so that she would not be a burden on him.

Pompeia Celerina Pliny's mother-in-law. He exchanges several letters with her but there is never any mention of her daughter's name. She owns an estate near Narnia, which Pliny enjoys visiting.

Regulus M. Aquilius Regulus, a lawyer and fortune hunter who began his nefarious career in Nero's reign. By informing on people who might be plotting against the emperor and being rewarded with a quarter of whatever was confiscated from them, Regulus built up a fortune. Pliny lambastes and ridicules him in several letters. The one misfortune Regulus did not deserve, Pliny says, was the death of his son. The childless Pliny would have felt that deeply, I believe.

FICTIONAL CHARACTERS

Demetrius The steward in Pliny's main house in Rome, in charge of day-to-day affairs. Technically he is a slave, but he would have been treated more like an employee. He has an Egyptian wife and two daughters.

Lorcis A former slave of Regulus. In the fictional world of my first novel, *The Flute Player*, she and the poet Martial have a daughter, Erotion, and have to smuggle the child out of Regulus' house. Lorcis and Aurora meet in that novel.

Lucullus Lucius Licinius Lucullus, cousin of Regulus' wife, Sempronia. After living in Antioch for some time, he returned to Rome to take up a consulship with Domitian as his colleague. Virtually every man in this branch of the Licinian family was named Lucius Licinius Lucullus.

Malachi Rabbi of the synagogue which Naomi and Phineas attend, and which Plinia also goes to on occasion and to which she donates money.

Merione A wet nurse from Regulus' household.

Miriam A Jewish woman who replaces Merione as wet nurse to little Joshua.

Naomi A slave who is Plinia's friend and confidante. She and her son, Phineas, were taken captive after the fall of Jerusalem in 70 and sold to Pliny the Elder.

Nestor/Jacob A Jewish–Christian slave who is Regulus' steward.

Phineas Son of Naomi, and Pliny's chief scribe.

Porcia Widow of L. Licinius Lucullus. The *nomen gentilicum* (family name) Porcius is well known because of several men like M. Porcius Cato, Caesar's enemy, but I don't intend for Porcia to be part of that branch of the family.

Sempronia Regulus had a wife, so technically she's not fictitious, but we don't know her name or anything at all about her. Pliny mentions Regulus' son in a couple of letters, but the only mention of his wife occurs in *Ep.* 4.2, when Pliny says that Regulus released his son from parental authority so the boy could inherit his mother's estate, meaning that his mother was dead. Purely for dramatic purposes, I have portrayed Sempronia as a lesbian, but there is no reason to think Regulus' wife actually was.

Thalia A servant woman in Pliny's household. Several mythological figures have this name. Servants were sometimes given mythological names from characters their owners liked or because they seemed to have a characteristic of that figure.

Thersites A clownish soldier who dares to speak up in an assembly in the *Iliad*. Odysseus uses his staff to drive him out.

GLOSSARY OF TERMS

Also see glossaries in previous books in this series.

apotheosis The event in which a person becomes a god. Such scenes become common in Roman art in the imperial period, usually with the person being carried or riding on the back of a winged figure.

Arch of Augustus Erected to celebrate Augustus' recovery of the legionary standards lost by Crassus when he was defeated by the Parthians in 53 B.C. It consisted of a central arch and two smaller arches, one on each side. Situated next to the Temple of Julius Caesar, it required anyone entering the Forum from the southeastern end to acknowledge the Julian family's absolute control of Rome. No trace of this arch remains, but we do have a representation of it on a coin.

Arch of Titus Erected around 82 by Domitian in honor of his brother's conquest of Jerusalem in 70. It depicts the triumphal parade held in 71 and shows some of the most important objects looted from the temple. Those objects were on display in the nearby Temple of the Caesars.

caldarium The "hot room" in a Roman bath. Bathers proceeded from a cold room (*frigidarium*) to a warm room (*tepidarium*) to the *caldarium*, then reversed the process. In a bath in a private person's home the cold room and warm room might be combined. The *caldarium* was kept so hot by means of ducts in the floor that sandals had to be worn to prevent burns on the feet.

caliga A sandal-like "boot" designed for Roman soldiers. It had a closed toe and heavy sole. The emperor Gaius Caligula got his nickname from a miniature soldier's uniform, complete with boots, which his mother, Agrippina the Elder, designed for him. The name Caligula would have sounded to the Romans like "Little Boots."

Centumviral Court A civil court that dealt with financial matters and inheritance cases. Pliny appeared before this court regularly during his public career.

compluvium An opening in the roof of a Roman house over the atrium. In Rome's earliest days, before the building of aqueducts, the *compluvium* allowed for the collection of rain water, which drained into the *impluvium*, a shallow pool in the floor directly under the *compluvium*. By Pliny's day people who could afford a private home could also afford to get permission to tap into the aqueducts and have water piped into their homes. The Romans did not easily give up their traditions, though, so they continued to build their houses with a *compluvium* in the roof. In addition to rain water, the opening also allowed birds, insects, bats and other small animals to have entry to the house.

cuirass A piece of armor, a breastplate. Alexander the Great and his men reportedly used a cuirass made of linen. Modern studies and reconstructions have shown that layers of cloth could be glued together to make a stiff breastplate, but there is no general agreement about how, or if, this was done.

denarii Silver coins, about the size of a dime; one was usually reckoned as a day's wage for a working person.

equestrian Member of the second wealthiest order (class) in Roman society. Originally named because they could afford to ride into battle on a horse, they became Rome's businessmen, since senators were prohibited from engaging in any business except agriculture. They wore a colored stripe on their clothing, similar to a senator's except narrower. Pliny and Tacitus were equestrians.

exhedra An outdoor eating area, usually at the rear of the garden of a wealthy Roman home, also spelled *exedra*. The *h* represents what's called a "rough-breathing" in Greek and, to some degree, in Latin. The emperor Hadrian was also called Adrian. The poet Catullus makes fun of a man with what we would call a "Cockney" accent who calls the Ionian Sea the "Hionian."

Falernian A type of wine highly prized by the Romans.

ianitor The man who answered the door in a Roman aristocrat's house.

Ludus Magnus The "Great School," where gladiators trained for their bouts in the Flavian Amphitheatre. It was built by Domitian next to it. Seats were provided for a small audience to watch the training.

salutatio The "morning greeting." The clients (dependents) of a wealthy man like Pliny or Regulus would gather in the atrium of their patron's house to greet him shortly after dawn. The patron would dispense small amounts of money, inquire about his clients' welfare, and receive their requests for help or favors.

Sicarii A group of terrorists who operated in Jerusalem before the war of 66–73 and into its early days. They attacked anyone they suspected of collaborating with the Romans and any Roman officials reckless enough to go into the streets of the city. Their method was to deliver a quick stab in the back and then blend into the surrounding crowd.

strigl A metal scraper, shaped like a letter *L* but with a rounded corner to it. In bathing, Greeks and Romans rubbed themselves with olive oil, usually scented, and then scraped it off with the *strigl*. They then rinsed and dried themselves and rubbed on more scented olive oil.

strophium A band of cloth or leather worn by Roman women to hold the breasts in place or to de-emphasize them. Overly large breasts were considered comical, while sagging breasts were seen as a sign of old age.

suffect consul During the first century A.D. it became common practice for a man to hold a consulship for a few months, then resign so someone else could be appointed to the post, a *consul suffectus*, or substitute. As the empire grew, more and more ex-consuls were needed to fill provincial posts. The suffect consulship wasn't quite the same honor as a regular consulship, but it met an administrative need. Pliny was appointed to a suffect consulship in 100 A.D. by the emperor Trajan. By that time it had become the custom for an appointee to deliver a speech in the Senate thanking the emperor for the honor. Pliny's *Panegyricus*, of which he was inordinately proud, is the earliest surviving example of this type of speech and our only surviving example of Pliny's oratory. It is interesting for its historical detail and, to those of us who admire Pliny, embarrassing for its boot-licking.

vigiles Even with a population of over a million by Pliny's day, the city of Rome did not have a police or fire department. The primary responsibility of the *vigiles* was to spot fires when they broke out and get people out of harm's way. They also carried out some of the basic responsibilities of a police force but did not do the kind of investigations a modern police force does.

AUTHOR'S NOTE

WHEN I WROTE *All Roads Lead to Murder* I never imagined there would be a seventh book in this series. I'm in my early seventies now. I have other projects on my bucket list, not all of them mystery novels. Perseverance Press has been an excellent outfit to work with. John and Susan Daniel and Meredith Phillips are congenial and supportive. I have a great deal to thank them for. But their list is small and exclusively mysteries, and I know I can't take up space intended for other authors with whom they work or expect them to publish books outside their field of interest.

For those reasons I've begun to do something I never thought I would do: self-publish. Two of my novels—*Murder My Love* and *Death by Armoire*—are already available on CreateSpace, thanks to the most capable assistance of my tech-savvy friend Judy Geary. I plan to put out several other books in that format, not all mysteries. I have to be realistic. If I did find an agent/editor/small press to do those other books, it would take at least two years from acceptance to publication. I simply don't have that much time left, I'm afraid. That was once my dream as a writer, but it hasn't happened and clearly isn't going to happen. (I did make enough a couple of years ago from my traditionally published books to pay for a modest remodeling of a bathroom.) I've derived great satisfaction from writing the books, though, and from the reaction that readers and reviewers have had to them. The occasional royalty checks that allow me to take my wife out for a nice dinner will have to suffice.

One of the joys of writing, for me, is working with my writers' group, the West Michigan Writers' Workshop. We meet every Wednesday evening in the Grand Rapids public library. That's right, *every* Wednesday. When I tell people that, they look at me like I'm (we're) crazy. A lot of writers' groups meet only once or twice a month. I don't see how they get anything done. I know that I have to have four double-spaced pages ready to present each week. And, of course, I try to write more than that in a week. That's over two hundred pages a year. That'll get a book done. I've been in the group since 2001, and I've produced thirteen books in those sixteen years. Group members have come and gone, but since 2011 we have established a core of ten or twelve people whose advice has proved invaluable to me. And I hope I have helped them achieve their goals. Several of them have published—books, articles, stories, and poems. Pliny may not have had a regular writers' group, but he did get critiques of his work from Tacitus and others, and he shared his comments on their work. What we wouldn't give to have a manuscript by Tacitus with Pliny's notes in the margins!

I was surprised to see that two reviews of the previous book in this series, *Fortune's Fool*, commented on its literary quality. That surprised me because I think of myself primarily as a storyteller. I may turn a nice phrase now and then, just as a blind squirrel occasionally finds an acorn, but I have no literary pretensions. For me it's all about the story and the characters and their relationships. I do love my characters. I hope readers do, too. As I did in the last two books, I've written some sections from Aurora's point of view. Those sections are in italics. Given enough time, I might even write a book from her P.O.V. Then I guess Pliny's sections would be in italics.

ABOUT THE AUTHOR

ALBERT BELL is a college history professor, novelist, and weekend gardener who lives in Michigan. He and his wife have four adult children and two grandsons. In addition to his Roman mysteries, Bell has written contemporary mysteries, middle-grade novels, and nonfiction. Visit him at www.albertbell.com and www.pliny-mysteries.com.

More Traditional Mysteries from Perseverance Press
For the New Golden Age

Wendy Hornsby
MAGGIE MACGOWEN SERIES
In the Guise of Mercy
ISBN 978-1-56474-482-1

The Paramour's Daughter
ISBN 978-1-56474-496-8

The Hanging
ISBN 978-1-56474-526-2

The Color of Light
ISBN 978-1-56474-542-2

Disturbing the Dark
ISBN 978-1-56474-576-7

Number 7, Rue Jacob
ISBN 978-1-56474-599-6

A Fine Wreath of Weeds
(forthcoming)
ISBN 978-1-56474-607-8

Janet LaPierre
PORT SILVA SERIES
Baby Mine
ISBN 978-1-880284-32-2

Keepers
Shamus Award nominee, Best Paperback Original
ISBN 978-1-880284-44-5

Death Duties
ISBN 978-1-880284-74-2

Family Business
ISBN 978-1-880284-85-8

Run a Crooked Mile
ISBN 978-1-880284-88-9

Lev Raphael
NICK HOFFMAN SERIES
Tropic of Murder
ISBN 978-1-880284-68-1

Hot Rocks
ISBN 978-1-880284-83-4

State University of Murder
(forthcoming)
ISBN 978-1-56474-609-2

Lora Roberts
BRIDGET MONTROSE SERIES
Another Fine Mess
ISBN 978-1-880284-54-4

SHERLOCK HOLMES SERIES
The Affair of the Incognito Tenant
ISBN 978-1-880284-67-4

Rebecca Rothenberg
BOTANICAL SERIES
The Tumbleweed Murders
(completed by Taffy Cannon)
ISBN 978-1-880284-43-8

Sheila Simonson
LATOUCHE COUNTY SERIES
Buffalo Bill's Defunct
WILLA Award, Best Softcover Fiction
ISBN 978-1-880284-96-4

An Old Chaos
ISBN 978-1-880284-99-5

Beyond Confusion
ISBN 978-1-56474-519-4

Call Down the Hawk
ISBN 978-1-56474-597-2

Lea Wait
SHADOWS ANTIQUES SERIES
Shadows of a Down East Summer
ISBN 978-1-56474-497-5

Shadows on a Cape Cod Wedding
ISBN 1-978-56474-531-6

Shadows on a Maine Christmas
ISBN 978-1-56474-531-6

Shadows on a Morning in Maine
ISBN 978-1-56474-577-4

Eric Wright
JOE BARLEY SERIES
The Kidnapping of Rosie Dawn
Barry Award, Best Paperback Original. Edgar,
Ellis, and Anthony awards nominee
ISBN 978-1-880284-40-7

Nancy Means Wright
MARY WOLLSTONECRAFT SERIES
Midnight Fires
ISBN 978-1-56474-488-3

The Nightmare
ISBN 978-1-56474-509-5

REFERENCE/MYSTERY WRITING

Kathy Lynn Emerson
*How To Write Killer Historical
Mysteries: The Art and Adventure of
Sleuthing Through the Past*
Agatha Award, Best Nonfiction. Anthony and
Macavity awards nominee
ISBN 978-1-880284-92-6

Carolyn Wheat
*How To Write Killer Fiction:
The Funhouse of Mystery & the Roller
Coaster of Suspense*
ISBN 978-1-880284-62-9

**Available from your local bookstore
or from Perseverance Press/John Daniel & Company
(800) 662–8351 or www.danielpublishing.com/perseverance**